Chutes and Adders

Chutes and Adders

Adders

Barbara Block

KENSINGTON BOOKS

Although the city of Syracuse is certainly real as are some of the place names I've mentioned, this is a work of fiction. Its geography is imaginary. Indeed, all the characters portrayed in this book are fictional and any resemblance to real people or incidents is purely coincidental.

KENSINGTON BOOKS are published by

Kensington Publishing Corp.
850 Third Avenue
New York, NY 10022

Library of Congress Card Catalog Number: 94-076701
ISBN 0-8217-4533-6

First Printing: August, 1994

Printed in the United States of America

For Larry, David, Noah, and Gary,
who couldn't finish the ride.

ACKNOWLEDGEMENT

I would like to thank Jane Driscoll, Bruce Coville, Barbara Russell, and Sherry Chayat for all their help and support.

One

I was in the small mammal room treating the baby ferrets to a couple of tablespoons of peanut butter when the buzzer sounded, but by the time I managed to extract myself from them and get up front, whoever had been out there was gone. There was just a parcel lying next to the cash register. No big deal I figured. The UPS man was running late and hadn't bothered waiting around for me to sign for it. He'd been doing that a lot lately.

It looked so harmless. In retrospect, it was as harmless as an open bottle of bourbon at an AA meeting, only I didn't know that then. If I had, I would have chucked the damned thing out. Instead I started to open it. But as I was peeling the tape off one of the sides, I caught sight of the name on the package and realized I'd made a mistake. The delivery wasn't for me. It was for John. So I did what anyone would have. I put the parcel down and went to get him.

He was working out back in the storeroom. The last room off the rear hallway, the storeroom was small, five by ten feet at the most. Before Murphy had bought the house and converted it into Noah's Ark it had served as a mud room. Now it

1

was a general catchall for livestock and supplies. I had to ma-
neuver my way around sacks of dog food, bags of cedar shavings, and cages full of ball pythons, corn snakes, and boa
constrictors to get to where John and Tim were cleaning out
Atilla's cage.

Tim was tapping on the outside of the aquarium glass to
distract the lizard, while John lined the bottom of the cage
with fresh newspaper. The fluorescent light emphasized his
receding hairline, his skin's greenish hue, and the pouches
under his eyes. Even though he was only in his early twenties,
John's features were already blurred under a layer of fat put
on by too many beers and too much fried food. The only good
thing about his face was his eyes. Brown with specks of gold,
they were usually fixed in an expression of sardonic amuse-
ment. By contrast, Tim's body and face were all angles and
planes: high cheek bones, almond eyes, a slash of a mouth,
sinewy arms, long blond hair.

I was thinking about how opposite the two men were—
beauty and the beast—when Atilla, bored with Tim's efforts,
charged at John's hands. But he was ready for the five-foot
monitor lizard—the move was one of her standard gambits—
and he deftly moved his hands to one side like a toreador with
a bull.

"I'll be glad when we sell her," Tim said as she smacked up
against the aquarium glass. "She gives me the creeps."

"Oh I don't know." John picked at one of his front teeth
with a fingernail while he watched Atilla hiss and whip her tail
from side to side in frustration. "I was thinking of buying her
myself. I like her attitude."

"Really?" Tim glanced up. "Well if you've got four hundred
dollars to spend on her how about giving me back the two hundred you owe me?"

"Actually, I was kind of hoping the boss lady would give

me a special deal," John replied, winking at me as he walked over to a cage full of mice that was sitting on a table by the far wall.

I took a cigarette out of my front pocket. "I can give you the standard thirty percent," I offered after I lit it.

"I was thinking more along the lines of fifty percent."

"Sorry. But you know I can't do that." The store was operating too close to the edge for that kind of giveaway.

"Murphy would have."

"But I'm not Murphy," I replied, trying to keep the irritation out of my voice.

John gave a sullen shrug. "Hey, can't blame a guy for trying." Then he opened the cage door, grabbed a couple of mice by their tails, and dragged them out. "Feeding time," he announced as he bore the squealing rodents over to Atilla's cage.

I turned and headed for the door.

"Yo, stay and watch the show," John called after me, an amused note in his voice. He thought it was funny that I didn't like watching the big lizard feed.

"Thanks, but I'll pass." I took a couple more steps before I remembered I hadn't done what I'd originally come in to do: tell him about the package.

When I let him know, John waved his hand absentmindedly in my direction, all his attention now focused on the spectacle that was about to unfold. "I'll get to it later."

"Whenever," I said and left. I was halfway down the back hallway when Tim called out to me.

"Hey, Robin, I forgot to tell you Maroney was here before you came."

I stopped and turned around. "What did he want?"

"The usual. You know, did I think you'd change your mind about selling the store?"

"Jesus. That man just won't take no for an answer."

Chutes and Adders

"That's probably why he's successful," Tim observed.

"Probably," I agreed. I stubbed the cigarette out on the floor—I was smoking too much again—and continued on down the hallway.

The truth was: I wouldn't mind selling the store. But it would be a stupid thing to do. The accountant had made that perfectly clear two weeks after Murphy had died. It was simple. If I sold the store, between the back sales tax I'd have to pay and the creditors I'd have to satisfy there'd be nothing left for me to live on. On the other hand, if I kept the store running and business picked up I'd be able to pay my bills and keep my house.

Of course that meant I'd have to stop working on my book, but then I wasn't doing too well with it anyway. And it had seemed like such a good idea when I'd started a little over a year ago. The topic had been hot: anatomy of the standoff at the St. Marie Indian Reservation. The story had been running in the national papers for months and it had everything: gun running, gambling, government malfeasance, Mafia involvement, two murders. And thanks to a couple of friends of mine I had the inside track. I'd sold the project in three weeks. Taken the advance, done the research, and was halfway through the first draft when I discovered that one of my main sources had been lying and the other had disappeared. Which meant I had to start all over again. So I was now six months behind.

What I should have done was do more checking at the beginning instead of quitting my job at the *Herald* and going free-lance. But I'd been temporarily blinded by ambition, seen the book as a way to jump start a ten-year lackluster career as a news reporter. I don't know. Maybe Murphy and I weren't so different after all. Both of us running after dreams. Both of us slipping. Only he wasn't going to get another chance. I was thinking about that, thinking about the fact that I was still having trouble believing he was dead—even though it had already been six weeks—as I went into the supply closet and started counting out crickets for the smaller lizards. Twenty minutes later I heard the scream.

I dashed out front. John was standing near the cash register, clutching his right hand with his left. His eyes were open wide in disbelief, the pupils dilated. His mouth was agape. His chest was rising and falling rapidly. When he saw me he raised his hand in supplication.

"Oh Christ," he whimpered. "You gotta help me. I've been bit by a saw-scaled." And he turned his head slightly toward the package that had come earlier. Only now it was open. And empty.

Tim and I both jumped back, scouring the floor with our eyes for the snake. Even though it was small, that species was aggressive and toxic as hell. But the viper wasn't there. It had probably already slithered through one of the holes in the baseboard.

"We'll have to look for it later," Tim said as he got his lock knife out of his pocket and grabbed John's wrist. "At least this should slow things down some," he added making two quick cuts above the bite.

John groaned as the blade sliced into his flesh. Blood trickled onto the counter. I ran to the bathroom and grabbed a towel. By the time I returned crimson dots were stippling the white formica.

"Listen," I told Tim as I wrapped the towel around John's arm, "I'm going to take him to the hospital. It'll be faster than waiting for the ambulance." We were only ten blocks away from St. Ann's. "You see if you can find the snake."

He nodded and reached for the broom while I grabbed John's good arm and propelled him across the floor. As I shut the front door, I could hear Tim crooning, "Come to Mama, baby. I've got something special for you."

Even though it was less than an eighth of a block, the walk to the parking lot seemed to go on forever. By the time we'd reached my Checker Cab John's brown hair was plastered with sweat and his breath was coming in gasps. My arm ached from supporting him. I could barely hold on to him while I opened the passenger door. Then I pushed him in, ran around to my side, and started the cab up. The engine roared.

"I'll be right there," I promised as I got out to scrape the ice off the windshield.

It only took me thirty seconds to clear a hole big enough to see out of, but it felt like thirty minutes. I got back in the car, shifted into drive, and zoomed onto the street.

"I don't feel so good," John whispered as I sped down Spofford.

"You'll be fine," I said, trying to convince us both.

But as I looked at the swelling creeping up his arm I knew that wasn't true and I think John knew it too. I made a right onto Gifford, squealed around the corner onto West Street, and went through the intersection without stopping for the light. A guy driving an '85 Camaro beeped and gave me the finger. I ignored him as I sped by. Out of the corner of my eye I watched a rope of saliva slide out of John's mouth and fall onto his lap. I touched his shoulder, but he shrugged my hand off.

As we passed the All Souls Pentecostal Church, I asked him if he knew who had sent him the package. He answered me, but his words were so garbled I couldn't understand them. He tried again, his mouth contorting with the effort. Nothing came out. The toxin was paralyzing his vocal chords.

I accelerated. Then as I was rounding the corner at Townsend and Clark I must have hit a patch of black ice because the car skidded out and I sideswiped a Jeep parked on the corner. I was straightening my wheels when I heard the wheezing. I glanced over. John's face had gone gray. His chest was heaving like a bellows.

"Hold on," I pleaded. "We're almost there."

This time he didn't brush my hand away. I don't think he could have even if he had wanted to.

As I made a sharp turn onto Ash, John fell against my arm. He shuddered and made a half gurgling, half barking noise. A stain spread over the front of his pants. The smell of feces filled the air. I said a prayer, put my foot down to the floor, my hand on the horn, and went up West Street at eighty miles an hour. I careened into the hospital parking lot, tromped on the brakes and ran hollering into reception. Suddenly people were lifting John out of the car. Everything was a blur of motion. A resident materialized beside me and I filled him in. When I was done, he started running down the hall after the stretcher.

"Was that John Blount?"

I spun around. A big sandy-haired man in jeans was talking to me.

I nodded.

"What the hell happened to him?"

But before I could tell him, hands were guiding me over to the receptionist's cubicle. She sat poised at her computer, a gum-chewing Cerberus with black fingernails. After we were done, a gray-haired lady introduced herself as Mrs. Goff and shepherded me back through the crowded waiting area to a private room. Then she closed the door and asked me if I wanted something to drink,

I think it was her solicitude that made me realize John was dead. They had put me in here in case I broke down. Only I wasn't going to. When I'd found Murphy lying in his car in the driveway I hadn't been able to stop screaming. After I'd woken up from the shot the doctor had given me, I'd vowed I'd never let myself get that way again.

"Is there someone we should contact?" Mrs. Goff asked, intruding on my thoughts.

I shook my head. I couldn't think of anyone.

She patted me on the shoulder. "I'll just go and find out how your friend is doing." And she closed the door carefully behind her, as if she were afraid something was going to break.

The room was small. There were no pictures on the walls, no magazines on the table in front of the sofa. I clicked on the TV. I got static. I turned it off and started pacing. I couldn't sit still. Whenever I did, I saw Murphy lying in the car, white powder clinging to his nostrils. I couldn't shake the image. I looked down at Murphy's watch. It was only four-fifteen. Somehow I'd thought it was later.

Then I rubbed the band, something I'd been doing a lot lately. The watch twisted around my wrist. Even though I had put the clasp through the last hole, the band still didn't fit. Murphy had been a big man, broad-shouldered, six feet two inches, one hundred ninety pounds, a man who took risks. Lots of them. That's one of the things that had attracted me to him in college. I'd loved his motorcycle. His air of assurance. We'd been glued together by passion. Except recently . . . in the past year, we'd. . . . No. I shook my head.

I wouldn't think about that now. Regrets were an expense I couldn't afford. I got up and walked out into the hallway. At first I stood in front of the door, then I wandered down the corridor. The walls were painted a sad shade of yellow. The place reeked of disinfectant and fear. The nurses and the interns talking to each other ignored me.

In the first treatment room, a bone-thin woman in dirty

jeans sat cradling a limp, small child. His face was flushed and his eyes shiny. Tears were running down the woman's face. I averted my gaze and walked on. The other treatment rooms were empty. Halfway down the hall, I saw Mrs. Goff talking to someone and started toward her, but before I reached her, she spotted me and came over. The man she had been talking to followed.

He extended his hand and we shook. "I'm Dr. Powers. I'm afraid I have some bad news."

"He's dead, isn't he?" I asked before he could say anything else.

"Yes. Yes, he is." The man looked as if he had been on call for the past forty-eight hours. Under his white coat, his shirt and pants were wrinkled. Deep exhaustion lines were etched around the corners of his mouth.

I asked Powers what had happened.

"He was dead when you brought him in." Powers spoke slowly, avoiding my eyes. He looked up at the lights and down at the floor while he talked to me. Clearly he had wanted to bring me good news and couldn't. He seemed like a nice guy, someone who honestly cared and I felt bad for him. "We threw everything we had at him. What can I say? Nothing worked. His lungs just gave out."

So that was that.

John was gone. I recalled him saying that he'd never make it past thirty. It looked like he'd been right.

I was turning to leave when it occurred to me that someone had to call the police.

"We've already done that," Dr. Powers said when I made the suggestion. "There's an officer waiting to talk to you in the lobby."

Two

The police want to talk to you.

I conjugated the phrase as I walked down the hall: the police want to talk to you; the police wanted to talk to you; the police will want to talk to you. Present, past, future. Then there was always the subjunctive, the pluperfect, and the conditional. Conditional. A good word. Also tenuous and fragile. Apt, not to mention applicable to the way I was feeling.

"He's over there." Mrs. Goff pointed past the nurses' station to the reception area.

Not that I needed Mrs. Goff to point him out. I couldn't have missed Murphy's friend, George Samson, if I tried. Nobody could. I always thought that one look at him and the criminals would just lie down and give up. First of all the man was huge. He was at least six foot four, weighed well over three hundred pounds, and all of that weight was muscle. Secondly, he was black—not beige, not cocoa—but black. Blue black. African black. And third of all, he scowled. A lot. Fortunately he also happened to be a really nice guy.

He broke into a big smile when he saw me and started across the floor. "Hey, kiddo, how you doing?"

"Okay." Amazing what habit makes you say.

Then when he was a couple of feet away, he stopped and folded his arms across his chest. "Do I have to wait until my twilight years for you to return my calls? I've been leaving messages on your machine for weeks."

"I've been meaning to." Embarrassed, I tugged on the waist band of my sweatshirt.

"But?"

I shrugged. "Things just got away from me." The truth was I hadn't spoken to friends or acquaintances since Murphy's funeral. I couldn't stand seeing the looks of pity on their faces.

"Anything I could do to help?"

"Not unless you can take out your magic wand and make the last couple of hours go away."

George's eyes widened. "Don't tell me you're the person they sent me down to talk to?"

"I'm afraid so."

"Shit." He rubbed his nose with his hand. "I'm sorry. You don't need any more crap."

"Hey, it's not like this mess is your fault."

George clapped his hand on my shoulder. "Listen, you look like you could use some grub. How about we go to the cafeteria, I buy you some food, and you can tell me what happened while you eat."

"Sounds good to me."

We talked as we went through the tunnel that connected the ER to the main part of the hospital. Different-colored arrows pointed in different directions. This way to X ray, that way to Internal Medicine, right to Radiation Therapy, left to the Mammography Suite, straight ahead to hell. As we walked, it struck me that maybe Murphy had been lucky to die at forty-two, that I was being selfish begrudging him his death. He wasn't the kind who would have aged gracefully, but then I didn't think I would either.

At the end of the tunnel we followed the orange arrow and turned left into the lobby and then right to the elevator bank. A prominent sign next to the buttons advised that stretchers had the right of way.

"What the hell is a saw-scaled viper anyway?" George asked as we got on the elevator.

"A small snake with a very nasty bite."

"I've never heard of them."

"They come from Southeast Asia."

"So it bought a ticket and took a plane here?"

I smiled. "In a manner of speaking. Lots of dealers in the States have import permits for them. Evidently people like to buy them. Go figure."

George rolled his eyes. "I've been in this job for ten years and people's stupidity still never fails to amaze me."

I silently agreed, thinking of Murphy dead from a cocaine overdose. We didn't say anything else until we stepped out into the cafeteria. It was a barn of a place. The fluorescent lights, pea green walls, and gray linoleum made it feel like a barracks. According to the sign over the red fire doors, the place had been designed for five hundred, but only a handful of people were sitting there.

"What do you want to eat?" George asked.

"A hamburger, a Coke, and a piece of fruit," I answered, suddenly realizing that I was in fact ravenous. It was after five and all I had had all day was a bag of Hershey's Kisses and what felt like ninety-seven million cups of coffee.

While George went to place the order, I collapsed onto a chair at a nearby table. Somebody had left a newspaper behind and out of habit I thumbed through it. The life style section was running a feature article I'd submitted three months ago on marriage counseling. I tried to read it but the letters wouldn't form themselves into recognizable words. Shock probably. Not that I needed to read it. I knew it was competent. But not inspired. An analysis which pretty much summed up my working years.

After college I'd been a substitute teacher in New York City for three years, but I'd gotten tired of the daily aggravations and given it up. Then I'd tried making it as a free-lance photographer. But I hadn't had the drive and when Murphy got a job in an ad agency up in Syracuse, I'd been glad to leave the city for Central New York. I'd done a little of this and a little of that for six months. Then I'd lucked into a job as a reporter on the *Herald Journal*. And stayed. I sighed and turned the page. I was reading my horoscope when George returned.

"You believe in that stuff?" He set down the tray.

"I don't disbelieve." I closed the paper. "How about you?"

George snorted and pushed the hamburger toward me. "Here. Your food's getting cold."

But suddenly I wasn't hungry anymore. The smell of the meat had made my throat close. It was a problem I'd been having a lot lately: being hungry and then not being able to eat. The only foods I seemed to be able to get down these days were yogurt and chocolate. I pushed the tray away, lit a cigarette in spite of the NO SMOKING sign on the wall, and asked him to start. I wanted to get this over with so I could go home and curl up in bed.

George squeezed my hand then took his notepad out of his breast pocket. He wrote down my name, address, and phone number, while I wound a hank of hair around my finger and studied it. It was carrot-colored. And I had the dead white skin to go with it.

When I was little I'd hated my coloring, my appearance: a

gawky, tall, blazingly white, carrot-topped stranger dropped in among a family of short, compactly built, dark-haired people. For years I thought I'd been adopted. The only features that told me otherwise were my brown eyes and the distinctive slight downward twist of my nose.

My father had kept telling me I'd be beautiful when I grew up, but I'd believed my mother who'd said I'd be attractive if I dressed properly and used makeup. I was wondering why I'd believed her and not him when George's voice cut through my thoughts.

"Now tell me exactly what happened," he urged.

I did and he wrote my answers down slowly and deliberately, pausing every now and then to make sure he had gotten my words right. The pen, the kind that came ten to a package, looked puny in his fingers.

"Were you expecting any merchandise of that sort?" he asked when I stopped talking.

"It wasn't addressed to me," I reminded him.

"That's right. I forgot." He tapped his pen on the table. "Tell me, how long has John been working in the store?"

"Since Murphy opened it four years ago. Then at some point—maybe a year, maybe less, he went part-time."

"How did he get along with the other guy who works there?"

"You mean Tim? Fine as far as I know."

"Any fights?"

"Not when I've been around." I picked up the orange George had brought and started peeling it. The oil left its scent on my fingers.

"How about with the woman?"

"Donna Sayers? They're going out."

"Really?" George raised an eyebrow. "Murphy never told me that. Not," he added quickly, "that there was any reason he should have. You want to clue me in on their relationship?"

"John and Donna's? I really can't tell you much. We didn't hang around together. For what it's worth, they seemed okay in the store."

"And outside?"

"Like I said, I don't really know. I never spent any time with them."

George leaned forward. "Then let me ask you this. What did you think of John?"

"He was okay I guess."

"That's pretty lukewarm. I gather you really didn't like him?"

"No. I didn't say that. It's just that sometimes I found him irritating," I said, thinking about our interchange over Atilla. "He always seemed to be looking for an angle. But he did know his reptiles. And he was really good with the animals. I have to give him that much."

George sighed. "Do you know if he was doing drugs? Had he gotten into a fight recently? Gotten somebody's girlfriend pregnant? That sort of thing."

"Sorry. But Murphy never talked about stuff like that and outside of work, John and I weren't what you would call conversationally inclined."

"Anything else you think I should know?"

I shook my head.

"Then I guess we're done." George closed his notebook. "Go home." He gave my arm a pat. The heat from his hand burned through my sweater. "Go home and take a nap. Forget about everything for a while."

God did I ever want to, but when I rang up the store to tell Tim about John I got the cops on the line instead and they told me to come over. They had some questions, they said, they wanted to ask.

Driving conditions had gotten worse since I'd brought John over to the hospital. The streets were glazed with a thin layer of ice and as I skidded my way over to the store I cursed my car, a Checker cab. Murphy had told me it wouldn't do well on the ice, but I'd been so enamored with it—remembrances of my childhood in New York City and all that—that I hadn't listened.

Tim was walking toward his VW as I pulled into the parking lot. He stopped when he saw me and I thought again of how small he was. He and I were both the same height, five foot seven. And I wouldn't be surprised if we even weighed about the same—one hundred forty pounds.

"John died in the cab," I informed him as I got out of my car. "He didn't even make it to the hospital."

"I know. The cops told me." Tim rubbed his hands together. He looked shrunken in the cold. He had lived in Florida until he was twelve and had never truly made the transition to Syracuse.

"How's Donna taking it?" She had been due in for work five minutes after I left for the hospital.

"I don't know if she knows. She never showed up."

"Did you find the snake?"

Tim shook his head. "The cops called the zoo. Some of the guys from there are coming down to see what they can do. Maybe they'll have better luck than I did."

"I hope so. God I don't want to go in there." I realized I was biting my lower lip.

"I don't blame you." Then Tim invited me over to his house when I was done with the police. I guess he didn't want to be alone either.

After he left I headed toward Noah's Ark.

The ice crunched underfoot as I half slid, half walked

across the parking lot. A yellow tape was tied across the stairs. I ducked under it and went inside. Two men looked up briefly and then went back to doing what they had been before. One was snapping photographs, while the other was taking notes. Both were wearing ski parkas, turtlenecks, and gray pants. The Bobbsey Twins. I noticed they moved cautiously, taking care to look where they stepped. Not that I blamed them. Most people would go Looney Tunes if there was a corn snake loose, let alone a viper.

Before I could say anything, the cop stationed by the door asked me who I was. When I told him he escorted me to the office, then left. A woman was sitting behind Murphy's desk. She had one of those hard, pinched faces that you saw on second generation Italian women over on the North Side. She looked familiar and as she extended her hand I remembered why.

I'd covered the press conference announcing Donnella Lorenzo's promotion to the CID. It had been a big deal because she was the first woman in the history of the Syracuse Police Department to make the unit. She'd come up the hard way I recalled. Onondaga Community College, then years of night school.

"Sorry to hear about your husband," she said as we both sat down. "I got some Jackson Chameleons from him last year."

I was impressed. In addition to ambition the woman had taste—at least in the reptile department. The goggle-eyed little lizards sold for over three hundred dollars a pair—when you could get them.

"He was very helpful."

He always had been, especially with women. "Flirting makes the day go faster," he'd said. "Where's the harm in it," he'd always wanted to know whenever I got upset. "And anyway it helps sales." Murphy's bottom line.

Lorenzo leaned back in her chair and settled her glasses on the bridge of her nose. Square, made of clear plastic, they did nothing for her appearance. "About the viper," she began.

"Yes?"

"I've called the zoo."

"Tim told me."

"Hopefully, they'll be able to take care of the problem."

"At least it's winter. He won't be going outside."

"Yes, that's something to be thankful for," Lorenzo agreed, favoring me with a chilly smile. Then she looked down at her notebook and back up at me. "Now, how about telling me what happened," she commanded, impaling me with her glance.

I repeated what I'd told George. "The bell rang."

"The bell?"

"It's a sensor, really. It rings whenever the front door opens."

"I see. And where were you?"

"In the mammal room giving the baby ferrets a treat."

"And how long would you say it took you to get from there out to the front?"

"Less than a minute."

"Fine. Then what?"

"Then I saw the package. It was lying on the counter."

"Nobody else was in the store?"

"No."

"Didn't that strike you as a little odd?"

"Not at the time. I figured the delivery man had gone out the side door."

"But you didn't hear that door close?"

"I wouldn't have. The sensor on that door is broken. It has been for several weeks."

"Go on."

I shifted in my seat. "There isn't much more to say. I started opening the parcel, realized it was for John, and told him."

"And where was he?"

"In the storeroom cleaning out a monitor lizard's cage."

"What did he say?"

"He said he'd be out in a little while."

"And then what did you do?"

"I went into the supply room and started counting out crickets."

Lorenzo stopped writing. "Is there anything else you want to add to your statement?" she asked, giving me a quizzical look.

"I can't think of anything."

"Are you sure?"

"I'm positive."

We stared at each other for a minute. I was the first to turn away.

"So you didn't notice that the wrapping paper the package came in had no stamps?"

I told her I hadn't.

"I guess you have other things on your mind these days."

"You could say that."

"Given your husband's death and all." Then Lorenzo handed me a sheet of paper that had been lying on Murphy's desk. It was the price list from Herp Inc.

"Do you do business with them?"

"Murphy did."

She pointed to a place three-quarters of the way down the

page. "Did you notice that seven different types of vipers are being offered for sale in this catalog?"

"So? Most reptile supply houses sell vipers." There were hundreds of different kinds. "Anyone can order one, if they know where to go. You should know that."

"That's my point. I know. You know. But most people don't."

I leaned forward. "Exactly what are you saying?"

"I'm saying that I think you know more than you're telling me."

"Why would I do that?"

"Because you have something to hide."

"Well I don't."

"I see." Lorenzo resettled her glasses on the bridge of her nose and folded her hands in front of her. "You're sure?"

"Absolutely."

"Then I suppose you're free to go . . ."

I shot out of the chair like a jack-in-the-box.

". . . For the time being," Lorenzo added. Then she smiled and went back to leafing through the papers on Murphy's desk.

That smile made my gut twist. I walked out of there feeling as if something very bad was going to happen.

Three

As I drove toward Tim's, I thought about my conversation with Lorenzo and decided I was being stupid to feel the way I did. The lady had just been trying to rattle me. See what shook loose. And nothing had. Nor would it. Because I hadn't sent the package. Despite her insinuations, there was no way she could connect me with it.

To get my mind off things I slipped a Rolling Stones tape into my cassette player and turned the volume up high enough so that people on the street could hear it. If there had been people. Which there weren't. The shops on South Salina were shuttered for the night. No one was out on State Street. Or Adams either. It was so cold, even the hookers were off Warren. The Merchants Association had finally taken down the Christmas decorations. The tinsel, the plastic candles, the reindeer, and all the other prepackaged good cheer were packed away till next year. The streets looked bleak under the lights.

Tim lived fairly close to the store. The houses there had been built one on top of the other. Most had small lawns and short driveways. Because of the proximity to St. Ann's, parking was always a problem. After circling the block several times, I gave up and pulled up in front of a fire hydrant.

The flat Tim rented was the lower one of a tired-looking two family colonial on Oneonta Place. The bottom porch step was missing a slat and the side railing wobbled when I touched it. From where I was standing, facing the front window, I could see the flicker of the television. Nobody was watching it. I rang the bell and waited. Next door a kid was carrying a keg up his walkway. Halfway there he slipped on a patch of ice and fell. The smell of cheap beer filled the air. He looked like he was going to cry.

"Yes?"

I turned around. Thomas Maroney was standing in Tim's doorway. He blinked several times when he saw me, obviously as surprised to see me as I was to see him, then recovered. He was in his fifties, average height, but he looked shorter because he was built like a fire plug. His receding chin gave his face a weakish cast, but his eyes countermanded the impression. They were cold and hard. He was a man who was used to getting his own way and it showed. I was just about to say something when Tim came out. He was followed by his dog, Merle. The dog came over and nuzzled my hand.

"I can come back if this is a bad time," I offered as I scratched the Great Dane behind the ears.

"No, stay." Tim shot Maroney a look. "Mr. Maroney was just leaving."

Maroney nodded. "Yeah. I was just on my way out."

"I didn't know you two knew each other socially."

"We don't," Maroney informed me. "I just bought this house and came by to renegotiate Mr. McDowell's lease."

"You certainly are keeping busy."

"I try."

Tim was starting to say something when his phone rang.

He excused himself and went to answer it and I stepped into the hallway.

"Heard you had some problems at the store today," Maroney commented as he took his coat, an expensive gray cashmere, out of the hall closet.

"That's one way of putting it."

Maroney slipped on the cashmere and smoothed down the lapels. "Tim give you my message?"

"Yes."

"And?"

"I've already told you I'm not selling."

"People have been known to change their minds."

"*If* I decide to, you'll be the first to know."

Maroney turned to the hall mirror and scrutinized the tufts of hair on either side of his head. He held his head first to one side and then to the other before turning back to me. "You know," he said, "you used to look real good. Real stylish. Hot. But look at you now."

I glanced down at myself involuntarily. I knew my jeans and sweatshirt were old but I didn't think they were that bad.

"I think you should take the money I'm offering and go on a vacation. Get a little sun. Relax. Have some fun. Maybe even meet someone. I hear Maui's real nice this time of year."

I didn't say anything.

"Listen, you've had a rough time. I feel bad for you. I'm trying to do you a favor."

I snorted. "Yeah, you're a real humanitarian."

Maroney shook his head in disgust and left.

As the door banged shut, I stood there twisting Murphy's watch around my wrist and wondering if Maroney was right and my accountant was wrong. If maybe I should just cut my losses and move on. Staying was so hard, but I didn't know if I had the guts to go. Damn Murphy for leaving me in this mess.

No, damn me for allowing it to happen. I was intelligent. I had good judgment. Except when it came to him. He was charming. He was handsome. He was exciting. He knew all the right words.

I'd never been able to say no to the man. He'd talked me into bed when I was seventeen. He'd talked me into supporting him through his MBA—which he'd never finished. He talked me into investing in a laundromat with him—which had gone broke. But it hadn't mattered. He just needed to find the right opportunity, I told my friends. For a while I thought the Noah's Ark had been it. And our sex life had been terrific. What else mattered? Except in the past year that had faded. We seemed to be drifting apart. And I didn't know why or what to do about it. And whenever I'd asked Murphy, he'd always said I was just imagining things. So that's what I told myself. Because it was easier. And because I was too scared to do anything else.

I sighed and walked into Tim's living room. It was sparsely furnished. On one side was a wall unit filled with books, records, and Tim's collection of skeleton specimens. A thirty-inch Sony and a pricey rack stereo system completed the list. Across the way, was a green-and-brown tweed sofa. In front of that was a kennel that was doing double duty as a coffee table. The walls were bare and white and there were no rugs on the floor. I put my pocketbook on the kennel, dug my cigarettes out, and lit up.

Then I walked over and studied the shelves. The books were mostly about reptiles and fish, the music was reggae and soul. A bottle of rum stood next to a brightly colored foot-high statue of a woman wearing a crown. I was just about to pick it up when Tim asked me if I wanted a Coke. I told him to make it a beer.

He cocked his head to one side. "Since when did you start drinking?"

"Since six weeks ago."

"What happened to the 'alcohol makes me sick' spiel?"

"It still does, but I decided I don't care."

"Fine with me. A beer it is."

He was back a moment later with a six pack, a bag of potato chips, and a jar of dry-roasted peanuts.

"I think one of us should call Donna and see how she's doing," I told Tim as he popped the tab on a Rolling Rock and handed it to me.

"You do it. I wouldn't know what to say."

"How about you're sorry."

But Tim just shook his head so I dialed. As the telephone rang I wondered what I was going to say. I still hadn't figured it out when her aunt picked up the receiver.

"So?" Tim asked after I'd hung up.

"She's not there. Her aunt said she's gone to the store."

"Maybe," he suggested, "the police are still talking to her."

"She wasn't there when I left."

"She probably arrived after you'd gone."

"That would make her, what? Over an hour late?"

"It's not as if she hasn't done that before," Tim reminded me as he took a swig of his beer.

"True." Donna, I had discovered in the six weeks I had been running the shop, was always late. She was a good worker once she got to the store. The operative word here was "once."

Tim and I drank in silence for a while. I fed peanuts, one at a time, to Merle. Doing that made me realize how much I missed my dog. I'd picked Elsie up from the ASPCA right after I'd graduated from college. Fourteen years. That's a lot of time together, almost as much as Murphy and I had had.

She knew all my stories. She'd died of old age in the middle of the living room floor seven months ago and I was still walking around that spot. Now the only thing I had left in my house was James, the cat. It made me regret more than ever that I'd never had a child. We'd kept putting it off, waiting till the time was right. But the right time had never come. Tim cleared his throat. I looked over in his direction.

"So what do you think about what happened to John?" he asked.

"Aside from the fact that I think it's a lousy way to die."

Tim looked bemused. "You mean there's a good way?"

"No." I twirled a lock of my hair around my finger. "I guess not. But this . . . I mean you have time to know what's happening."

"Maybe that was the point."

"Maybe." Merle lay down and put his head on my knee and I scratched behind his ears. "I'll tell you something though."

"What?"

"The more I think about it, the more a snake strikes me as an odd murder weapon. I mean if you want to kill someone why not use a gun? Or a knife? A snake is so iffy. He may bite. He may not."

"Saw-scaled vipers are aggressive. They go after anything that moves. That's what they're famous for."

"But their bite isn't always fatal. If you can get someone on a life support system they can pull through."

"So what are you saying?"

"I guess I'm saying that maybe the snake was meant as a warning. Otherwise why not use something like a sea snake? A bite from one of those and you're dead in five minutes or less. Period. End of discussion."

"*If* they bite," Tim reminded me. "They may be deadly but

they're mellow. Fishermen out in the Indian Ocean handle them all the time and never get bit."

"Whatever." Suddenly I didn't feel like discussing the subject anymore. I didn't feel like discussing anything. I was too tired.

"I tell you one thing though," Tim said as he reached for the remote and turned up the sound on the television, "John must have really pissed someone off."

It was an unarguable statement. We spent the rest of the evening watching sitcom reruns and drinking beer.

I looked at my watch when I woke up the next morning. It said seven-twenty. Tim must have thrown a blanket over me at some point, but I don't remember when. In fact, I didn't remember much, period. I just knew that I'd had too much to drink. God, did I feel lousy. My shoulder was wet from dog drool, my head was throbbing, I had a rotten taste in my mouth, and my legs ached. What I needed was a shower, a decent cup of coffee, and some fresh clothes. In other words, I needed to go home.

As soon as I pulled into the driveway, James came trotting out to greet me. He'd been born under a house in the country and clung to his outdoor ways. I scooped him up and buried my face in his fur. It was thick and shiny and cold. The hairs tickled my nose. With my free hand I fished yesterday's mail out of the box, got my key out, and opened the door.

The radio was still playing in the kitchen. I turned it off, set James down on the counter, and placated him with a saucer of milk. Then I watered my jade tree, made myself a cup of coffee, ate a couple of chocolate bars out of the fridge, swallowed a handful of vitamins, grabbed the day's newspaper, and listened to the messages on my answering machine. Three were from various friends wanting to know why, for all practical purposes, I'd dropped off the face of the earth, the fourth was from my editor at Prestige asking me when I'd have my manuscript done, and the fifth was from George. I rewound the machine and went upstairs. I'd call everyone back later when I wasn't as tired.

I went upstairs, threw my clothes on the bed, and started running the water for a bath. I love my bathroom. It's got green tiles on the floor, blond wood on the walls, a pedestal sink, and an enormous sand-colored bathtub. I dumped in some lily of the valley bath oil and got in. As I watched my skin turn rosy red, I relaxed for the first time in twenty-four hours. I opened the paper and lit a cigarette.

John had made the front page of the metro section. Most of the article dealt with the snake and the fact it had yet to be found. Great. With that kind of publicity nobody would ever walk into the store again. I turned the page. The cops had made another drug arrest on the West Side. They had gotten a couple of grams of coke and a few joints. Basically, pretty minor stuff. The only thing of interest was that I knew the people arrested. They lived down the block from the store. I read Ann Landers, then turned to my horoscope. It said I should try to get along better with an irritating person in my life. I was not encouraged. I put the paper on the floor, stubbed out my cigarette, flicked the butt into the toilet, and closed my eyes.

I was just drifting off when the doorbell rang. Probably Jehovah's Witnesses. It rang again. I sank lower in the water. Somebody started pounding. There was a pause, then more pounding. Finally, I gave up.

"All right," I yelled. "Hold on. I'm coming." I hopped out of the tub and shrugged on Murphy's bathrobe.

The doorbell rang again. I slammed down the steps two at a time, leaving a trail of wet footprints behind me.

"What is it?" I threw the front door open. The doorknob hit the wall.

I caught my breath when I saw who was there.

My stomach churned.

Something told me this wasn't going to be a good day.

Four

Lorenzo and some guy I didn't recognize were standing on the doorstep. Lorenzo's nose was red from the cold. A line of snot ran down past a small black mole to her lip. She wiped it away with the back of her hand.

"We have some more questions we need to ask you," she told me.

"Forget it." I started to shut the door. "I'm calling my lawyer."

"Fine. Tell him to meet you downtown."

"With pleasure."

"Wait," her partner cried. He jabbed the air with his finger for emphasis. "Why complicate things? We're not charging you. All we want to do is clarify a few more facts." He was a weedy-looking man with a receding chin and a surprisingly deep voice. When he smiled I noticed he had a mouthful of bad teeth. "Come on, give us a break. This way we get this over with and we can all get on to other pleasanter things."

I decided the man was probably right. After all, what was the harm? I was in the clear. What did I have to be afraid of? Lorenzo probably had a suspect and just wanted to tie down a few loose ends before she made the collar. I'd answer their questions and they'd leave and everything would be fine. So I told them to come in. Dumb, right? Especially from someone who had been a card-carrying radical in the sixties. I should have known better. But sometimes I just like to believe in fairy tales and happy endings.

Lorenzo and her partner handed me their coats in the hallway. The material smelled of winter, of frost and smoke. When I hung them up, the hairs from the wool scratched my fingers. Lorenzo's shoes left little trails of salt on the Oriental runner as she walked down the hall into the living room. James raised his head and yawned when we entered. He looked like a miniature panther. Dark patches of hair marked the last places he'd slept on the beige sofa. I hadn't vacuumed recently and it showed.

"Big cat," Lorenzo observed as James put his head back down and closed his eyes.

"Twenty-three pounds." I sat down and started stroking his back. "Nasty too." Lorenzo pulled one of the wicker chairs up close to the sofa and planted herself in it. Her partner strolled around the room, picking things up and putting them down.

I nodded in his direction. "Does he have a name?"

"Cunningham. Officer Cunningham," Lorenzo said as she took out her notebook and resettled her glasses on the bridge of her nose. Her skin was still blotchy from the cold.

I watched Cunningham walk over to my bookshelves and started looking through the piles. I had been in the middle of sorting and cataloging them when Murphy died and I'd never had the heart to finish the job.

"You have lots of books on reptiles here," he observed.

"My husband was in the business."

"Did you read them too?"

"No. I just liked to look at the pictures."

He gave me a quizzical glance but before I could say any more Lorenzo coughed and I turned to her.

"Let's get back to yesterday," she said, referring to her notebook. "In our previous conversation you stated that you never saw the person who delivered the package. Is that correct?"

"Yes." I pulled Murphy's robe tighter around my knees and tucked my legs up under me. I wanted a cigarette in the worst way, but they were upstairs.

"You also stated there's a bell that rings whenever anyone comes into the store."

I nodded. From the kitchen I could hear the sound of the Mamas and the Papas on the radio. They were singing "California Dreaming." The West Coast seemed like a real good place to be right now.

Lorenzo clicked her tongue against the roof of her mouth. "But according to his statement, your employee, Tim McDowell, said he didn't hear the bell. How do you account for the discrepancy?"

Thank you, Tim. "Maybe he wasn't listening."

I could hear the weatherman on 94.5 FM announcing the forecast. Cold, sleet, and snow for the next three days.

"Or maybe it didn't ring," Lorenzo said.

"It did."

"Funny, but all we have is your word on that. In fact, all we have is your word that a 'person,'" she stressed the word "person," "left the package with the snake on the counter of your store. Nobody else saw or heard anything."

"Meaning what?" I asked even though I could see where the conversation was headed.

Right then is when I should have told them to leave, but I

couldn't. I had opened the box. Now something compelled me to see what was inside it.

"Meaning, there's no reason why you couldn't have left the package for Mr. Blount yourself."

Cunningham turned away from the mantel and looked at me expectantly.

"I didn't," I said stupidly. It was the best I could do and I could see from Lorenzo's expression it wasn't nearly good enough.

She leaned forward. Her hands gripped the brown wicker chair. "How do we know that?"

"The address wasn't in my handwriting."

"You could have had an accomplice."

"I took John to the hospital."

"So what?" Lorenzo shrugged her shoulders. "You knew he was going to die anyway. You just did that to make yourself look good."

"If I had wanted to kill him," I snapped, "why wouldn't I have just dropped the thing off at his house and saved myself all that trouble?"

She leaned even farther forward. We were now almost nose to nose.

"*Did* you want to kill him?"

I jumped up. "Get real."

Lorenzo leaned back slightly and put her hands on her thighs. "Oh, but I am," she said enunciating each word. "Very real."

I heard a harsh, rasping noise. It took me a few seconds to realize it was me breathing hard. It was the only sound in the room. Cunningham turned back to the mantel and picked up my Leica.

"This yours?"

I nodded, glad for the distraction.

"Nice camera. Expensive. You shoot lots of pictures?"

"At one point."

"Professionally?"

"I've had them in print, if that's what you mean."

"You're a real talented lady. You write. You take pictures. What else do you do?"

"Nothing that would interest you."

"Don't be too sure." Then Cunningham turned away from me and moved toward the oak table and paisley armchairs that flanked the fireplace, brushing everything he passed lightly with his fingertips.

"Sit down," Lorenzo ordered.

When I lowered myself back down on the sofa James opened his eyes and twitched his tail, a sign he was feeling peevish. He leaped off the sofa, jumped onto the windowsill, and stared at a blue jay sitting on a branch of the maple in my side yard. James was the reason I no longer had a bird feeder.

"How well did you know Mr. Blount?" Lorenzo asked abruptly.

"Not well at all."

"But you did know him?"

"He worked at my husband's store."

"Spend time with him?"

"As in how?" I tucked my feet back in under me.

"Lunch, dinner, a beer."

"No."

Cunningham came up behind me. "You sure?" he whispered in my ear. The hair on the back of my neck stood up.

"I'm sure," I answered.

"Why?" Lorenzo demanded. "Didn't you like him?"

I hadn't. Though I hadn't said that to George the other day when he'd taken my statement. But there had been something about John, something off-kilter that I couldn't put my finger on. Maybe it was because I always felt as if he were smirking at me. As if he knew a secret I didn't.

And I wasn't real fond of the pleasure he seemed to take in watching the big snakes eat.

It gave me the creeps.

And since I'd taken over the store I'd had the feeling he was doing business on the side. But when I'd asked him, he'd denied it and stalked away leaving me feeling foolish. So I'd dropped the matter because I wasn't sure. Even though I suspected I was right. But I certainly wasn't going to say that to Lorenzo and give her something, no matter how thin, to work with. Instead I told her I didn't know him very well.

Lorenzo raised an eyebrow indicating her disbelief then turned a page in her notebook. "Let's go on to something else. Did you and your husband have a good relationship?"

"Yes."

"Are you sure?"

"Of course I'm sure. Not that I see where that's any of your business."

She leered. "Everything—and I do mean everything—about you is my business now."

I barely managed to keep myself from smacking her across the face.

"So, you two talked to each other?"

"People usually do when they live together." A lie. In the last year we'd always seemed to be passing each other. If he was going in, I'd be going out. And vice-versa.

"You discussed your work with each other?"

"When we had the time." For some reason my palms were sweating while my feet were freezing.

"Then maybe you can answer a question for me?"

"What?"

Lorenzo handed me a sheet of typing paper. It was filled

Chutes and Adders   **35**

with doodles and scribbled phone numbers. "Do you recognize the writing on this?"

"Yes. It's mine."

She took it back and held out three sheets of yellow legal paper. "Now I'd like you to look at these."

I scanned them hurriedly. Each paper was divided into two columns labeled A and B. Column A listed a variety of snakes and lizards, some of which I noticed were illegal to import into the States, while column B stated their prices.

"Do you recognize the writing?"

"It's Murphy's."

"And these." Lorenzo handed me two more sheets.

"I think," I replied after I scrutinized them for a minute, "that John wrote these."

"Thank you." Lorenzo took the sheets of paper back. "You know what you've been looking at?"

"Price lists?"

"Very good."

"Did you also happen to notice that every reptile on these pages is either venomous or a protected species?"

"I noticed. What of it?"

Lorenzo tapped the papers with her nails. "The reptile curator found these papers in the heat vent while he was looking for the saw-scaled viper." Lorenzo paused. "They were wrapped around fifty grand. Now, what do you have to say about that?"

I was too stunned to say anything at all.

Five

"Don't want to talk?" Lorenzo asked. "That's okay. I will. I'll tell you what I think happened and when I'm done you can tell me whether I'm right or wrong." She took a Kleenex out of her pocket and wiped her nose. "Now the way I read the situation is that you and Murphy and John were running a racket. You guys were selling reptiles off the books—all kinds of reptiles. Whatever people wanted you got for them."

"You're nuts," I said even though I could see Murphy doing what Lorenzo was describing. He'd always been free and easy when it came to legalities.

"Am I?" Lorenzo replied. "I don't think so." Then she continued. "For a while everything went along perfectly. It was the perfect scam. Big bucks, minimal risk. Then Murphy OD'd and the shit hit the fan. Now I don't know what happened between you and John." Here Lorenzo looked at me. "Maybe you two had an argument. Maybe you just got greedy and wanted all the money for yourself . . ."

"But . . ." I interjected.

"No. We know you and John weren't getting along after your husband's death."

"We?"

"People talk. Tell us things. We have signed statements to that effect."

"Well then maybe those people told you that the only differences John and I had centered around the direction the store was going to take."

Lorenzo held up her hand. "Let me finish. In any case, I'm guessing that at some point after your husband's death you took the fifty Gs and hid it."

"I didn't even know the money was there!" I protested.

"Naturally," Lorenzo continued, ignoring my interruption, "John wasn't going to just sit by and watch his money go south and after a while you must have realized that too so you decided to send him a little present." Suddenly Lorenzo leaned forward, clasped my hands, and fixed me with a gaze of luminous sincerity. "Tell me what really happened. If you do, I think I can promise that the DA will reduce the charges."

"Get out." I yanked my hands away and stood up. I was trembling. Lorenzo stood up too, all the while shaking her head sadly like a mother troubled by a recalcitrant child. "You're making a mistake."

"No," I replied. "My only mistake was letting you two in my house in the first place."

"No. Your mistake is thinking you can get away with this."

The moment Lorenzo and Cunningham left I ran into the kitchen and called my lawyer. Fortunately he was in. When I told him what had happened, he was briefly silent, overcome no doubt by the enormity of my stupidity. In retrospect so was I. But grief had made me slow in more ways than one.

"So you don't know anything about the snake?" Joe demanded a minute later.

"No. Of course not."

"And you had no reason to want to kill John?"

"What kind of question is that?" I couldn't believe what I was hearing from him. "You're as bad as the cops."

"Relax. Listen, I had to ask. It's my job. I have to know what I'm dealing with here."

"Well you asked and I told you."

"Fine. Now let's go on to something else."

James jumped up on the counter and rubbed himself against my arm. I scratched him under his chin and he closed his eyes.

"The paper Lorenzo had, the one in your handwriting . . ." Joe continued.

"What about it?"

"You're sure it was your handwriting?"

"I'm positive."

"Did you get a look at the phone numbers?"

"Really nothing more than a glance. Lorenzo took the paper back pretty fast."

"Did you happen to recognize any of them?"

"No."

"I see." Joe made a clicking noise with his tongue.

James jumped back off the counter and stalked over to his food bowl. "You know what I bet happened?"

"What?"

"That paper was probably from an article I was working on. Murphy must have picked it up by accident. You know how sometimes if you're in a hurry you can grab a whole bunch of stuff off a desk." I had a bad habit of leaving trails of paper wherever I went.

"Forget about the paper for a moment," Joe said. "The paper isn't what's worrying me. We can explain that away. I think."

"Then what is worrying you?" I asked, afraid to hear the answer.

"The fifty thousand dollars the cops found."

"Why?"

"Because it provides a solid motive for John's murder."

"But I didn't know anything about the money."

"We're going to have to prove that."

I shifted the phone to the other ear. "Forgive me, but don't you have this backwards? Isn't there such a thing as presumption of innocence? Aren't the cops the ones who have to prove that I knew about the money?"

Joe sighed. "Theoretically yes. Practically speaking no. What the cops have to prove is that there is a strong possibility you knew about the money. That you were in a position to acquire the snake. That you gained from the crime. Then they can take their case to the D.A., he takes it to the Grand Jury, they indict, and we get to fight it out in court. Which you don't want to happen, right?"

"Right," I echoed weakly.

"Then here's what I want you to do. First of all, don't say anything to anybody about any of this."

"I won't," I promised.

"Because whatever you say, no matter how innocent you think it sounds, can come back to haunt you in court. Not that we'll get there, but it's always better to be on the safe side. Second: from now on in, the cops want to talk to you, call me."

"I will."

"Good."

"What else?"

"Have you come across any other records of this business Murphy and John were allegedly involved in?"

"No."

"Nothing?"

"Nothing."

Joe clicked his tongue again. "Well, start looking for them. The more we know about what Murphy was doing, the better our chances are of turning up something to refute Lorenzo with." And with that he hung up.

I gripped the receiver until a recording came on and told me to please hang up. I did as I was told and went upstairs. A bitter, metallic taste lay on my tongue as I slipped on my sweatshirt and jeans and pulled my socks and sneakers out from under the bed. I put them on, took a deep breath, walked over to Murphy's closet, and opened the door.

And I thought I had known this man. Well. I knew he was into shortcuts. I knew he liked to skate along the edge. God how could I not? But as I said that's the thing that had attracted me to him in the first place. That and his looks. In a college full of clean-cut collegiate types, he'd been the one with the three-day stubble, the dark glasses, and the motorcycle boots. He'd been the antithesis of the nice Jewish boy. And when he'd flirted with me, I'd practically waltzed into his bed.

Of course over the years I learned he flirted with everyone. But I hadn't cared too much. In a sense I'd even liked it. It was an ego thing. Because I was the one who had him. I was the one he came home to. I was the one he talked to. Or so he said.

I tossed an armful of khaki pants and blue shirts onto the bed so I could get to the cartons on the back shelves.

We had been good together. Our relationship had worked. Or so I thought.

I carried a carton out and tipped it onto the floor by my bed. But the truth was I didn't know what to think anymore. About anything. It was as if somebody had tipped my world upside down the same way I'd tipped the carton over. I picked up an old *Hustler* and tossed it down. Better not to think about things. Better to just attend to business. I thumbed through the old magazines Murphy had been saving. But there was nothing there. No scribbled pieces of paper, no notes in margins. No nothing. The next six cartons yielded the same results. I went through Murphy's old sneakers, the bags of newspapers, the scuba gear, and the high school jackets Murphy had sworn to me he had already thrown out. Zip. When I was done two things were obvious: the closet was empty and what I was looking for wasn't there.

I searched Murphy's dresser drawers. Zero. In a frenzy I moved on to the linen closet, the guest room, and the work-shop down in the basement. I pushed around furniture, pulled up cushions, and even ran my hand behind the refrigerator. An hour later, I stood in the middle of the kitchen, hair plastered to my face, hands black with soot, with *nada* to show for my efforts. There was only one more place I could think of to look—the tree house. I put on my ski jacket, stopped to water my spider plant with the remains of yesterday's coffee, and went into the backyard.

Even in the summer the hill out back is steep enough to make for a hard climb. Now, covered with a glaze of ice, it was nearly impossible. I had to hold on to the chain link fence and pull myself up hand over hand. When I was almost to the top, I let go and half scrambled half slid straight across, grabbing onto tree branches for support as I went. Finally I reached the elm.

The tree house was perched in a fork formed by two of its larger branches. Built by a Mr. Savior for his sons, it was one of the reasons Murphy had bought our house. When the weather was nice, he had read the paper out there. I hadn't joined him, because I don't like heights—a fact I was reminded of when I looked at the ladder going up. Actually it wasn't a ladder so much as pieces of wood nailed to the bark of the tree.

My hand slipped off as I grabbed hold of a slat. It was covered with ice. I picked up a rock lying near my feet and hammered. The ice shattered. I took a deep breath and started up. Finally I got to the top. I pushed the trapdoor open and slithered in. The place smelled of tobacco and smoke—just like Murphy had.

My eyes filled with tears as I gazed at the view from the four windows. Clusters of houses, punctuated by evergreens, dotted the white streets. Plumes of smoke rising from the chimneys of houses drifted into the sky. A pair of cardinals, the male a slash of scarlet, flew by. Then the feeling passed and I got down to work.

It took me less than five minutes to find what I'd come for. The manila envelope was wrapped in a plastic bag and shoved underneath a pile of cushions. I noticed that my hands were trembling slightly as I opened the flap and peered inside.

But there were no papers, no invoices.

What there was were two thick wads of bills and a gun.

I drew the .38 out slowly.

"Just holding it for a friend," Murphy had told me after I'd found it in the hall closet a few months back.

When I'd reminded him that guns made me nervous—it was one of our ongoing arguments, him wanting to have one and my saying absolutely not—and asked him to get it out of the house, he'd agreed. Too bad I hadn't specified off the property. It was typical Murphy. I didn't know whether to laugh or cry as I weighed the gun in my hand. After a minute I put down the revolver, picked up the money, and began counting. The bills felt worn in my hand. They were all fifties and hundreds, twenty thousand dollars worth of them.

First the fifty thousand and now this. As I refastened the

rubber bands around the money, I kept on thinking of all the scrimping and saving I'd done since Murphy had quit his job at the ad agency and opened Noah's Ark. The trips not taken, the books not bought, the movies and plays not seen. "Go ahead," I'd said, "if it makes you happy, it makes me happy," I'd said. "We're a team."

What a fool I'd been.

And I couldn't even yell at him.

I felt betrayed.

And angry.

And sad.

Then I remembered Lorenzo and panicked. Now was not the time for self-pity. I could feel sorry for myself later. Now was the time to get this stuff the hell out of the house because if Lorenzo came back with a search warrant and found it, she'd probably arrest me on the spot. I stuffed the money and the gun back in the envelope and half slid, half ran down the hill. As I climbed the porch steps I thought about calling Joe, but nixed the idea on the basis of taking care of first things first. I'd talk to him after I'd put the envelope in a safe place. And maybe I'd just tell him about the gun. Not the twenty thousand I'd just found. After all this was Murphy's money. And I was going to need it. Especially if I had to pay for Joe's services. And even if I didn't have to, I was still entitled to it. I figured I deserved it for what Murphy had put me through.

The phone was ringing as I came through the door. I ignored it as I looked for my car keys. After four rings the answering machine clicked on. One of my friends came on the line and asked me to call her so we could go out to a movie together. Or something. Kate was just finishing up when I spotted my keys peeking out from a pile of junk mail. I grabbed them and started toward the door. I figured on heading for the store. I could hide the package there. It was the last place the cops would look, given that they had already searched it. I only hoped the place wasn't still roped off. If it was I'd just have to put the envelope in my locker at the *Herald*.

I backed my car out of the driveway and took a right on Crawford, a left on Scot, then another left onto Genesee. For some reason I caught every red light. I was waiting for the one at the corner of Cherry and Olmstead to turn when I noticed Donna walking out of Fay's. She was using a cane. Her shoulder-length brown hair was disheveled. Fatigue had made her sharp features even more angular. She was one of those women who reach their high point at eighteen and then go downhill from there.

I pulled over to the side of the road and got out of my car. I hadn't talked to her since John had died and I felt guilty about that. The very least I could do was to tell her how sorry I felt and see if there was anything I could do. As I got closer I noticed there was a bruise under her right eye.

"What happened to you?"

"Nothing much. I just slipped on some frigging ice going into my aunt's house. I hurt my ankle and got this." She put her fingers up to the bruise and touched it gingerly.

"Do you need anything?"

"I'll be okay." She gave a resigned shrug. "The police talk to you?"

"Twice."

"Did they ask you about some business that Murphy and John were supposed to be involved in?"

I nodded. "I don't know anything about it. Do you?"

"No." Donna raked her hair with her fingers. "Well, I'm getting cold standing out here. Guess I'd better get going."

As I watched her walk to her car I realized I hadn't believed her answer. But I couldn't tell you why that was. And then I stopped thinking about it. At that point I had other more important things on my mind. Like a .38 and twenty thousand dollars.

Six

The air was beginning to smell of snow as I drove across town toward Noah's Ark. The closer I got to the West Side the smaller and cheaper the houses became. Cunningham had called the area a Spanish neighborhood. Spanish yes, neighborhood no. What the area was, was a collection of down-at-the-heel houses, grocery stores with bars on the windows, and liquor stores where the proprietors sat in cages and the customers roamed free. If you didn't live around there, you didn't visit.

A dried out Christmas tree shedding tinsel and decorations lay in the middle of Orlando Street. A group of kids were setting off firecrackers next to it as I passed by. I made a left on Spoon, drove two more blocks, then parked in front of the store. A sprinkling of gawkers were milling around on the sidewalk. Crime scene tapes seem to attract people the same way fruit attracts flies. It took me a moment to spot the plain-clothesman. He was sitting across the street in an unmarked maroon Mustang drinking coffee and thumbing through the paper. I walked over, identified myself, and asked if I could get inside the store.

He shook his head and turned the page. "Sorry, babes. No can do. You got to talk to the boys downtown." Then he yawned and went back to the sports pages.

I walked next door to El Gordito's to make the call. The grocery store's blue walls were splattered with graffiti, its two narrow front windows covered with chicken wire. The sign above the door had fallen down two years ago and never been replaced. A tall, thin Cuban named Sam Ramirez ran the place. A former professor of literature at the University of Havana, he had come to Syracuse via Miami and New York and stayed because, as he had said, he had nowhere else to go.

The door banged shut behind me when I walked in. The steel plate reinforcing it made the door heavier than it should have been. Before I could say hello, Sam popped his head out from the back to see who was there. I unzipped my jacket. With two space heaters and a radiator going full blast, the place felt like a sauna.

"Mind if I use the phone?" I asked.

"Mi casa es su casa," he replied gravely before withdrawing into the back again.

I took that as a yes and dialed the Public Safety Building, PSB for short. Ten minutes and three people later I'd learned that—yes, probably, maybe, it was very likely that the tape would come down tomorrow. Unless it didn't, of course.

I was quietly cursing when Sam came back out carrying two cups of coffee. "You look like you could use this," he said, handing me one.

As I gratefully sipped the strong, sweet, milky brew I thought once again of how Sam reminded me of a Spanish don. He had the fine features for one—the high cheekbones, the high-bridged nose, and the well-formed mouth. He should have been riding a horse instead of wearing an apron.

Sam combed his mustache with his fingers and tsk-tsked.

"First your husband and now this." He fixed me with his gaze. "You must be careful, *querida.*"

"Why?" I asked, suddenly alarmed. "Are you saying I'm going to be next?"

"No. No. No. Nothing like that."

"Then what are you saying?"

"Just that it is a well known fact that like attracts like. Good calls to good and evil to evil."

"Sam, if you know something . . . anything . . ."

"I know no facts . . ." he insisted shaking his head from side to side to emphasize each word.

". . . then you've got to tell me what it is."

". . . I am only telling you what I feel." He struck at his chest with his fist. Then he bowed, picked up the cups, and headed out toward the back.

"Sam," I called after him, but he didn't even turn around.

I told myself he was just an old man prattling on about nothing. The trouble was: I didn't believe it.

I was still thinking about what he had said as I walked outside. The promised snow had materialized. Little flakes swirling down from the sky melted on my eyelashes and lips. I put my hands in my pockets, buried my chin in the collar of my parka, and hurried toward the cab. I was almost there when I crashed into Manuel Riojas.

"Hey watch it." Manuel rubbed his shoulder. Even though he was sixteen, at five feet four inches he was small for his age. The reedy mustache and skimpy goatee he'd managed to grow warred with his rounded chin, small nose, and delicate jawbone. In spite of the facial hair he looked about ten. Only his brown eyes, nervously darting back and forth, made him look older.

"Sorry."

The kid was blue from the cold. The windbreaker he was wearing was better suited for a spring day.

"No problem." He took a couple of steps forward, stopped dead, then turned around and hurried back over to me. "You know," he said, "my shoulder is hurtin' bad from where you bumped me." He worked his face into a wince. "How about you giving me a lift home? It's the least you can do."

I managed not to laugh out loud. "You've got to be kidding."

Then I spotted Jamal Williams sauntering up the block and understood Manuel's request. Jamal was wearing a triple fat goose down coat on his body and a mean expression on his face.

I looked back at Manuel. His face had turned ashy. "What the hell does Jamal want with you?" I asked him.

"Nuthin."

"Nothing?" I raised an eyebrow.

"I just owe him some money. It's no big deal." He touched his ear. Then he began twirling one of his earrings around. He had three: a star, a diamond stud, and the one he was playing with, a skull and crossbones.

"Well, if it's no big deal then I guess you don't need a lift."

"Come on, Robin," Manuel pleaded, grabbing hold of my arm, the time for playing cool apparently past. "That dude's gonna beat the shit out of me."

I didn't disagree, because from what I'd heard of Jamal he would have. It was what he did.

"Please."

I relented. Manuel might be a pain in the butt, but he didn't deserve to have his jaw wired up for the next six months.

I nodded toward the car. "Okay, let's go."

We were just a couple of feet away from the cab when Jamal spotted Manuel.

"Hey, Manuel," he cried and put on a burst of speed.

Manuel and I ran.

"Hurry up," Manuel yelled from inside as I struggled with the cab door lock.

"Fuck you. You want to do this?" The key turned. I wrenched the door open, slid in, and started up the motor.

Jamal was less than three feet away when I pulled out from the curb.

Manuel rolled down the cab window and stuck his head out. "Hey," he yelled to Jamal as we took off. "I'm getting your shit now." Then he fell back in the seat. "I hope he believes me," he added glumly.

"For your sake I hope he does too."

As we went back past the Rite Aid Pharmacy, Manuel pulled a pack of Camels out of his shirt pocket, offered me one, and took another for himself.

"Damn." He patted his pants pockets.

I looked over. "What's the matter?"

"I'm just lookin' for my lighter."

I handed him my matches. "Here. Use these."

He lit up. "Yo . . ."

"Yes?" I replied as I turned on the radio.

"You guys ever find that viper?"

"Not yet."

"That guy Karkoff tells me that snakes go for hot water pipes. Maybe you should be looking there."

I shot Manuel a curious glance. Ken Karkoff was the head curator of the reptile and bird section of the Burnett Park Zoo. Not exactly a person in Manuel's usual social sphere.

"My last community service," he explained as he drummed

his fingers on the door handle. "John fixed it up for me. He was nice that way."

I wondered what Manuel had done for him in return. In my experience, the word "charitable" had not been a part of John's vocabulary.

"Yeah, John was an okay dude."

"If you say so."

Manuel's drumming got louder. I stopped for a red light.

Suddenly Manuel opened the cab door and stepped out into the street. "Thanks for the lift," he said. And then before I could say anything he took off. Weird kid.

I watched him half jog, half run across Oswego Street, dodging the cars as he went. He ran past Christo's record store, turned the corner, and disappeared. When the light turned green, I continued on to the *Herald Journal*. I had been planning on taking Manuel home, but in truth I was just as glad to see him go. The sooner I got rid of the money and the gun sitting in the glove compartment the better I would feel. I took a right on Dale and headed toward Clinton Square. I figured on putting the envelope in my locker down at the *Herald*.

Then tomorrow I'd pick the envelope up and hide it somewhere in the store.

It was a good idea—one that would have worked.

There was only one problem.

After I got downtown and parked the car, I discovered the envelope had disappeared.

Seven

I couldn't believe it.

I stared into the glove compartment hoping the envelope would somehow magically reappear.

It didn't.

I searched the car. The envelope wasn't there. Not that I thought it would be, because I knew where I had put it. I just couldn't think of anything else to do except keep looking. I was like a robot on automatic pilot. Then on my third pass through I found the lighter, a fancy gold one with three diamonds on it, lying all the way under the front seat.

And I remembered.

I remembered Manuel saying he had lost his.

And I remembered something else.

When Manuel and I had gotten into the car back at Noah's Ark, I'd had to stop and unlock my door while Manuel had scooted right in. But I was positive I'd locked both doors before I'd gone into Sam's. Which meant somebody had been in the car.

And then I recalled one last thing: when I'd bumped into Manuel, he'd been coming from the direction of the cab.

I hit the steering wheel with my hand. No wonder the little bastard had practically jumped out of the car when I'd stopped for the red light. If it hadn't been for Jamal, Manuel would never have gotten in the cab in the first place.

I was in a grim mood as I nosed the car out onto West Genesee. Was this what Sam had meant when he'd told me to be careful? When he'd said that good attracted good and bad attracted bad?

Goddamn.

The kid had my money and the gun.

I had to find him.

I spent the next couple of hours checking everywhere I could think of, but nobody had seen Manuel, or if they had, they weren't saying. I continued searching, circling the same areas again and again. But I didn't have any luck. For the moment Manuel had disappeared. Finally I pulled into the 7-Eleven over on Village Place to get a pack of cigarettes. As I walked by the trash cans, two half-starved German shepherds stopped pulling apart the plastic garbage bags long enough to watch me. Empty milk cartons, orange rinds, coffee grinds, and chicken bones lay spilled out on the snow. I stepped around the mess, went inside, and bought a pack of Camels and a couple of Snicker Bars. As I was paying, I noticed a sticker on the cash register. It said VISIT THE BURNET PARK ZOO.

And I recalled what Manuel had said about Karkoff.

The zoo wasn't that far away from where Manuel had run out of the car. Maybe the kid had gone up there. It was certainly worth checking out.

Even though the snow had picked up, the streets were still clear. It took me about twenty minutes to drive over. As I went up the hill, a line of four school buses passed. Two kids in the back of the last one waved. I waved back. When I was a kid, my father had taken me to the Bronx Zoo every Sunday. It had been our thing. We saw the bears, watched the seals, visited the lions, then had lunch in the cafeteria and went home. He'd died when I was eight and I'd never set foot in a zoo again until last year when I'd been hired to write a series of articles about the renovation at the Burnet Park Zoo. I'd needed the money too much to say no.

The psychologist I'd gone to about three weeks after Murphy died said I was taking his death so hard because I'd never resolved the loss of my father. He said I had a lot of grief work to do. When I'd replied I'd rather work as a waitress he hadn't been amused. So I left. Being there hadn't been my idea anyway. I figured I'd just muddle along and sooner or later everything would work itself out. And if it didn't, what the hell, I could always end it.

I parked as close to the entrance as I could get. The zoo had been built right on top of a hill and in the winter the wind turned sharp and mean. If Manuel was up here, he'd be somewhere in the buildings. The woman sitting behind the ticket counter was wearing two sweaters and a down vest. I described Manuel, told her I was supposed to meet him in the entrance area, and asked her if she'd seen him.

She glanced up from the Harlequin Romance she was reading. "We get so many kids running around here each day, I can't keep track of them all." She held her place open with her thumb. "Do you want to talk to someone in security?"

I leaned on the counter and favored her with a smile. "Maybe I just misunderstood," I lied. "Perhaps if I could just walk around and check . . ."

"I don't see why not," the ticket seller said and went back to her reading.

I went through the turnstile down a corridor labeled ADVENTURES IN ANTIQUITY. The walls were covered in fiberglass modeled to simulate the rocky inside of a cave. Plaques hanging along the exhibits traced the evolutionary path from fish to reptiles. I paused at the anaconda's cage.

The snake, all thirty feet of it, lay curled up in its pool of water. A couple of weeks ago, I'd heard it had nearly snagged a keeper who had walked in there by herself. Being four foot eleven and weighing less than one hundred pounds was a definite disadvantage on a job like that. Fortunately, she had turned out to be a fast runner; otherwise she would have been a half digested bulge in the snake's belly. A staff member went by and I asked where Karkoff's office was.

"He's in his lab. Through there," he said, waving his hand toward the bird room before he hurried on.

I went in. The large room gave off the same air of sadness that pastel-colored houses in the tropics did on a gloomy winter's day. The ceilings were high, skylights supplied most of the light. A narrow path meandered between the trees. A plaque at the entrance listed the birds in residence. Most seemed to be sleeping, except for two orange kingfishers, their color garish in the grayish light, who were engaged in a noisy territorial squabble. Beneath them an egret was methodically emptying the contents of his food dish into the water. I continued on.

In the next area, a mother, father, and baby gibbon were sitting on a tree branch, desultorily picking at bits of food. Their cage was bare except for a few ropes hanging from the ceiling. So much for the promised enriched environment I'd written about.

"They don't seem happy, do they?" a voice behind me asked.

I turned. It was a pale-faced woman with a toddler in hand.

"No, they don't," I agreed. I walked on, feeling guilty. She had clearly wanted to talk and I didn't want to be bothered.

I found a door marked STAFF around the next corner, opened it, and slipped inside. The zoo, I realized once again as I walked down the hallway, was really a theater. The exhibitions were the stage, the animals were the actors—albeit unwilling ones—and the real work was done out back.

I paused to read the notices tacked up on the bulletin board. There was an announcement of grants being given for travel to Australia and Africa; the date and time of the staff Christmas party; a variety of job notices from all over the country. Nothing much of interest. At least not to me. I went on.

Gray walls, gray linoleum floors, I could have been walking down any office corridor. The place was so quiet I could hear the hum of the heating system. No one seemed to be around. Either everyone was in a meeting or they'd gone home. Karkoff's lab, which was where I'd interviewed him, was one of the next three rooms. I just couldn't remember which one.

The first door I tried was locked. The second opened. I stepped inside. The room was good-sized, but cluttered enough so that care had to be taken walking through it. Three of the walls were lined with metal shelving. The fourth was taken up with a big sink and a number of garbage cans.

A person was emptying the contents of a paper bag into the garbage can. When I came in, he stopped what he was doing and glanced up. His eyes narrowed. But I smiled because I'd lucked out. It was Karkoff. He was dressed in a white shirt and black pants, just like the last time I'd seen him. The pants were too tight, calling attention to his high waist and long skinny legs. His face was round, his skin almost gleamingly clean. His eyes were blue and moist, his lips so chapped that they were cracked and scabbed. A few wisps of mud brown hair stuck out of his Alaskan trapper's hat, the kind men wore in the Gold Rush days. He'd been wearing it when I'd interviewed him last year too. Only today the ear-flaps were up. Then they'd been down.

"Remember me?" I said to him in my most cheerful voice.

"Of course." He put the bag down and came toward me. His expression was less than friendly. "Robin Light. Wife of the late, not always lamented, Murphy. Writer of puff pieces for that rag they laughingly call a newspaper. Present proprietress of Noah's Ark."

"Are you always this insulting?" I asked him as I struggled to keep a lid on my temper. I was here to learn something, I reminded myself. Not get into a fight.

"Insulting? Oh dear. And I believed I was just being truthful."

Asshole, I thought but I took a deep breath and asked him if he'd seen Manuel. After all, that kid was running around with my twenty thousand. The last thing I wanted to do was get into an argument with someone who might know his whereabouts. But I needn't have bothered restraining myself because Karkoff didn't know diddly. At least that's what he said.

"Oh, dear me no," he replied as he stroked his chin with his hand. "The lad hasn't been around here in months."

"He said he used to work for you."

"He did help me out once in a while, but nothing more. Unfortunately I had to let him go. He turned out to be a rather unreliable sort."

"Unreliable?"

Karkoff's fingers closed around a misting bottle. "I don't like to talk about people behind their backs."

Right. "So you haven't seen him."

"I already told you I haven't."

Then Karkoff went over to a wooden box painted drab olive and opened the door. An impossibly bright green snake sat on a branch. It opened its mouth and hissed. "Emerald tree boa," Karkoff informed me as he misted the snake. "We're trying to get a breeding colony started. Very hard to do, because they're a canopy species. They live in the treetops," he explained. "Nasty things." He pointed at its mouth. "You get bitten by one of those and you'll need a plastic surgeon. Of course, if you get bitten by a saw-scaled viper you'll need a mortician." He laughed at his own joke, a high-pitched whinny that lasted for a few seconds, before he got himself back under control. "Most snakes are really quite docile unless disturbed, but those little saw-scales will go right for you."

"Frankly, I don't think this particular one is going to be going anyplace," I replied. "I think he's dead. From the cold."

Karkoff closed the door and went on to the next box. "Is that what you think?"

"Yes it is," I answered.

"Well for your sake I hope you're right."

"I hope so too. You seem to know a lot about those particular snakes."

"I know a lot about all snakes. Obviously reptiles are my special passion. They are a marvelous, much maligned species. Of course most people don't share my enthusiasm. I find they have an absolutely irrational fear of reptiles. Do you?"

"No, not at all."

"Really?" Karkoff smiled as he put the second snake back in its box and latched it. He looked genuinely happy. Then he walked over to a closet door on the far wall and beckoned for me to follow. "Come," he said. "I want to show you something."

I was about two feet away when Karkoff opened the door. At first I didn't see anything but a water bowl on the floor and a tree branch running diagonally up to the ceiling. I stepped closer. A dark mass on the floor uncoiled itself and slithered

Chutes and Adders   **59**

upward. It looked down at me, fixing me with its eyes. Then it spread its hood.

"It's a king cobra," Karkoff said proudly.

"I know what it is." I kept my voice even. I wasn't going to give this man the satisfaction of seeing how scared I was.

The snake's tongue flicked in and out, seemingly keeping time with my breathing.

"I call him Rajah." There was real affection in Karkoff's voice. "Don't you want to say hello?"

"Not really." I concentrated on staying still. If I didn't move fast, the odds were I wouldn't upset him—which was the last thing I wanted to do. I calculated that baby had enough venom in him to kill me plus two or three other people. Very, very slowly, I put my right leg back and then my left.

Rajah moved slightly forward. I froze.

"He won't hurt you," Karkoff said.

"If you don't mind, I think I'd prefer not to take a chance."

"He can feel the fear you told me you haven't got. All those little vibrations you send out. He can sense every one. As I was saying before, snakes are marvelous examples of adaptation to their environment. They're almost perfect in that regard. Did you know that they rarely miss their prey?"

"Let's just skip the nature lesson."

Rajah hissed. His hood fanned all the way out again.

"I'd keep my voice down if I were you," Karkoff remonstrated. "We don't want to get him upset, do we?"

"No, we don't," I murmured. "Could you please close the closet door."

But Karkoff went on as if he hadn't heard me. "We got him about four months ago. He was in awful condition then. Had ticks, parasites, the whole nine yards. It took hours of work to get him back in shape. His scales are so beautiful now, so shiny."

I didn't say anything, couldn't say anything. I was frozen in fear, conscious only of my own breathing, my own smell.

"The police found him during a drug bust. He was sitting on two bags full of cocaine. His cage was filthy. It hadn't been cleaned in months."

I took a quarter step back. Rajah's tongue flicked in and out. He was smelling me, but he didn't move.

"Too bad John and your husband didn't take more pains checking out their buyer's character. But, after all, they had their five thousand dollars. What did they care? I can't abide people like that. Even though from time to time I've been forced to deal with them."

"Why blame me for what my husband did?" I protested as I took another small step back. Rajah watched, but stayed still. Soon—if all went well—I'd be out of the snake's striking range. "I didn't have anything to do with his business."

"You knew."

"You're out of your mind." I took another step. And another.

"Stop lying."

"I'm going to report you for this," I said when I was on safe ground. My voice was shaking with anger.

But Karkoff didn't answer. I watched in horror as he glided over to the closet. The snake turned his head and looked at him. Karkoff held out his arm. "Come to Mommy," he crooned. Rajah hesitated for a minute and then slithered onto Karkoff's arm and worked his way across Karkoff's chest. Karkoff waited until the snake was within easy reach of his other hand before he grabbed him by the neck.

"Come, say hello."

I looked around. There was no place to go. I couldn't go forward. Karkoff was blocking my path. I couldn't go sideways. I had a wall on my left and shelving on my right. So I did the only thing possible. I went backward. For every step I took back, he took another one forward. We were a couple locked in a dance. Finally I couldn't go any farther. My path was blocked by garbage cans and a table.

Karkoff lifted Rajah up.

"Time to get acquainted," he said as he draped him across my shoulders.

Eight

The cobra arched his body and stared at me. He stayed that way for a thirty-second eternity. Then he dropped back down and started swaying slightly. I stopped moving. I stopped breathing. The snake reared up again and brought his head under my chin. He began poking at the neckband of my sweatshirt. Then he raised it and slithered inside. I could feel him, cold and heavy, moving between my breasts as he made his way down to my waist.

"The only way to understand snakes is to hold them," Karkoff was saying from what seemed like a long ways away. "I've even slept with mine."

Rajah's head poked out of the bottom of my sweatshirt. He started back up my torso. When he got to my shoulders, he draped himself over them, a heavy weight bearing down on me. Beads of sweat ran down my forehead. Rajah's face came up level with my eyes. We stared at each other. His eyes were cold and flat. I remember thinking this is what a mouse feels like before the cat pounces. Then Rajah hissed and drew his head back to strike.

Karkoff grabbed him before he did.

He smiled. "Wasn't it you who wrote that a trip to the zoo should be an educational experience? Oh, by the way," he continued. "You might like to know that Rajah is defanged. Unfortunately, he came to us that way."

I edged my way around the table and ran for the door.

"Hey," Karkoff called after me, "can't you take a joke?"

After I finally managed to light a cigarette—I had trouble because my hands were shaking so violently—I sat in the car and watched the snow fall and told myself that I was fine, that Karkoff was just an asshole with a sadistic sense of humor. That he'd been getting back at my husband through me. That I'd learned something: he disliked both Murphy and John. But none of that mattered. I was still trembling with rage when Karkoff came out of the zoo ten minutes later.

He walked fast, almost trotted, looking neither right nor left. The flaps on his hat bobbed up and down in the wind. He reminded me of a bird, one of those large ones with small wings. God how I wanted him to turn toward me. I wanted to see the expression on his face when I drove toward him. I'd stop maybe an inch away, maybe less. Or maybe I wouldn't stop at all. Seeing his expression would give me pleasure. A lot of pleasure. Perhaps I'd tell him how he had to learn to love cars by experiencing them.

I was still thinking about doing it when the son of a bitch got into a rusted out, gray station wagon and took off. *Next time, babes,* I thought as he tore out of the parking lot. *Next time you're mine.* I watched him blow his turn onto the access road, hit the divider with his rear wheel, and skid to the other side before regaining control.

This was a man in a hurry. Too much of a hurry. Then it hit me. Maybe, when I'd talked to him I'd pressed one of his buttons without knowing it. Maybe he knew where Manuel was.

After all, he hadn't said that he didn't. He'd just said that Manuel wasn't there. Maybe he was heading to him right now. Maybe Karkoff had given the viper to Manuel and Manuel had delivered the package. That would certainly explain why Karkoff had acted the way he had. Yes, it certainly would.

I put my foot on the gas and went after him. I took care to stay well behind. Not that it mattered because snow was covering the wagon's rear window, but I did it anyway just to be on the safe side. As Karkoff went skittering down the icy twisting park lane, I realized that I was as crazy as he was for going that fast. At one point, it looked like he was going smack into a tree, but he pulled out of the slide at the last second.

I caught up to him at the West Geddes exit. Karkoff waited for a spot to open in the traffic and then went. I hung back a ways, then followed him onto the avenue, taking care to stay three or four cars behind. The snow was coming down harder now, big wind-driven flakes of the stuff, covering everything, making the road greasy with slush. It was fender-bender weather. In some ways, though, the storm made things easier for me. Without it, Karkoff might have noticed my car, it not being exactly inconspicuous.

As it was, we drove up Geddes more or less in tandem for the next several blocks. Traffic was slow, down to less than twenty miles an hour, with lots of stopping and starting as everyone groped their way along. I was fiddling with my heater, trying to get some more hot air, when Karkoff put his blinker on and switched lanes. I followed without looking.

There was a loud honk. A yellow snowplow loomed up alongside me. I jammed on my brakes and it roared through. Three more cars passed before I could get into the left lane. By then, Karkoff had turned and I was stuck, cursing, behind a red light.

Fortunately, he hadn't gone very far. I spotted him haloed

under the streetlight midway down Oswego Street. We were back in Manuel's neighborhood. I felt a surge of excitement. Maybe, I'd been right. Maybe, I'd hit pay dirt. I parked in back of a Ford pickup and watched. Karkoff walked up to a house located in the middle of the block and banged on the door. It opened almost immediately and he slipped inside.

I sat in the car watching the flakes slanting in on the wind. A car drove by me, another fool out on the road. On the radio, the announcer was busy telling everyone to drive carefully and to avoid Route 81. There was a ten-car pileup around Tully, but then again there was always a ten-car pileup around Tully.

Finally I slipped the can of Mace I carry in the car ever since I'd been mugged into my jacket and got out. At least this time, if something else happened, I'd be prepared. I'd had enough surprises for one night. The wind whipped the snow into my eyes and mouth. I reached behind me, fumbled for my hood, and put it up. By the time I got to the house, my cheeks were stinging from the cold.

The steps were slick, with snow on top and ice underneath. I had to put my hand out to keep from falling. The house's air of desolation was almost palpable. The porch railing was missing most of its wooden posts. The bottom windows were boarded up and covered with torn plastic. An old sofa, hemorrhaging springs, sat off to one side. A multicolored kite with a tail made out of an old stocking lay frozen across it. It would be spring before it thawed out.

The house number, 2559, was written on a new piece of paper with a blue ballpoint pen and taped to the mailbox. The numerals were shaky, as if someone's hand had been trembling when they wrote them, and the two had an odd slash across the top. I leaned closer, trying to read the name. But the paper it was written on was old and weathered and the writing was smudged to near illegibility. The first letter looked like an "r" or maybe it was a "b." The second was definitely an "a," while the third was an "m." Or maybe an "n." I gave up.

I was standing on the porch, finger on the buzzer, trying to work up the nerve to ring it, when I thought I heard Manuel's voice floating in the air. I looked up and saw two figures down the block. As they came nearer, I realized it was Manuel and his friend Shannon. Seeing both of them together didn't surprise me. In the last six weeks, I'd rarely seen them apart. I'd spotted them smoking cigarettes outside of El Gordito's, shooting hoops in the covered court outside the Boys' Club, and running from the truant officer.

Two weeks ago while driving home from work I'd noticed both of them spray-painting their names on the walls of the Brighton overpass. When I'd yelled out to them, they'd run.

But not this time.

Because this time they weren't going to see me.

I crept back down the steps as quietly as possible.

They kept coming closer. I held my breath and prayed.

They were under the streetlight now. Little snow speckles dusted Manuel's hair and jacket. He looked wet, cold, and miserable. But then who wouldn't be? Even a penguin would have tucked his head under his wing by now. I stepped onto the pavement and grabbed his arm.

Manuel's head snapped up. His eyes widened. His mouth dropped open.

"I think you and I have something to discuss," I said, tightening my grip.

Unfortunately, I hadn't counted on his strength. He moved his arm up, twisted it, then brought it down hard. I could feel my fingers loosening and then his arm was free. I made another grab for it, but it was too late because by then Manuel and his friend had turned and were sprinting up the alley between the two houses.

I went after them, but by the time I got to the end they had disappeared. As I stumbled over a garbage can lid someone had left lying out in the driveway, it occurred to me that this was Manuel's territory, not mine and that he was wearing sneakers and I was wearing boots.

I stood there panting, watching my breath turn white, and thought about what to do next. Basically, it came down to three choices. I could go left, right, or straight. I had decided on left, possibly a political rather than a tactical decision, when I heard a meow. A skinny, ginger tabby padded out from beneath a cast-off pile of lawn furniture and began rubbing herself against the side of my boot.

I leaned down and gave her a pat. The cat lifted her head and I scratched her under the chin. Her ears were torn and ragged and she had a large, festering cut above her left eye.

"Sorry, bud, got to go," I whispered and straightened up.

The cat's eyes widened even more. They glinted in the light.

"Scat."

She wove herself around my feet instead. I was pushing her away with my boot when I noticed something I should have seen before: footprints in the snow—two sets of them. Maybe Manuel wouldn't be so hard to find after all. Of course, the prints didn't have to be his, but then again who was to say they weren't. And anyway, what option did I have?

The waffle-patterned prints turned right and so did I. The cat trotted along beside me. I let it, figuring it would take off when something better presented itself. I avoided piles of old tires and dented garbage cans as I went through one postage-stamp-sized backyard after another. The house and streetlamps threw irregular pools of light onto the snow-covered ground, illuminating some patches to a blinding white and leaving others in the shadows.

As much as possible, I kept to the shadows. This wasn't the kind of neighborhood where people would take kindly to someone roaming around in their backyards at night. At best they'd call the police and at worst they'd come out with a knife or a gun. I was skirting the remains of an old refrigerator when I heard a crash up ahead. I stood still for a second and waited, hoping to hear Manuel's voice, but there was nothing, just silence. The cat meowed. I shushed it and was taking another step forward when someone grabbed hold of my jacket.

I whirled around.

It was Go-Go Nelson, one of the neighborhood's sleazier inhabitants. His smell, a combination of alcohol and vomit, washed over me. He was a tall ruin of a man, with caved-in cheeks, and a body that could have done stand-in duty for a skeleton.

I told him to ease off as I wrenched the cloth away from his grasp.

"Fuck you. I want my money."

"What money?" I asked, taking a step back.

"The money you owe me." He coughed and spat up a big ball of phlegm.

"I don't know what you're talking about."

"You're full of shit."

"I think you're talking to the wrong person."

But Nelson wasn't listening. He was too far gone in his own private alcoholic fog.

"I want what you promised me," he shrieked.

Then he lunged at me. I didn't even have time to scream as his hands went around my throat. I kneed him. He let go. I started to run. But I didn't get very far because a moment

Chutes and Adders   **69**

later I felt his hand on my shoulder. He spun me around, then took his free hand and swung it toward my face.

I saw the punch coming and ducked, but I wasn't quite fast enough. His fist grazed my chin. Before he could try again, I let loose with a kick. This time I connected with his knee. He let out a strangled gasp and dropped my arm. I started running again. He tackled me. As I hit the ground, I remembered the can of mace in my jacket pocket.

Nelson was on top of me by the time I finally got it out. He grabbed my hand with both of his. As we wrestled, I managed to push down the button. The spray went wide, but some of it must have hit his face, because he jerked back, put his hand up to his cheek, and began moaning. I scrambled up and ran. He ran after me lurching along like Frankenstein.

"You . . ." he cried out, holding out one hand while he clawed at his cheek with the other, "you owe me."

I skirted an old chair, sprinted through another yard, turned into a driveway and crouched, panting, beneath a staircase that led up to a second floor. A moment or two later, he came by sputtering obscenities.

After he passed, I sat on the ground and wondered what the hell Nelson had been talking about. Then the cat jumped on my lap and kneaded my leg with its claws. That and the fact that my sweat was freezing on my skin made me abandon my hiding place and leave.

The driveway I was now standing in belonged to one of those large buildings that house three or four families. I looked up. Lace curtains hung in the windows, the woodwork had a fresh coat of paint, and the shrubbery had been bound in burlap to protect it from harsh temperatures. Somebody was making an effort which was nice to see, that being the exception rather than the rule.

The cat meowed again and butted my ankle with her head.

I picked her up and zipped her into my jacket. What the hell. She needed a home and I needed all the good karma I could get. When I hit the street I realized I'd run in a big semicircle. I'd ended up almost back where I started from. I was standing just two doors down from the house Karkoff had gone into. I was about to walk to my car when the front door opened.

I melted into the darkness and waited. I didn't want to meet Karkoff. I'd had more than enough aggravation for one night. People were laughing. I heard Karkoff's voice and somebody's I couldn't identify and then somebody's I could.

I took a peek out just to make sure.

There was no doubt.

I recognized the ponytail.

Nine

Maybe there was a good reason for Tim to be gabbing with Karkoff, but I couldn't think of any.

And I wasn't going to try to either.

In fact I didn't want to think at all.

Tim had been the last unpleasant surprise in a day filled with too many of them.

Instead I went home, fixed the cat some temporary quarters, made myself a giant hot toddy, took a bath, and collapsed into bed.

I awoke the next morning to the sound of the telephone ringing. It was my friend Lynn calling to invite me to a dinner party at her house on Friday. I told her I couldn't go. It wasn't that I didn't like the people she'd invited. I did. They were all nice, but I just wasn't in the mood for polite social chitchat these days. I tried begging off, but Lynn wouldn't take no for an answer. It would be good for me, she kept insisting. Finally, against my better judgment, I yielded and she hung up. The day hadn't even started and I was already in a rotten mood. I hate it when I allow myself to be talked into doing something I don't want to do.

I got dressed, brewed myself some coffee, ate two chocolate bars, swallowed a handful of vitamin pills, and called the PSB to find out when I could get back into Noah's Ark. The animals had to be taken care of. After a fair amount of wheedling and threatening, the guy on the other end of the line, one Vince Barbino, promised me—no fooling around—the tape would come down early that afternoon. Which meant I had about three hours to spend searching for Manuel. I put on my jacket and went out the door.

Who knew? Maybe this time I'd get lucky. After yesterday, I was due for some. It had snowed some more during the night. About six inches of white powder covered my driveway and the guy who plowed hadn't come yet. Fortunately it was the powdery, light kind so it didn't take me that long to shovel. After I was done I went into the garage and greeted the cat. She clawed at me as I was putting her in the car.

I guess she was pissed because I'd locked her in there last night, but I hadn't had a choice. I didn't trust James enough to keep the new cat in the house and since I'd left her food, water, and a litterbox, I figured she really didn't have that much to complain about—an opinion she obviously didn't share. The cat and I spent the rest of the morning driving around the West Side looking for Manuel. But once again I came up empty-handed. Nobody knew anything. I was almost developing a sympathy for the police. Around one o'clock I decided I was hungry and stopped at Burger King.

I placed my order—a couple of hamburgers, a large french fries, and a medium Coke—took it back to the car, and shared it with the cat. As I was pulling out, I happened to get a look at myself in the mirror and winced at the sight. I did not look good. In the daylight, the black-and-blue mark on my jaw stood out like a neon sign. It's true that Nelson's fist had just grazed me, but I had the type of skin that bruised easily and took a long time to heal.

A year ago I would have immediately driven to the nearest drugstore and gotten some coverup, but I didn't have time for that nonsense now. I felt like I had back in college during finals: you got up, put on clean clothes, brushed your teeth, washed your face, ran a comb through your hair, and that was it. Anything else was not relevant to the task at hand.

As I drove out of BK's parking lot and headed for the store, I realized that since Murphy's death I'd slipped back into my college mode and that I was acting as if this were final exam time. And maybe I was right. Maybe it was. And maybe Lorenzo was giving the test. And maybe, I decided as I pulled up in front of the store, I'd better ace it.

The tape was gone. Barbino had been true to his word. I could go in. I tucked the cat in my jacket, got out of the car, and scrambled up over the snowbank to the sidewalk. Then I walked through the snow to the door, opened it, and went inside. Everything looked the same. But it felt different. John's murder had torn a hole in this little corner of the cosmos and let a whole host of things, things I'd rather have not dealt with, in.

"This is it, kiddo."

I unzipped my jacket and plunked the cat down on the counter. She meowed. Even though she'd had half of my hamburger I decided she was probably still hungry. She looked like she had three months of eating to catch up with. I went into the storeroom, dug out a can of mackerel, some dry cat food, three stainless steel bowls, and brought everything back inside. I filled two of them with food, the third with water, put them down on the floor behind the counter, and watched the cat eat.

She gulped the fish down then started on the dry food,

casting furtive glances over her shoulder every other minute. Pickings must have been slim out in the back alleys. It looked like the store had a cat again. She'd take care of the mice, while the geckos ate the roaches. The last cat we had had in here was BJ. He was big and black and had disappeared last May. Since then the rodents had gained ground. Maybe this one would last longer. I ruffled the cat's fur and she purred.

I was taking off my jacket when the phone rang. It was Tim wanting to know if he should come in. I told him to make it tomorrow instead and hung up. I still hadn't sorted out the significance of what I'd seen last night and until I did I wasn't sure I wanted him around.

Maybe I was being unfair.

Maybe what I'd witnessed didn't mean anything.

Maybe the meeting was just coincidence.

Or maybe it wasn't.

I just didn't have enough evidence to make a decision. I *was* going to have to talk to Tim. But not then. I didn't have the energy. I began feeling overwhelmed. There was too much going on.

Little steps for little feet, big steps for big feet, I reminded myself. It had been one of my father's favorite sayings to me. Now it was my mantra.

Translation: one thing at a time.

I made a list of what I had to do.

First I'd take care of the animals, then I'd go back to looking for Manuel, and after that I'd continue my search for Murphy's records. Tomorrow I would deal with Tim. Somehow just having a plan to follow made me feel better. It was like having a map through the land of chaos.

The cat kept me company while I worked. Feeding the fish, testing the water, and making sure the filters were running properly took me over an hour. I spent another couple of hours taking care of the birds. Then I checked on the reptiles. The cornsnake and the ball python were fine, but the heat rock in the anoles' cage was no longer functioning. I found a new one in the storeroom and put it in. Then I tossed ten crickets in the cage and watched the show. Ten minutes later there were none left and the little lizards were back smugly basking under the heat lamp. I continued on, methodically working my way down the rows of cages while Murphy's and John's ghosts scritched and scratched around the edges of the room.

It was so quiet that when the phone rang, I jumped.

"This Noah's Ark?" a deep voice on the other end asked.

I said that it was.

"Well this here is Flying Tigers out at Hancock. You got a package just come in from Herp Inc., down in Fort Myers."

"I didn't order anything." Unbidden, the thought of the package with the saw-scaled rose. A chill ran down my back.

"Well someone did." Then I realized I was being silly. This was just a regular shipment. Something John or Tim had ordered. They'd just forgotten to tell me. "The freight is eighty-five dollars."

"Eighty-five dollars? What the hell is in there?" Eighty-five dollars was about double the normal shipping bill.

"Look, lady, I just work here. You got a beef, you got questions call the company."

I looked at the clock. It was after five. The people down at Herp Inc. would be long gone. They started their day at seven and left by four-thirty.

"So you coming or what?"

I told him I'd be down in a little while and hung up.

So much for my list. But what else could I do? If I didn't pick up the reptiles they'd probably freeze to death, airport hangars not being noted for their high temperatures, and I didn't want that on my conscience. I hurried with the rest of my chores. I finished the reptiles, did the mice, and was filling up the water bottles in the gerbils' cages when I thought I heard a noise on the second floor.

I told myself it was my imagination. There was nothing up there but four rooms full of pet food, cages, gravel, filters, and the like. I started feeding the rabbits. One of the lop-ears hopped over and gently nibbled on my fingers. His nose tickled. He was already sold to a little girl. He was her surprise birthday present. I knew, because I'd helped her mother pick him out. I was thinking about how nice it must be to have a child to make a birthday party for when I heard the sound again.

This time it was an unmistakable thud. I told myself one of the windows had probably broken loose in the storm and was banging against the wall. The latches on the frames were all rusted through. Any stress could cause them to break. I had almost convinced myself of that when I heard the thud a third time. Shit. I had to go up and close that window. Otherwise the snow blowing in would soak through the bags of feed we had stored up there and damage them.

I got out a flashlight. There was no light in the room with the windows. The switch had shorted out months ago and typically Murphy had never gotten around to fixing it. The ceiling light swayed back and forth as I went up the steps to the attic. By the time I reached the top step, my heart was pounding away like I was in the twentieth mile of a twenty-six-mile marathon. I knew I was being silly being scared, but that didn't make me feel any less nervous.

For some reason I thought about my Aunt Rose's farm out in Saratoga. I had been six when we first visited. I had liked everything except the outhouse. At night, I waited until I couldn't hold it anymore. Then I would race down the path and back as fast as I could, not stopping until I was safe back in my bed again, where the night monsters couldn't touch me with their cold, probing fingers. We had gone there every summer for ten years, but I'd never changed my mind about how I'd felt.

It took me a couple of minutes to work up enough courage to push the door open. A weak glint of light from the parking lot washed in through the bank of four windows on the opposite wall. From where I was standing, I could see one of the middle windows moving back and forth.

I breathed a sigh of relief as I hurried across the room.

But three-quarters of the way over, I tripped over something lying on the floor.

Ten

It was Manuel.

He lay sprawled out on his stomach. His arms and legs were splayed out like a starfish. His head was tilted to one side. His eyes and mouth were open. He seemed surprised, as if he hadn't expected whatever had happened to occur.

I thought he was dead. I reached out and touched his hand. It was cold. But when I groped for a pulse, I found it. Under the flashlight's beam, the hair on the back of his head looked wet. I bent down. The coppery scent of blood filled my nostrils. Little white bone fragments stuck out of a gash as long as my hand.

For one sickening second, I had the feeling I could reach out, take Manuel's scalp and pull it off his skull. I gagged, fought down the impulse to vomit, then ran downstairs and dialed 911. After I told them what had happened, I grabbed the throw off the office sofa, and raced back up the stairs. While I was tucking the blanket around Manuel the cat came in and sat down next to his leg.

I leaned over and put my lips almost to his ear. "Manuel, can you hear me?"

He didn't stir.

"Manuel," I whispered, "what did you do with the money and the gun?"

I felt a stab of guilt at asking the question, but I had to know.

But Manuel didn't answer. He couldn't. Looking down at him, I wondered if he'd ever be able to. I forced myself to go through his pockets, but all I found was some loose change. It looked like I was out of luck. Permanently. Unless of course Manuel had stashed the envelope up in the attic. I'd have to look tomorrow in the daylight. What the hell had Manuel been doing here anyway?

Manuel groaned. I squeezed his hand.

Minutes passed like plinking drops of water. Finally I heard sirens. The sound got closer. The rescue squad was coming.

The front door down below banged open.

"Where are you?" A man yelled.

"Up here," I hollered back.

A few seconds later two paramedics ran in and elbowed me out of the way. One knelt by Manuel and began taking his pulse while the other snapped opened his emergency kit.

"He got hit in the back of his head," I told them.

"When?" the one kneeling down asked.

"I don't know. I came up here and found him like this."

"How about some light?"

"There isn't any." I handed the one with the kit my flashlight.

More footsteps on the stairs. Suddenly it was darker. A body was blocking the light from the hallway. "What have we got?" It was one of the ambulance crew.

"Head injury." The guy on the floor slipped an oxygen mask over Manuel's face and started an IV.

The man in the hallway turned and ran back down the stairs. His feet pounded on the steps.

The parrots shrieked.

I crept closer to the circle of light. "How bad is he?" I whispered.

"Bad enough," the guy holding the IV answered. He didn't turn his head when he spoke.

The paramedic came back through the door with the body board. He put a cervical collar around Manuel's neck and then the three men log-rolled Manuel onto the board and strapped him in. They lifted the board up and moved it through the narrow door and down the stairs. Through the open front door I could see the flashing red lights of the rescue squad, the ambulance, and the police car. In Syracuse they always came together, three for the price of one.

"Is he going to die?" Stupid question, but I asked it anyway.

The guy holding the IV bag told me he didn't know.

I started following them, but a policeman blocked my way.

"You want to tell me what happened?" He had his hat tipped back, his pad out, and he looked bored with me, with Manuel, with the whole thing. Another spic kid bashed over the head—big fuckin' deal. Since I'd been down here, I'd become familiar with the attitude.

"That's it?" he said when I got done.

"That's it," I repeated.

He nodded his head in the direction of the stairs. "Show me where you found him." He was so obviously going through the motions I was surprised he had bothered to ask.

I climbed the steps again, slowly this time, with the cop at my back.

"No light?" he asked when we were inside.

"No light." I explained about the switch.

He took out his flashlight and turned it on. The beam washed over the puddle of blood left by Manuel. He crossed the room to study it. I stood by the door, waiting for him to finish, determinedly studying the wallpaper on the landing. It bubbled out where the glue was coming loose. There were water stains where the roof had leaked.

Smudged handprints partially obscured the pictures of the brown puppy and the white kitten huddled together under a scalloped pink umbrella. Somebody, probably one of the children for whom the paper had been intended, had drawn big, bushy tails on several of the puppies. Then he had written his name, Eddie, under the kitten's feet. A penciled-in arrow pointed down to the baseboard. I traced it with my finger. Right above the pink border, someone else had written "Susy was here." Susy and Eddie. They probably had grandchildren by now.

"Hey!"

The policeman beckoned me over to the open window. I stood in front of it, shivering, as snow blew in. It was snowing again. I wondered when it had started.

He pointed to the splotches on the floor. "Looks like he got in here." Then he leaned out the window. "You had any problems with anyone climbing up this trellis before?"

I shook my head.

"You know the victim?" the cop asked. He could have been talking about a stolen bike for all the interest his voice displayed.

"His name is Manuel, Manuel Riojas."

"Address?"

"Number 277 Otisco Street."

"Any idea why he came here?"

"None."

First he had run from me and then he had come back here.

Why? It didn't make any sense. Then I wondered what had happened to Manuel's friend, Shannon. Was he lying somewhere with his head bashed in too?

The cop grunted. He played his light over the rest of the room. There was nothing to see except bags of dog, cat, and rabbit food, cedar shavings, cat carriers, and boxes of different-sized leashes. "What's on the rest of this floor?"

"More of the same."

He snapped his notebook shut. "Mind if I take a look?"

"Be my guest."

He was through in less then five minutes. "I guess that's it," he said, putting his notebook away. "Detectives will probably want to talk to you at some point or other." Then he left.

I didn't think there was any "probably" about it.

But if Lorenzo wanted to talk to me, she was going to have to find me first. I scooped the cat up and locked the store. She'd been meowing and rubbing up against me since I'd been talking to the cop and I didn't have the heart to leave her alone. What the hell. At least I'd have company on my trip out to the airport.

Under the streetlights you could see the snowflakes being whipped this way and that by the wind. It looked like one of those old Christmas scene paperweights that someone had shaken up. I went down Oswego. Two blocks later the street was filled with Department of Public Works trucks and backhoes fixing a water main break. I couldn't go any further. I made a U-turn and went down Shonnard. As I passed Clifford Place, I remembered the C&S Social Club—it was one of Manuel's hangouts—and wondered if maybe Shannon was holed up there. It was worth a quick detour to find out. After all, I was practically there already.

I put the car in reverse, went back about six feet, made a right on Clifford, drove down half a block, parked the cab in

Chutes and Adders   **83**

front of the club, and got out. Rap music spilled out onto the sidewalk. The Club, a misnomer if ever there was one, was set in the middle of a vacant lot. Constructed from cheap tar paper shingles, it was so flimsy that if the Big Bad Wolf had had a go at it, he could probably have blown the place down with a couple of puffs. A sign from the last tenant, boasting the lowest VCR prices in town, still hung in the grimy window. Vacant lots filled with trash ringed the place. The other houses on the block were mostly SROs filled with people whose next stop would be the street, jail, or the psychiatric ward.

I figured I wasn't being terminally stupid going inside, because while I wasn't a homegirl, I'd been around the area long enough for the kids to know my face.

But when I walked in I wondered if I'd been wrong. Everyone stopped talking. Someone clicked the radio off. It was suddenly very quiet, too quiet. The boys, mostly Latinos with a sprinkling of Anglos, Blacks, and Indians, were clustered around a pool table in the center of the room. A couple of stained sofas were pushed off to one side. The walls were pasted over with pinup shots. A keg sat by one wall. Paper cups and cigarette butts littered the floor. The place smelled of cheap stale beer, grass, and mildew.

"What you want here?" a skinny kid with a mop of curly hair that came down to his shoulders asked. He wore spiked wristbands that looked like the real thing. A peace sign was carved into his hand.

I kept hold of the doorknob. "I'm looking for Shannon."

"This is members only," a beefy-looking Indian said.

"I know."

"So how come you're here?" the skinny kid demanded as he drifted toward me.

"I already told you." I kept my tone level.

The Indian kid started closing in on the other side. "That's not good enough."

Everyone was watching.

"A friend of his got hurt." I gripped the doorknob harder. I hoped I hadn't miscalculated the situation or my currency in it. "I wanted to let him know."

"Yeah, like who?" Curly was right in front of me now. He hooked his thumbs in his pants loops and started rocking back and forth on the balls of his feet.

"Manuel Riojas."

"Manuel?" a voice from the back piped up. I looked. It was one of Manuel's friends, the tall one with the teeth that stuck out sideways, the one they called Rabbit. He moved forward a little. "What happened to him?"

"He got hit on the head."

"Holy fuck!" the Indian shook his head and scratched his balls. "Head stuff is bad, man, real bad." He looked like he probably had enough experience to know.

"So, any of you seen Shannon?" I asked again.

No one replied.

"Hey, why the fuck should we tell you?" The skinny kid pushed his face in mine. He seemed to have one mode of expression—belligerence. The others were merely apathetic.

"Because I think he's in trouble."

"Yeah, right," the skinny kid muttered. But despite what he said he must have believed me because instead of saying anything else he ambled over toward one of the sofas, flung himself down on it, and began cleaning his nails with the blade of a pocket knife.

"Shannon ain't got no home," Rabbit informed me. "He just crashes."

"That's right," somebody else said.

"You think maybe he'll turn up here tonight?"

Chutes and Adders   **85**

Rabbit shrugged.

"If he does, tell him Robin Light wants to talk to him."

Not that I thought Shannon would come find me even if he got the message. Why should he? If I were him, I know I certainly wouldn't.

Eleven

The storm had gotten worse since I'd been inside the social club. I knew I should go home—to hell with the reptiles—but I didn't want to. Movement gave me the illusion of doing something and right then doing anything was better than sitting home and doing nothing.

As I drove along Route 81, I thought about Manuel and what he'd done with the envelope; I thought about why Karkoff had acted the way he had with me; I thought about Tim and Karkoff; I thought about John's death and the business he and Murphy had run, and I wondered how all of it fit together.

It was as if somebody had dumped a big jigsaw puzzle on the table and told me to put it together, but all I could connect up were a couple of pieces. Then I stopped thinking and concentrated on my driving. The road was even worse than I thought it would be. At the Liverpool intersection, a tractor trailer leaned into a ditch. Five miles further up another car was off the road, its front end stuck in a snowbank. I turned on the radio.

Snow squalls and blowing and drifting snow were predicted for the rest of the night. Evening activities were being canceled all over the county. The announcer was telling everyone to stay home.

"Hear that, cat?"

She opened her eyes and closed them again. Curled up on the pile of skirts and sweaters I should have brought to the cleaners three weeks ago, she was obviously uninterested in our transportation difficulties.

About five miles before the airport exit visibility suddenly improved. I got onto the road leading to Hancock. Everything on either side of me was white. In another mood I might have found it pretty. Now I felt as if I were driving deeper and deeper into the Arctic tundra. And then the road would end and I'd keep driving until I sank under the snow and suffocated.

The feeling persisted all the way to the Flying Tigers' office. I left the cat in the car—she didn't even lift her head up when I got out—and went up the steps to the office.

Nobody was there when I walked in the door. I pressed the bell and waited. The walls were painted an anemic light blue, the carpet was industrial beige and a sign on the desk informed me that all transactions would be recorded by video camera for my own protection. I made a circuit of the office and studied the potted ivy on a white formica table. It was plastic too. The table was flanked by two pseudo-Scandinavian chairs. I sat down on one of them. It was uncomfortable enough to keep me awake if I'd been tempted to doze off.

The place was not what I had expected. The name Flying Tigers had conjured up visions of stubbled men in leather jackets landing B 52s in the middle of jungle fields. I had expected their office to be old and gritty. I had expected empty Scotch bottles in the trash basket. I had expected a secretary with scarlet nails and a short tight skirt. I had expected romance instead of plastic.

I got up and pressed the bell again, this time twice. A minute later a door in the back opened and a man ambled in. He was short and stocky. His paunch pushed up against the quilted vest he was wearing under his jacket. He had pulled down his ski cap over his ears, emphasizing a bulbous nose. If the sleeves on his jacket had been any longer, he would have reminded me of Dopey.

He looked me over. "Had a rough night, huh?"

I glanced down at myself. Manuel's blood was on my hands, my jeans, and my shirt. With my black-and-blue jaw and uncombed hair, I looked like somebody *I'd* cross the street to avoid.

"In a manner of speaking."

He clicked his tongue against the roof of his mouth in sympathy.

"I'm here to pick up the package for Noah's Ark."

"About time." He motioned for me to follow him. "You Murphy's wife?" he asked as we went back out the door he had come in through.

"What makes you say that?" When we stepped into the freight hangar I could see why he was wearing a vest and hat. If possible, it was colder in there, than it was outside.

"The red hair." He went over to a desk and started rummaging around through piles of paper and old coffee cups. "Tough break. Young guy too. How old was he?"

"Forty-two. What are you looking for?" I asked, changing the subject.

"The manifest. It was here a moment ago. You call the company?"

"It was too late. I'll have to do it tomorrow."

He shrugged his shoulders and kept digging. "Tain't my money."

I glanced around. The place was as big, if not bigger, than a high school gym. Other than two desks, a chair, and a heater, the rest of the space was filled with boxes.

"Found it," Roy said a moment later as he extracted a yellow sheet and attached it to a clipboard.

We started walking.

"Your husband was a real nice guy," Roy remarked. "Always had time for a chat. Used to give me a bottle of Canadian Club at Christmas and Easter every year, regular as clockwork."

Listening to him talk about Murphy hurt, but I didn't want him to stop. It was a little like having a scab on your knee when you where a kid. You kept picking at it even though it bled.

"But them other two bozos . . ." he continued.

"Tim and John?"

"Yeah. Especially that guy John. They was always in a hurry. Never have time to say so much as a thank you. Manners, manners is real important. But folks these days tend to forget that."

As we walked, Roy continued nattering away. He was obviously one of those people who liked to talk. "When I began, I had the other shift, but I like this one better. It's more peaceable, especially at home. My wife, she's getting up when I'm going to bed. Works out better. Guess that's why we've been married for thirty years now." He shook his head in amazement at that fact.

I wondered if Murphy and I would have lasted that long.

Roy poked his fingers back up under his cap and scratched his upper ear.

"Well, this here is it." He pointed to a carton lying on the floor. A sticker saying LIVE, HARMLESS REPTILES was plastered on the front. He stuck out his hand. "Money please."

I forked over the eighty-five dollars and Roy carried the

carton over to a nearby table, then handed me the bill of lading. I quickly scanned it. Standard stuff. Nothing on the manifest seemed big enough to justify the freight charges I had just paid. I'd definitely have to call Herp up in the morning.

"Roy, you got a knife?"

"Sure." He took a box cutter out of his jacket pocket and handed it to me. "You gonna check the shipment out?"

"Doesn't everyone else?"

"Not all the time."

Especially not if it had been illegal stuff, I thought as I slit the tape and opened up the cardboard flaps. Inside the carton was a styrofoam container. I lifted the cover off. A sharp odor stung my nose. Followed by a hint of what? Something rotting? One of the snakes must have died. Terrific.

Four knotted bags nestled between gobs of crumpled up newspaper. Three were cloth. The fourth was plastic. I took the one closest to me out and put it onto the desk. It was warm to the touch. Good. That meant the heating blocks on the bottom of the carton were still working. Otherwise the snakes and the lizards would have been dead a long time ago. As I started to unknot the bag, Roy went over to the other desk, opened the bottom drawer and took out a bottle of Rye and two dirt-streaked jelly jars.

"Have one?" he asked, lifting the bottle.

"Sure, why not?" The alcohol would sterilize the glass.

Roy poured till both glasses were half full. Then he set one down next to me. "Enjoy." He took a gulp and wiped his mouth with the back of his hand. "You wouldn't believe some of the things I've seen come through this here terminal."

"Like what?" The damned knot was tied so tightly I was having trouble loosening it.

"An ocelot."

"An ocelot? Who the hell got an ocelot?"

"Fella lives out in Clay."

I raised my eyebrows. "I wonder what his neighbors think."

"Beats me."

I picked up my glass and took a swallow. The stuff was awful. It smelled bad and tasted worse. When I was a girl, the drunks lying on the sidewalk had stunk of this. I put the glass down.

"Of course, three weeks after that he got himself an alligator. I wonder if he's married?" Roy drained his drink, then poured himself another and topped mine off. "My wife would throw me right out on the street if I came home with things like that."

Finally I pulled the knot apart.

Roy stepped back several feet, which made me wonder if he knew something I didn't.

I opened the bag and peered in. A golden tegu glowered at me. Even curled around in the confines of the bag, I could see that the lizard was a big boy, at least four and maybe five feet. His tongue flicked in and out. He hissed. I moved my face back just as he leaped out of the bag. A pile of papers fell onto the floor as he landed on the desk. I'd forgotten they could jump.

"Guess he didn't enjoy the trip too much," Roy said.

"Guess not." I put my hand out and the lizard lunged for it.

"I'd be careful, if I was you."

"No kidding."

The thing had claws that could rip the skin off my hand and the disposition of a Sumo wrestler deprived of his beer. I moved to the other side of the desk and the lizard turned with me. The creep wasn't going to let me get in back of him. "You have a towel and a pair of gloves?"

Roy was back a few minutes later with the requested items. He watched me roll up the towel and put on the gloves.

I said a short prayer and held the towel in front of the tegu. He battened on to it with a death grip. While his front was occupied, I reached around and picked him up by the tail and dropped him in the open bag.

"You did good," Roy allowed after the tegu was safely confined.

"Thanks, but it would have been better if it hadn't happened at all." I licked the blood from the cut above my wrist, where the lizard had nicked me. The salty taste lingered in my mouth. It was not unpleasant.

Roy handed me a Band–Aid. "Everybody has accidents."

"Well I've been having too many to suit me."

"At least yours ain't fatal."

"You didn't like John much, did you?"

"The way I see it is: If a man goes around handling cactus, he's going to get hisself poked. That's just the way it is."

I started on the next bag. The three Haitian boas didn't give me any trouble—they looked half dead. I picked each one up. They barely moved. They hadn't fared nearly as well as the lizard. I put them back, retied the bag, and went on to the next one.

It felt like it weighed fifteen, maybe even twenty pounds. I hoped it wasn't a big snake like an anaconda or a python. I didn't like handling anything over ten feet by myself. Too dangerous. Roy refilled his glass as I struggled with the knot. When I finally got it undone, I found another plastic bag inside.

Roy moved back. "Boy, that sure does smell bad."

The odor was familiar, but I couldn't place it.

I untwisted the tie top.

The smell made my eyes water. God, what the hell was in here? Roy moved back even farther. I turned my head, took a deep breath of fresh air, opened the bag, looked inside, and froze.

At first I couldn't believe what I was seeing.

I thought it was a fake.

One of those rubber mask jobbies that they advertise in horror magazines.

Because things like this just don't happen in real life.

I told myself it was just a bad joke from someone with a sick sense of humor.

Then I took another look, a closer one, and knew I was wrong.

It wasn't a joke. The thing was real. I gagged and reeled back. I could feel the bile in my stomach rising. Sweat ran down my sides.

I tried to run to the bathroom. But I never made it.

I threw up where I was standing.

Twelve

I closed my eyes and rested my head on the cab's steering wheel. It didn't help. I could still see the head, obscenely nestled in its black plastic shroud. Visions of the blond, spiked hair, the milky eyes, the leathery skin, kept replaying themselves in my mind. And then there had been that odor, sharp, hard, almost medicinal. It was familiar, but I couldn't name it.

"A-r-r-row." The cat insinuated herself between my armpit and my arm and crawled into my lap.

I stroked her back and she began to purr. The taste of vomit was still in my mouth. I popped a Lifesaver, leaned my head back against the seat, and studied the cargo area. There was nothing to see, just a block-long row of anonymous, square buildings, an empty parking lot, and the landing strip out back. It was a bleak vista. I willed myself to think about something else. I pretended I was lying in a hammock on a beach in the Caribbean. The sand was fine and white. Two little girls were down by the shore looking for shells. My pulse rate began receding. Then Roy stuck his head in the window.

"Nasty weather for sitting around like this."

I turned my head slightly. "Cold makes me feel better."

"Drinking's not good on an empty stomach," he advised.

When I'd thrown up over the bag, I'd told Roy it was because I hadn't eaten anything all day.

"I always down a quart of milk a day myself. Helps line the old gut." He stuck his head further in the car and sniffed. "If I was you, I'd put that box in the trunk. Otherwise you're going to end up with a smelly car."

"I can't. The lock's frozen." I put the key in the ignition and started the cab.

"You forgot this when you ran out." He held out a pink slip of paper. It was my copy of the manifest.

I took it and tossed it on the front seat. "Thanks. I have to go."

But Roy didn't move. "Now I'm an easy goin' guy. I don't rightly care what comes through this terminal. Your husband knew that." My heart started pounding. Had he seen the head? "But the people that run this place ain't like me," Roy continued. "They're sticklers for regulations. Now me"—he pointed to himself—"like I said, I believe in being nice to people, especially when they're nice to me."

The light dawned. I reached into my jacket, took out two twenties and handed them to him. He held them up to the streetlamp.

"They're real," I snapped.

"I'm not saying they ain't." He tucked them into his shirt pocket and poked his head back in the window. "Amazing, how expensive everything is getting these days."

Greedy bastard. I handed him a ten. "This is all I have."

"Thanks. Much obliged." He tapped his nose. "Anything else I can do for you, you let me know. Just ask for Uncle Roy."

"Right." I shifted into drive.

He must have missed the sarcasm, because he was still

waving as I pulled out of the parking lot. Hell, why shouldn't he wave? I had just given him fifty bucks. Uncle Roy my ass. I clicked on the radio. The radio announcer was nattering on about the plans for expanding St. Ann's. I reached over and turned the damned thing off. I needed to concentrate. I had to decide what to do next. As far as I could see there were three possibilities: I could call the cops; I could send the head back; or I could get rid of it.

I briefly considered the first possibility, before rejecting it. If Lorenzo found out about this, she would nail me to the wall. I pictured the encounter.

"First," she would say, "somebody dies in your store. Then we find fifty thousand dollars you tell me you don't know anything about. Two days later a kid gets his head bashed in in your shop—which you also tell me you know nothing about. And now someone sends you a severed head and you still don't know anything?"

I'd be lucky if she didn't book me on the spot. Choice number two didn't have much going for it either. Not only would I have to repack the damned thing, but there was always the possibility of the package being traced back to me. And how would I explain that?

"Well, you see, officer, I had this minor problem. Someone sent me something I hadn't ordered and I was just returning it."

No, I thought not.

Which left me with choice number three. I turned off the main road and onto Hoytville Avenue. It had stopped snowing. The plows had been out. The street was salted and cleared. The shops lining Mattydale's main street, the usual collection of strip stores, were shuttered for the night. There had to be a dumpster around somewhere. I slowed down and started searching. Nothing on the left. I looked right, inadvertently glancing at the rear view mirror while I did.

Something was moving in the back seat.

My mouth went dry. The skin on my scalp prickled. I kept my eyes straight ahead.

I was afraid to look back, afraid of what I'd see.

Then I heard the scratching.

I told myself it was the golden tegu getting restless, but I didn't believe it. Heart pounding, I made a sharp turn into the parking lot of the Vineyard Restaurant, skidded to a stop, and jumped out.

I squatted on the tarmac, cupped my hands over my mouth, and blew into them. Flecks of snow landed on my hair and my hands. In a few minutes, the constriction in my chest eased. My pulse rate began going down. I stood up, gathered the tattered remnants of my nerve, and went over to the car. When I peered in the window, I didn't know whether to laugh or cry.

The cat was pawing at the box. That's what I'd seen.

I opened the door and shooed her out.

She trotted over to the front of the car, jumped on the hood, and began sniffing the air. I had wanted to go farther, but this was going to be it, this was as far as I could go.

I glanced at the restaurant. I hadn't eaten there in years. It was the kind of place you went when you were young, in love, and poor. It had red-and-white checkered tablecloths, Chianti bottles doubling as candle holders, and red sauce over everything. I looked around the parking lot. The dumpster was over in the left hand corner. I put the cat back in the car and drove over to it.

All you have to do, I told myself, *is take the bag, throw it in the trash, and get out of here.*

For a moment, I thought about grabbing the whole carton

and tossing it in, but I couldn't. The name of the store was written on the front in big black letters. If I tossed the box in and anyone found it, I would be in even worse trouble than I was now. No, there was only one thing to do.

I got out of the front and opened the back door. I coughed as the stench hit me. The odor's name was on the tip of my tongue, then it skittered away and I gave up trying to identify it. In spite of the cold, rivulets of sweat were running down my armpits.

He's already dead, I told myself. *Whatever happened, happened. What you're doing doesn't make any difference.*

But that little voice deep inside me, the one that everyone has, wasn't buying. Nobody, it whispered, deserved to end up in the trash.

I ignored it and opened the carton's flaps. The cat jumped into the back and butted the box with its head. I swatted at her and she meowed in protest.

I lifted up the bag and holding it as far away from me as possible, went over to the dumpster and tossed it in.

"Rest in peace," I murmured as it disappeared.

If there was a hell, I was going to burn for this one, that I knew.

I turned to go back to the car and almost fainted.

A cop was watching me.

Thirteen

I'd been so intent on what I'd been doing that I hadn't heard the squad car driving up.

"Can I ask what you're doing, ma'am?"

I blurted out something really stupid like throwing things away.

"May I ask what you were disposing of?"

"I was cleaning out my car," I said, trying not to let my voice shake.

"At this time of night?"

"I just spilled my coffee over everything." This man had to know I was lying. Given my behavior how could he not?

"We've had a lot of problems around here with people disposing of unauthorized items in the dumpsters."

"Really?" I stood there paralyzed.

The cop walked toward me. When he was about a foot away he stopped and pointed to my jacket. "What's that? More coffee?"

I looked down. There were dark stains near the zipper. Blood. Manuel's blood. I must have wiped my hands on my jacket after I'd found him. I'd been too upset to notice. I looked back up. The cop was standing there, tapping his foot, waiting for my answer.

"Ketchup."

But I could tell from the way his hands tightened on his belt that he had doubts about my story. He had just opened his mouth to say something else, probably something like, "let's take a run downtown" when the cat meowed.

"Where'd the kitty come from?" he asked, inclining his head in the animal's direction. She was sitting on the hood of the cab licking a paw.

"I found her a little while ago."

"Is she how come the coffee spilled?"

I nodded.

"She don't look so good."

"I know. I was taking her home."

His face softened. "Poor thing." The cop went over and scratched the cat between her ears. "We always had cats when I was a kid. But my wife, she's got this allergy. We can't have them in the house."

"That's too bad."

"Yeah, isn't it." He picked the cat up and held her against his chest. "God, she's all skin and bones. I bet she doesn't weigh more than six pounds."

"More like four."

He handed her over to me. "Go on. Get out of here." I felt relief flowing through my veins. "Go home and give the cat something to eat."

I didn't have to be told twice. I took the cat and got back in the cab. I wanted to peel out of the parking lot, but I made myself go the legal limit. The last thing I needed was more trouble. As I drove back home, my mind kept wandering to what I'd found. Who had the head been meant for: John or Tim? Tomorrow, I'd call up Herp Inc. and see who'd placed the order. That, at least, should give me a clue. And then I began wondering if the head was tied to John's death in some way, and if so, how? I kept speculating, trying out this pattern, then that one, until finally I couldn't think at all and I decided the only thing to do was forget about everything for the time being. Maybe tomorrow things would make more sense.

I got off 81, took 690 East, and then exited at the Teall Avenue exit. As I was driving up toward Genesee Street, my stomach started rumbling and I realized that with everything that had been going on I'd forgotten to eat. At the next light I made a left on Teall, drove two blocks, parked in front of the 7-Eleven on the corner of Erie and Taylor, and went in.

I had picked up a couple of containers of yogurt, a pint of Breyer's coffee ice cream, and the last remaining edition of the morning's *New York Times* when I heard, "Hey, Robin, how things going?"

George. I almost dropped the things I was carrying. I couldn't believe it. What was it with that man? He had an almost psychic ability to appear when I didn't want to see him.

"Where have you been?" He took a bite out of one of the two chili dogs he was holding. "I've been trying to get hold of you all evening."

"I've been running errands." Which in a way I had been.

"Want one?" He offered me the uneaten hot dog.

"Thanks, but I think I'll stick to yogurt." I started toward the counter.

"Listen, you free Thursday night?"

I allowed as how I was.

"Good. Let's get together. How about we meet at The Orange at nine?"

I agreed, but as I watched George amble back out to his patrol car, I couldn't erase the nagging feeling that the meeting he'd proposed wasn't just a social encounter, that he had something on his mind he wanted to talk to me about, and that I wasn't going to want to hear what he had to say.

"That it?"

I looked up. The cashier was standing behind the counter fingering one of his dreadlocks.

I picked up two chocolate bars and put them on the counter too. "Now it is." Then I paid for my stuff, drove back to the store, set up the reptiles, and went home to bed.

I had a night filled with bad dreams. The next morning when I woke up, I felt as if I'd been poleaxed. Every joint in my body ached. When I sat up, I felt dizzy. The flu had struck. With a vengeance. I scrounged up the phone and called Tim and asked him if he could handle things down at Noah's Ark by himself. When he said yes, I was so grateful I could have kissed him. Even if he was a murderer. Because at that point, as long as he could take over for me I honestly didn't care what he was. Next I crawled downstairs, made sure both cats had enough food and water, changed their litter boxes, then went back upstairs, took four Advil, climbed into my bed, and slept straight through the next twenty-four hours.

When I got up the following morning, all my aches were gone. I guess all I'd needed was a good night's sleep. For the first time since I didn't remember when I wanted something besides chocolate and yogurt to eat. I searched the refrigerator. Nothing there except stuff that should be thrown out. I slipped on my jacket. It looked as if I was going out to eat.

The minute I opened the garage door, Pickles, as I'd come to think of the cat I'd found the other night, ran over to me and rubbed herself against my legs. I deposited her in the car and pulled out of my driveway. She sat, half on and half off my lap, while I drove.

It was a pretty day. The sky was blue instead of gray and the smattering of snow that had fallen since I'd been asleep made everything look soft and fluffy and white. I stopped across town at a little dive of a place on the corner of Oswego and Shonnard Street. The restaurant was run by a Dominican woman and what it lacked in atmosphere, it made up for in its food. The coffee was strong, the toast came thick and well buttered, and the scrambled eggs were creamy. I skirted the pool table sitting in the middle of the room and brought my order over to one of the six small tables set out along the left-hand wall. Except for Angelina, the owner and cook, I was the only person there.

I had just started eating, when Sam came in. He gave me a half wave then turned back and placed his order. Five minutes later he came over, carrying a plate in one hand and a mug of coffee in the other. I put down the paper I'd just picked up, unopened and unread. He sat down, reached across the table for the hot sauce, and sprinkled it on his eggs.

"I heard about Manuel," he said as he took a bite. "You should have called me. Perhaps I could have helped."

My appetite suddenly vanished. "Thanks, but I don't think there was anything anybody could have done."

"*Verdad?* You might be surprised." He chewed and swallowed. "Manuel's aunt called me from the hospital this morning. She was there all night."

"How's he doing?"

"Not so good. He is in a coma."

"Did she tell you what the doctors said?"

"They said there is nothing to do but wait and see."

"That's awful."

"Perhaps the offering I will make for him will help."

"Offering?"

"When you light candles and pray," Sam quickly said. He

patted my hand. "Don't worry, Manuel will be fine. I can feel it."

"I hope you're right." I began playing with my eggs.

"So do I," Sam said. "So do I."

I was going to ask him what he meant when the restaurant door opened and two kids ambled over to the pool table. Dressed in starter jackets, jeans, and sneakers, they looked no more than fourteen. One lifted the cue sticks off the wall, while the other racked up the balls. There was a crack as the first kid broke. Bad luck. The eight ball fell into the pocket. The second kid laughed and said something in Spanish. They started over. I looked at Sam. He was following the proceedings with interest.

"In the old days, in Havana, I was very good," he said softly, almost to himself. "For many years, I support myself through school doing that." He nodded toward the game. "It needs both the eyes and the brain." He tapped his head. "You have the eyes, but I have seen much more than you in my life. Perhaps it is time that we talked."

"About what?" I asked.

"About the things that have been happening in your place."

"The other day you told me you had nothing to say, remember?"

"Yes. I remember."

"And now you do?"

"I thought there were certain things it was better for you not to know. Now I think perhaps I was wrong."

"What made you change your mind?"

"Manuel." Sam took a sip of coffee.

"So you're saying you'll answer my questions?" I asked, not quite believing what I was hearing.

"If I can. But first you must help me with mine."

Ah. I cut my eggs into little cubes while I thought about what I should do. I desperately wanted to hear what Sam had to say. I knew whatever it was he had to tell me was going to be important. But he wouldn't talk until I did. The problem was Joe had warned me not to talk to anyone about anything connected with the case.

"Well?" Sam was waiting for my answer.

I decided to give him an edited version of the story. Only it didn't work out that way. I ended up telling him everything. Once I started talking I couldn't seem to stop. Words tumbled out one after another. Through it all, Sam remained silent, giving little murmurs of assent now and then to show he was listening. I felt like I was in a confessional. Or a psychiatrist's office.

"Your turn," I said when I was finally done.

But instead of talking Sam pushed his chair away from the table and stood up.

"Where are you going?" I demanded.

"Out. We will talk later." And with that he put on his coat and left.

I sat there stewing. I didn't know who I was madder at: me, for letting myself get taken or him for doing it?

Tim looked up from the cash register as I walked in the store.

"Busy morning," he announced. "I think everyone's coming in hoping to see the saw-scaled viper. Go figure."

I was still so angry from my conversation with Sam that all I did was grunt.

"Well, you know what they say," Tim rattled on, oblivious to my mood. "Any publicity is better than no publicity at all."

I hung up my coat, opened a can of cat food for Pickles, dragged out a bag of pine chips, and started changing the rabbit's bedding. At least here was a task I couldn't screw up.

"And Donna called," Tim continued. "She said she'd be in to work after John's funeral. I guess we can manage till then."

I gave the mini lops and the dwarfs fresh water and food and fed them some carrot tops as a special treat. Their noses tickled as they took the greens out of my hand.

"So what were you, sick or something?"

"Or something."

"I don't feel too good myself."

"Really?"

"Yeah, I've been feeling I'm coming down with something for the past couple of days."

"Now that's interesting."

"Why's that?" Tim stopped counting out change.

"Because you looked fine when I saw you talking to Karkoff the other night." So much for my good intentions.

He closed the register drawer. "Exactly what are you saying?"

I didn't answer his question. Instead I asked him what he had been doing there.

"I was visiting my uncle, not that it's any of your business."

"And Karkoff just happened to be there?"

"That's right."

"I thought your family lived down in Florida."

"My brother lives in Florida, my aunt and uncle live up here."

"What did you two talk about?"

Tim folded his arms across his chest. "Football."

"Yeah. Right," I sneered.

"Are you calling me a liar?"

"You said it, not me."

The muscles at the bottom of Tim's jaw clenched. He took a step toward me, then turned and walked toward the back room. A moment later I heard the side door slam. He was gone.

I lit a cigarette and smoked it while I thought about how I shouldn't have called Tim a liar, even if I thought he was one. Then I thought about how I hadn't handled things too well over the last couple of days and about how, if I knew what was good for me, I'd better get a grip on myself. This was most definitely not the time for me to come apart. And believe me I knew what I was talking about. I'd done the hospital bit once—right after I'd graduated college. Too much acid. It was the kind of experience you never forgot and didn't want to repeat. I'd never dropped another tab since then—or taken a drink. Until recently.

"I need some fish food."

I looked up. A customer was standing in front of the counter tapping her fingers. So much for introspection. It was time to get to work. There was a steady flow of customers for most of the afternoon. Finally around four, traffic eased off, and I had a chance to call Herp Inc. I was more than anxious to see if I could get a line on the other day's delivery. At first things looked promising, but then the person I was talking to came back to tell me she couldn't find the manifest. She promised to call back if it turned up, but she wasn't too optimistic. It seemed they were shorthanded and the temp they'd hired to file, had "filed" a whole batch of things in the trash.

This was definitely not turning out to be a good day.

I put the receiver down and watched Pickles unravel a roll of toilet paper around the office. She was having such a good time, I didn't have the heart to stop her. Well, if I couldn't do things one way, I'd just have to try another direction. I picked up the phone and called Joan Pavic on the *Fort Myers Sentinel*. We'd met in New York City when I'd first graduated college and somehow we'd remained friends ever since.

"Hey, kiddo, how you doing?" I asked when she came on the line.

"Busy. Let me call you at home."

"Wait a minute." And I told her what I needed.

"Psycho killers are a little out of your line, aren't they? Don't you usually do social issues type stuff? Or have I got the wrong person?"

"I'm diversifying."

"You sound like a company."

"Do you think you can help me out?"

"Sure," Joan said. "No problem. As soon as I'm off deadline, I'll see what I can dig up."

I hung up and passed the time killing off the last of Murphy's Scotch and making a list of the things I knew, the things I didn't know, and the things I thought I knew. The column in the middle was by far the longest. Just looking at it got me depressed. I closed up the shop and went home. I could just as easily wait for Joan's call there.

It was ten before she rang me back.

"Find anything?" I asked.

"Yes and no. Which part do you want first?"

"The negative."

"Fine," she said. "I checked the police reports and there's no mention of any headless bodies turning up anywhere in this area."

"How far back did you go?"

"Four weeks."

"Are you sure?"

Joan made an exasperated noise. "Yes, I'm sure. This isn't Miami, you know. We don't get a corpse a day around here. Something like that would be noticed."

I drummed my pen against the desk. "Well, the damned thing had to come from somewhere."

"True. But not from around here."

"Great." So much for that idea. "So what's the good news?"

"I got to talking with Eduardo Duarte, one of the guys on the desk, and he told me something you might find interesting." I waited. "What do you know about brujería?"

"Isn't that the Latino version of witchcraft?"

"I'm impressed."

"Go on."

"Well according to Duarte, the *palero* . . ."

"*Palero?* Doesn't that mean stick in Spanish?"

"*Palo* means stick. *Palero* means witch."

"Are you sure?"

"Of course I'm sure."

"Because . . ."

"Listen," Joan interrupted, "do you or do you not want to hear what I have?"

"Yes. I do."

"Then please let me talk."

"I'm listening."

"Good. Now, as I was saying the witch gets his power from something called a *prenda*. To make it you need all sorts of good things like grave dust, herbs, blood, animal carcasses, and—here's where we come to you—the head of a dead person."

I doodled skulls on the pad in front of me. "Can you be a little more specific here?"

"What I'm saying is that maybe somebody sent the head up there for the same reason you used to bring me cilantro when we lived in New York City and I had an apartment on the East Side and you had one down in Chinatown."

"You mean it's an exotic ingredient?"

"Exactly."

"Somehow I find that explanation difficult to believe."

"Well actually so do I," Joan admitted. "But I thought I'd run the idea by you anyway."

"I mean why not just dig a head up from around here? It would be a hell of a lot simpler than mailing it to someone."

"I don't know. Maybe the guy who was supposed to get it is someone who doesn't like getting his hands dirty. Maybe he's into shortcuts."

"Yeah, and maybe there's even someone out there who's running a catalog business for witch doctors. Six hundred dollars for a head. Five hundred for a hand. Two hundred fifty bucks for a thigh bone. Delivery guaranteed within forty-eight hours or your money back."

"Hey, weirder things have happened."

"True," I conceded. I was going to say more but a burst of static crackled in my ear.

"Jesus," Joan grumbled when the line cleared a few seconds later. "Nothing works right anymore. Sometimes I think I'm in fucking Romania. Anyway," she continued, "not to change the subject or anything, but how *are* things going with you?"

I gave her the edited version. Then we spent the next three-quarters of an hour chatting about this and that. I was yawning by the time I said good night.

Fourteen

When I got off the phone with Joan I went straight to bed, but I couldn't sleep. I kept thinking about what she'd told me. Brujería in Syracuse. It was an incredible thought. People here went to the State Fair and the Apple Festival. They spent Saturday afternoons at the mall and Saturday evenings at the movies. The closest they got to Latino anything was Taco Bell.

But still.

By last count there *were* eight thousand Hispanics living in the city.

Mostly Puerto Ricans, Cubans, and Dominicans.

Islands where Santería held sway.

Which meant there was also brujería.

The good and the bad.

Like Christianity and witchcraft.

Two sides of the same coin.

And then I thought about Sam again and the things he'd promised to tell me—but hadn't—and wondered whether some of this stuff figured in his tale. Somehow I thought it did. And I decided that first thing in the morning I'd corner him in his store and I wouldn't leave until he told me everything I wanted to know.

Only things didn't turn out that way.

For openers Sam wasn't in his store when I went to work. A sign in the window said he'd be back in a little while. Only he wasn't. I kept calling El Gordito's and calling Sam's house throughout the morning. But I didn't get an answer at either place. A couple of times I'd look up from waiting on a customer and think I saw Sam's old Ford pick-up cruising down the block. But then the truck would continue on and I'd realize I'd been mistaken.

I started to go nuts, patience never being my strong suite. Around two o'clock I called the paper and talked to Bob Cowin, the Life Style editor down at the *Herald*, figuring that maybe he'd heard something about activity like that somewhere in the city. He hadn't.

But the idea intrigued him.

He thought it would make a great feature.

I should do it if I got any leads and—Oh, by the way—where was the feature I'd promised him on suburban teenage prostitutes?

I told him I was working on it, hung up, gnashed my teeth, and bit my nails.

Finally around four-thirty the store emptied out and I decided to close up early because I wanted to take a run down to the Shining Crystal Bookstore. I knew they had books on tarot and magic. I was hoping they had books on brujería as well. Or maybe I'd luck out and there'd be someone there who could tell me if stuff like that actually went on in Syracuse. And if so where?

But I didn't go there immediately because while I was getting in my car it occurred to me that I already knew someone who might know what I wanted to find out.

As it turned out I was right. Angelina did know something. Unfortunately she just didn't want to tell me what it was.

She was doing the dishes when I walked into the restaurant. I ordered coffee and we started to talk. Everything was going fine until I mentioned the word 'brujería.' Then her English deserted her.

"No comprendo," she said as she picked up a glass and began drying it.

I repeated myself. Her drying motions became more vigorous. I explained again, this time in pidgin Spanish.

"You go now." She made shooing motions with her hands.

I tried explaining again. She put down the glass, turned to the two men sitting at one of the side tables, and let go with a burst of rapid-fire Spanish. They put down their coffee cups and pushed back their chairs.

"You go now," she repeated, giving the men a meaningful look. They glared at me.

I left before they threw me out.

I just hoped I'd have better luck at my next destination.

The drive over to the bookstore took twenty minutes. The place was sandwiched between a supermarket and a pizza store on the corner of Dell and Cherry. The area, three blocks long and five blocks deep, was in a perpetual identity crises, occupied as it was by college students, punks, poor blacks, and an enclave of sixties radicals that had never made it through to another era.

I started sneezing the moment I walked into the shop. It was the incense. I'm allergic to it. While I waited for the clerk to make his or her appearance, I looked over some of the books. They were grouped according to subject matter. I picked up something on astral projection, put it down, and browsed through a book on finding "your inner path." Right now I thought, laying it back down, I'd be happy with any path at all.

I drifted over to the middle of the store and studied the crystals and stones on the countertop. They were heaped in separate sparkling piles; quartz, agate, tiger's eye, turquoise. A greenish stone with pink around the edges caught my eye. It was held in a silver mount. When I turned the price tag over, it read seventy-five dollars. I liked it, but not seventy-five dollars' worth.

"That's a bloodstone. It calms and soothes, as well as protecting the wearer against negative influences. Buy it and I'll throw in the chain for free."

New Age or not, everyone hustles. I turned around. An anorexic-looking teenage girl with black hair tipped green at the ends, a pierced nose, and a metal chain that went from her lip to her ear was doing the talking. But she had a nice smile and warm eyes. In spite of the facial hardware, I liked her.

When I told her what I was looking for she didn't even raise an eyebrow. "Just a sec," was all she said. A few minutes later she was back with three books, all of which, she informed me, had chapters on the subject I was interested in. I took them all, plus the stone on the principle that I could use all the help I could get.

"You into this stuff?" I asked her as she rang up my purchases.

She shook her head. "I'm strictly New Age."

"Do you know anybody who is?"

"Nope. I have a couple of friends who are into goddess worship but that's about as far as it goes."

"Because I'm doing an article."

"Sorry I can't help." She put my books in a bag and handed the bag to me.

"You sure?"

"Yes."

"Well, if you hear of anything." I gave her my card and told her to give a ring.

She promised she would. I was halfway to the door when she called me back. "I don't know if this will help but I do remember one thing."

"What's that?"

"One of my friends heard someone she knows talking about this store on the West Side that sells oils and candles and herbs and those little statues of saints. I'd ask my questions over there if I were you."

I wanted to but as it turned out the girl didn't know the shop's name or location and the friend who'd told her was off trekking in Nepal.

So I did the only thing I could think of: I went straight home and called Sam again. But he still wasn't in. At that point I began to get a little worried so I dialed up Tim and asked him if he knew where Sam was. He said he thought he'd overheard one of our customers telling another one that Sam had gone off to New York on some sort of family business and that he would be back in a few days.

Tim's news put me in an even worse mood. I had just sat there and let Sam walk away from me. Why had I done that? I asked the cat. Why hadn't I followed him outside and insisted he talk to me? James didn't answer. When I repeated my question, I knew I was losing it so I put on my jacket, went outside, and shoveled my sidewalk off. I was a lot calmer and a lot colder when I came back inside a half hour later. I made myself a pot of coffee, got a couple of chocolate bars out of the fridge, sat down at the kitchen table, and began doing what I should have done in the first place, which was reading the books I'd just bought. Two were paperbacks. One was hardcover. The paperbacks had been printed in Florida, the hardcover in New York City. I had never heard of either press, not that that meant anything. All three had African motifs on their covers. I opened them up one at a time. The paper was cheap, the bindings glued. They hadn't been made to last.

I started with the thinnest volume. It was slow-going. Santería was much more complicated than I thought. There were over fourteen gods and each one had two names: Christian and Yoruban. Like the Greek and Roman ones, each god had its own particular likes and dislikes, its own spells, its own requirements, its own powers. I kept reading. Somewhere around page eighty I got to the part on brujería. That's when I saw the photograph of the stick and did a double take. The staff was long and thin. Tied on top were three feathers and a stone I couldn't identify. The caption underneath read, "Protection against the evil eye." I had seen one of those before. At Angelina's restaurant to be precise.

I shrugged on my jacket and grabbed the book. Angelina and I were going to have another discussion.

And this time I wasn't going to take no for an answer.

She was closing up as I walked through the door. No one else was in the place. She stopped sweeping when she saw me. "What you want?"

"To talk about this." And I pointed to the stick hanging on the wall.

"I don't know nothing about that. It was here when I move in."

"It's a protection against the evil eye. Look." I opened the book I'd brought with me to the proper page.

She shrugged and repeated what she'd told me before.

I came closer. "Why won't you talk to me?"

She put one of her fingers to her head and made a curling motion. "Ever since your husband die, you have become a crazy woman, a *loca.*"

"Maybe. But at least I'm a citizen."

Angelina turned pale. My shot had gone home.

"Why you come in here bothering me?" she screeched, clasping the broom handle tightly to her chest. "What I ever done to you? You leave me alone. Go talk to your friend."

"My friend?"

"The Cuban. You go talk to him. He tell you what you want to know."

It took me a moment to realize she meant Sam.

I decided to try his place one more time.

Maybe he was back home by now.

It was a little after seven when I got there. The street was quiet. Except for a few cars driving by, nobody was out. It had started snowing again. The store was closed, but I could see Sam's pick-up parked in his driveway. Tim had been wrong. He was home. For a moment as I walked down the driveway to Sam's apartment I thought I caught a glimpse of Lorenzo driving by, but then I decided I must have been mistaken. I just had the woman on my brain. I turned and rang the bell.

No one answered.

I tried again.

When no one answered this time, I tried the door handle. It turned. The door was open. I walked in. At that point it never occurred to me not to. That's how obsessed I'd become. The hallway light was on.

"Sam?"

Nothing. Maybe he hadn't heard me. Maybe he was upstairs. I realized as I started down the corridor that in the five years I'd known Sam, I'd never been in his house. The walls were covered in flocked red velvet paper. I pushed open the first door I came to. It was the living room. The furniture was all ornate dark wood. The sofa and loveseat were covered in green velvet. Lamps that looked like they could have been

Tiffanys sat on two end tables. Bookshelves covered the far wall. They were filled to capacity. Piles of books stood alongside the chairs and sofa. I lit a cigarette before I glanced at their titles. They seemed to be equally distributed among Spanish, English, and German. A cup of coffee sat on top of the TV. I touched it. It was cold.

I walked into the next room. It was a library. More bookshelves crammed with good leather-bound editions took up every available inch of wall space. I crossed to the desk. A yellow legal pad was sitting on the blotter. The top page was covered with doodles of sea shells and flowers and clusters of arrows that pointed this way and that. In the middle I spotted Donna's name and mine and the name of the store nestled in among three snakes with wings coming off their backs. I studied the page for a moment before deciding that it was nothing more than random jottings, the kind you make when you're involved in a boring telephone conversation. I continued on.

The kitchen was small, but arranged for maximum efficiency. Brass pots hung over an old gas stove. The pine table by the wall had been set for two. Three pink carnations sat in a peach-colored ceramic bud vase.

"Hey, Sam," I yelled again.

The house wasn't that big. He should have heard me by now.

Something was very wrong. I could feel it.

I mounted the stairs slowly. From the top of the landing, I could see three rooms.

"Sam, it's Robin," I called out again.

Again there was no response. The silence was absolute. Even my footsteps were muffled in the thick pale blue carpeting. I crossed over to the room on the left and looked in. It was a bedroom done in varying shades of tan. The place was pristine, so perfect I had the feeling I was looking at a movie set. I opened the next door. The room was clearly Sam's bedroom. I closed my eyes for a second before I went in. A faint odor of something I couldn't identify hung in the air. The blue drapes were drawn. There was no clutter on top of the double cherry dresser. The bed was made, the white chenille bedspread carefully folded over the two pillows on the queen size bed. A pair of trousers lay in the middle of the bed next to a fresh white shirt and a gray V-neck sweater. On the floor was a pair of newly shined wingtips. Sam had laid out a change of clothes. But he hadn't put them on. Why?

Then I spotted something that made me stop wondering about that and start wondering about something else. In the corner of the room off to one side was a chrome and glass table. On it was a wooden bowl filled with small, oval, highly polished black stones. Next to that sat a double-edged ax beaded in white and red with six cowrie shells in the center. Both objects, according to the books I'd just read, symbolized Chango's power. It was hard to believe, but maybe Angelina had been right. Obviously Sam was a follower of Santería. Maybe he was a follower of the other path as well.

I thought about that as I crossed over to the bathroom and stepped inside. The room still smelled of soap and aftershave. A razor and a topless can of shaving cream lay on the wooden shelf above the sink. I touched the shower curtain. It was wet. Sam had showered not that long ago. As I was standing there I noticed the little recessed window set into the back wall. On it was another bowl. In the bowl was the branch of what looked like an evergreen. Certain kinds of evergreens, I recalled from my reading, were used to soak up the evil spirits. Then I remembered something else. I remembered seeing Sam sell a branch like that to a woman. When I'd asked him what that was for, he'd just shrugged and changed the subject.

As I walked back to Sam's room, I recalled what the clerk at the Crystal Lights had said about a store on the West Side that sold things for Santería and I wondered if the store she'd been referring to was Sam's. Now that I thought about it, he'd always sold different-colored candles and packets of strange-smelling herbs with names I'd never heard of and he'd never been willing to explain. And then what had he said to me about Manuel? Something about making an offering? What kind of offering? I was standing near his bed, staring off into space, wondering exactly what Sam had been referring to, when I felt the draft.

A window was open.

I pulled the drapes back.

One of the French doors was slightly ajar. Sam had installed them in the fall, when he'd refurbished the little balcony off his bedroom. He had told me he was looking forward to sitting there in the summer.

Instead of closing the door, I opened it and stepped out onto the tiny terrace. The cold hit me like a slap and I shivered. Bare tree branches stood out against the grayish black sky. Smoke streamed out of chimneys from the surrounding houses. I gave a quick glance around. Besides a small white plastic table and chair sitting off to one side there was nothing here. But as I was turning to go back inside, I caught sight of the snow on the balcony floor.

It was freshly trampled. Even in spots I hadn't been standing in. Sam had obviously been out here fairly recently.

So where the hell was he?

Then a cat meowed below and I looked down and had my answer.

Because Sam was lying on the ground. He'd been half hidden by the shadow cast by the house. That's why I hadn't seen him right off.

Fifteen

I ran outside, but I could have taken a leisurely stroll for all
the difference it made. I was a couple of feet away, when I saw
the dark stain smudging the back of Sam's bathrobe. I covered the rest of the distance slowly, afraid to know and afraid
not to know. When I reached Sam, I crouched down and
touched the dark spot. It was wet, just like I knew it would be.
Sam's gods hadn't been powerful enough to protect him from
death. I stifled a sob. Whatever Sam had been going to tell me
was his to keep.

I wanted to scream, but the sound swelled in my throat
and died. For a split second, I was back with Murphy, cradling
his head in my hands and pleading with him to speak to me in a
strange mewling voice I didn't recognize as my own. I shook
my head and the vision passed. Reflexively, I tucked Sam's
bathrobe around his legs. It seemed to be the least I could do.
In spite of the cold, his skin was still warm to the touch. I
shuddered. He hadn't been killed that long ago.

Poor Sam. Like my father, all he'd wanted was to go back
home. But they'd both died alone in the dark. I patted his
hand. Tears began trickling down my cheeks. I wiped them

away with the back of my sleeve, unsure of whether I was crying for Sam, my father, or myself. I'm not certain how long I sat that way. It could have been one minute or it could have been an hour. Maybe I'd still be there if I hadn't heard the sounds of footsteps crunching on ice, laughter floating in the air as people walked by El Gordito's.

I stood up. A downstairs light winked on in the house across from Sam's backyard. A shadow of a man drifted across the half-drawn window shade. A moment later the light went out and the shadow was gone. I knew I had to get out. This time I'd been lucky. This time the person across the way had been getting a snack or looking for the *TV Guide.* But next time he might glance out of his window and when he did he'd see Sam. And then he'd call the police. I didn't want to be around when they arrived.

"Descanse en paz," I whispered to Sam.

Then I turned and sprinted up the driveway. I was panting with fear by the time I locked Sam's front door. As I shot the bolt home, I could feel the hairs on the back of my arms prickle, my heart racing. I cupped my hands over my mouth and forced myself to take long, slow, deep breaths. All I wanted to do was get in my car and get as far away from this place as possible. But I couldn't. At least not if I wanted to be walking around tomorrow afternoon. There were a few things I had to do first. I went over them in my head. I had to get my jacket and wipe my prints off the things I'd touched. And if I was smart I'd also see if I could find anything that would answer some of the questions Sam had never gotten around to clarifying. In the abstract, it was a simple enough list to accomplish. I just wasn't sure I was up to doing it.

My footsteps echoed on the wood floor as I walked over to the coat rack. I lifted my jacket off the hook, put it on, and took my gloves out of my pocket. I intended to use them in place of a rag. The house's silence underlined each movement I made, lending it an importance it might not otherwise have had.

The living room seemed darker than it had fifteen minutes ago. I stood in the doorway while I tried to recall what I had touched. But I couldn't. My mind was as blank as snow in the Arctic. The phone began ringing. I counted. Fifteen rings in all. Then quiet. Whoever was on the other end had given up. I forced myself to recreate what I had done when I had first entered Sam's house. I remembered touching the end tables and picking up a few of the books. I hurried over and gave everything a swipe.

Feeling like Lady Macbeth, I repeated the same ritual in the library. I didn't know if what I was doing would work, but I had to try. The consequences of not doing anything were too great. When I was done wiping, I crossed the room to Sam's desk and ripped the piece of paper with my name on it off the pad and put it in my pocket. Then I put on my gloves and opened up the desk drawers.

There was nothing unusual in any of them, just stamps, stationery, pens, pencils, a check ledger, all neatly arranged. I felt a stab of disappointment. I'd wanted to check Sam's calendar. See if there was anything of interest to me in it. But it wasn't there. I closed the desk drawer. Maybe it was upstairs or maybe he didn't keep one. Maybe he was one of those people who kept all his dates in his head. My father had been like that. Up until the time he died, he'd had a perfect memory. He used to brag that he never forgot anything. Ever.

The phone started ringing again. The sound went through me like a hot poker through tin. I wanted to go into the kitchen and rip the damned thing off the wall. Only, of course, I couldn't. By the time I got upstairs the caller had stopped. The climb up the stairs seemed to go on for too long a time. It was chilly on the second floor landing. For a moment I just stood there staring at the wallpaper, thinking I don't know what. Then I walked over to Sam's bedroom and went inside.

The room was as cold as a marble slab. The white voile curtains billowed in and out. A few snowflakes drifted in through the open window, the one I'd forgotten to close when I ran down the stairs. I forced myself out onto the balcony and erased my footprints with the side of my boot. I tried not to look down, but I couldn't help it. My eyes were drawn to Sam. I forced them away, closed the French doors, and turned back toward the room. I decided to take a few more seconds to look for Sam's calendar. Then I would leave. It was time.

I located it almost immediately.

It was in the oak night table next to Sam's bed.

I rifled through the pages looking for something. Anything that would give me an idea.

What I found was that Sam had been a busy man.

He had gone to the symphony and Syracuse Stage and the opera.

He'd been an active member of the Spanish Alliance and the Hispanic Coalition.

He'd been on the board of the Metropolitan Arts Council.

I wondered if any of the names written down was the one I was looking for, the one I had come to ask Sam about? If any of the people in the book I was holding had information that could help me out of the mess I was in?

But I'd probably never know.

Because now that Sam couldn't tell me, there'd be no way I'd ever find out.

Unless I spoke to every single one of them.

I put the calendar in my pocket on the theory that I might. Then I turned to go and that was when I noticed something lying on the floor by the curtain, something I'd missed before. I went over and picked it up.

For a moment I simply stared at what was in my hand. I couldn't believe it.

It was my address book.

Then I told myself I'd made a mistake. It just looked like mine. Every stationery store in town sold them. I opened the red cover with trembling hands. No, there was no mistake. It was mine, all right. There was my name and address right on the front page. Shit. I couldn't believe it! I looked twice more to make sure. But no matter how much I wanted it not to be, my name was still there. It hadn't disappeared. It seemed that Walt Disney was wrong. Wishing didn't always make it so. Just to make triply sure I flipped through the pages. Yes, there were the flowers I had doodled across the "l's" and the "w's," the blot of strawberry jam in the middle of the "d's."

My mind started doing cartwheels of terror. Round and round it went, spinning out of control.

What was my address book doing on the floor in Sam's bedroom?

I knew I hadn't taken it with me. I had left it on Murphy's desk.

Or had I?

I didn't remember. Had it been in the front seat of the cab? I closed my eyes and tried to recall when I had last used it, but it was useless. I was too panicked to concentrate. Then I thought about why my address book had ended up in Sam's bedroom and I felt even more terrified.

There could only be one reason.

Somebody was setting me up.

I tried to think of other possibilities.

Nothing else came to mind.

I stuffed the book in my jean pocket and headed for the

stairs. I had to get out of Sam's house before the cops arrived. Because there was at least one thing I was certain of. They would come. And soon. Whoever had killed Sam, would make sure of that.

I was halfway down when the buzzer rang.

"Try knocking," I heard someone on the other side suggest.

Shit.

I ran back up to the landing.

The banging intensified.

"Hey, Mr. Ramirez, open up. It's the police."

Whoever was talking had the voice of an unoiled buzz saw.

More banging.

"Mr. Ramirez. We need to talk to you."

Under the circumstances, there was only one thing I could do.

Sixteen

Jumping off the balcony had made perfect sense when I thought of it, but now that I was actually going to do it I was having second thoughts—lots of them. The truth is, I've hated heights ever since I was eight years old and Michael Hastings pushed me out of a tree we were both climbing in. Perhaps, I decided as I looked down, I had been a tad hasty. Maybe I should stay and explain everything to the police. And Lorenzo.

But then I thought: explain, what?

Why I hadn't called them when I'd found Sam's body?

Why I had his calendar in my pocket?

Why I was here in the first place?

Why did I think they wouldn't listen to my explanations? Was it because I wouldn't have either?

"Mr. Ramirez," the cop with the buzzsaw voice yelled. "Answer the door."

"Or I'll huff and I'll puff and I'll blow your house down," I muttered. Then I giggled and clapped my hand over my mouth to stifle the sound.

The wind picked up. The gusts tossed the branches of the

spruce over by the edge of the yard into strange shapes. An eyeless head leered out at me, then a dog without a tail. As I shivered and glanced away, I heard another car drive up and screech to a halt.

"What have we got?" a new voice asked.

"A possible 126."

It didn't take a genius to figure out what a "126" was, but I wasn't going to stick around and see if I was right. Academic curiosity only went so far. I grasped the balcony railing with both hands and vaulted over it. For a few brief airborne seconds I felt like Indiana Jones. Then I landed. Because I'd locked my knees instead of bending them I hit the ground with a bone rattling thud. My left ankle gave way and I toppled over into the snow.

When I tried to get up, a stab of pain shot through my ankle. I fell back down. I tried again, this time putting my hands out in front of me and using them to take some of the weight off my legs. That helped somewhat and I managed to get myself into a standing position. Then I put my full weight on my foot. Big mistake. I'd never actually seen stars before. Up until that moment I thought it was just an expression. A moan escaped my lips.

Shut up, Robin. Not a sound. Make it to the car and you're golden, I told myself.

But five agonizing steps later I remembered something I'd conveniently forgotten. I was parked out front.

I sidled up to the edge of the house and peeked around the corner. A police cruiser was nosed up behind the cab. I quickly flattened myself against the wall.

"Let's go," I overheard one of the cops say.

There was the sound of wood splintering as the police rammed Sam's door open. It was definitely time to leave. I half ran, half hobbled across the yard. But as I ducked through a hole in Sam's fence and onto Mrs. Garcia's driveway, I saw something that froze me to the spot. I'd left my footprints in the snow—a line of them.

I might as well have painted a sign saying "Here I am, guys. Come and get me."

I stood there waffling between going back and trying to erase my prints or continuing on. I had just decided to turn back when my eyes fell on the ground I was standing on. It had been shoveled. I was standing on macadam. No prints. I blessed Tony Garcia and ran on. God must have been feeling sorry for me because Terry Street was shoveled too. Now all I'd have to do was get rid of my boots—the sooner the better. I could almost see the smile of delight on Lorenzo's face when she told me that the soles of my boots matched up with plaster casts of the footprints in Sam's backyard. It was a pleasure I was determined to deny her.

When I hit Gifford Street, I realized I was running and slowed down so I wouldn't attract attention—the last thing I needed at the moment. In the distance, I could hear the blare of police sirens as they drew closer to El Gordito's. It wouldn't be long before the blue and whites would be out blanketing the area looking for Sam's killer. And once they ran a make on my car's plates I'd be their prime suspect. I just wanted to be home when they caught up with me—it would make the alibi I'd come up with more convincing.

I slowed down long enough at the corner of Gifford and Rose to throw everything I'd taken from Sam's house down the sewer grate. I'd made a mistake taking the stuff. I'd realized that as I'd gone off the balcony. The risk just wasn't worth it. At least now if the police picked me up, I wasn't holding anything that would link me with Sam's house. I kept to the shadows as I limped along. Cozy lights lit up the houses on either side of the street. Occasionally, through a window, I'd catch a glimpse of someone walking across a room and I'd wish that someone was me. Then I stopped looking and concentrated on just putting one foot in front of the other because my ankle was throbbing and the more I walked, the more it hurt.

By the time I reached Pine Street I realized I wouldn't be able to go much farther. Unfortunately my house was still several miles away. I ducked into the nearest doorway and rubbed my arms and tried to figure out how the hell I was going to get back home. I couldn't walk. My ankle wouldn't let me. Calling a taxi would be the height of folly especially if the cops canvassed the cab companies, and I didn't want to call a friend and get them involved in this mess. And of course I couldn't drive because my car was surrounded by police cruisers.

I smoked a cigarette while I tried to come up with some sort of plan. But the pains shooting around my ankle made it difficult to think. Then, just as I was about to give up, I saw a bus going down the street and—*pow*—I knew what I was going to do. Take Centro. There was a bus stop around the block on North Street. I could catch one from there to downtown, then transfer to the Salt Springs line and get off two blocks from my house. I started walking again. My limp was getting worse. I decided to cut through the vacant lot midway down the street and save myself a couple of blocks. The huge Victorian mansion that had sat on that site was no longer there, having burned to the ground several months ago. The blaze had lit up the night for blocks around. Now there was only a rubble-strewn lot filled with scorched boards, blackened furniture, and melted plastic.

I could still smell the smoke as I picked my way through the tangle of broken boards, strewn clothes, used condoms, and old newspapers. New garbage had been added to the old. Halfway through the lot, my ankle gave out again and I had to rest. I was leaning against a dresser, trying to talk myself into getting going, when I realized that the pile of boards I'd been staring at wasn't a pile at all. It was some sort of ramshackle tepee-shaped structure. Somebody was living back here.

I was wondering who it could be when I heard a noise, then caught a glimpse of someone threading their way through the debris. He was holding a bag in one hand and his head was down, otherwise he probably would have seen me. When he was about six feet away I cleared my throat. His head snapped up.

It was Shannon.

"Who's there?"

"Me." I stepped forward. "Robin Light."

Even in the dimness I could see his eyes growing big. Then, before I had time to say anything else, he dropped the bag, bent over, and came back up holding a hunting knife, the kind with the serrated edges that hunters gut deer with.

"Don't come any closer," he cried. "Cause I'm gonna cut you if you do. I don't wanna but I will."

"Shannon . . ."

"I promise I will," he shrilled as he shifted the knife from his right hand to his left and back again.

I did as I was told. He was as scared as I was, which frightened me even more. Fear and weapons, like pills and booze, are a lethal combination.

"I should cut you for what you did to my homey." He choked back a sob. "That just wasn't right, man."

Oh Jesus, I thought, *this is it. I'm going to die in a vacant lot for something I haven't done.* But then instead of coming toward me Shannon spun around and ran away.

I watched him go, too shaken to follow him, even if I could have.

And then I realized the implications of what he'd said. He thought I was the one who hit Manuel over the head.

Which meant either he hadn't been with Manuel when the attack had taken place or he hadn't seen the attacker. Otherwise he would have known the person wasn't me. Either way he didn't know what happened to the money or the gun.

Great. I hobbled across the lot. When I came to the place where Shannon had been standing, I stopped and picked up the paper bag he had been holding. I was hoping against hope and logic that my money was in it, but when I saw the McD's logo I knew it wasn't. I looked inside anyway just to make sure and saw a Big Mac, a large fries, and an apple pie. My mouth started watering. I guess my body wanted to be fed, even if my mind didn't know it. For a moment all thoughts vanished as I tore into the hamburger. Then as I ate the fries, I began to think about the tepeelike structure I'd just discovered. Had Shannon been coming home to eat? It was extremely possible. After all, Rabbit had said the kid was living on the street. And then it occurred to me that maybe Manuel had stashed my envelope in there and that I would be wise to check the place out. Which is what I did after I polished off the last of the apple pie.

The ceiling was so low, I had to hunch over to get inside. A lit kerosene lamp sat on a packing crate. Next to that was a sleeping bag, a skate board, and an expensive Walkman. Tapes, copies of *Mad Magazines*, and dirty clothes were scattered over the floor. The funk of dirty socks and sweaty sneakers hung in the air. I searched the place and found nothing but a couple of nickel bags of grass and a report card in the name of Shannon Dalton. He'd gotten all F's, except for an A in English. I briefly wondered what his life would be like if he'd been born on the other side of town before I put his report card back where I'd found it.

Well one thing was for sure. The envelope wasn't here.

Not that in my heart of hearts I'd expected it to be.

Because by now I was pretty much convinced that whoever had hit Manuel and taken my twenty grand was the same person who had killed John and Sam—actions that were way out of Shannon's league.

The question was: were they out of Karkoff's or Tim's?

Seventeen

The bus trip back home was long and dismal, just me and five other down-and-outers swaying along together through the frigid night. Even though it was only a little after ten-thirty by the time I put my key in my door lock in my soul it felt like four in the morning. By now my ankle was thrumming with pain. All I could think about was getting inside and sitting down. I had just swung the door open when I felt a hand on my shoulder. My heart jumped. I whirled around, positive I'd find Lorenzo. But it was George. And he didn't look happy.

"Forget something?" he growled. Even though it was twenty degrees out, he was wearing a T-shirt, jeans, and a flimsy yellow nylon windbreaker.

I put my hand over my mouth. What I'd forgotten was that I was supposed to have met him at the Orange Grove earlier in the evening.

"Sorry, the cab died," I murmured, feeding him the same story I'd concocted for the police even though I felt guilty about doing it.

Which didn't make any sense. Because even though this man had been a friend of Murphy's, even though I liked him and he liked me, when all was said and done he was still a cop.

"It was probably the starter," I hurried on. "At least that's what the guy down in the garage said the last time it did this." Which was true. "I guess the car belongs in Florida. It just doesn't like the cold."

"You should have called me. I would have given you a lift."

"It didn't occur to me."

"So how did you get home?"

"I took the bus." I stepped inside my house. George followed right after.

"What happened?" George pointed to my ankle. "You're limping." I'd been trying not to, obviously without succeeding very well.

"It's nothing. I slipped on the ice."

Liar, liar pants on fire.

"Let me take a look."

I refused, but George kept on insisting and finally I capitulated. Getting home had used up every last available ounce of my resolve. I didn't have the energy left to argue.

"The first thing we have to do," George observed as I hobbled down the hall to the kitchen, "is get your boots off."

I hit the light switch on the kitchen wall as we went inside.

And burn them, I silently added while I pulled out a kitchen chair and sat down.

The relief was so great I groaned with pleasure. I leaned over, pushed another chair closer to me, and put my foot up. Then I tried pulling the boot off my left leg, but I couldn't. My ankle was too swollen.

"Let me." And then before I could say anything, George had whipped a knife out of his pocket, steadied my leg against his thigh, and was slicing through the leather. The blade he was using was long and narrow and sharp and I kept very still while he worked.

"Nice," George commented, scrutinizing the boot he'd just cut off.

"I thought so."

They'd been brown, Italian, and expensive and I'd bought them the last time I'd been in New York. Murphy had had a fit when he'd found out how much they'd cost. Now I was sorry I hadn't bought a couple more pairs in different colors.

"What do you want me to do with them?"

I pointed to the garbage can over by the sink. "Throw them in the trash."

George lobbed first one, then the other in. Funny, I reflected as he did, how sometimes things take care of themselves.

"Now," he said, "let's see what we've got. I rolled down my sock and we both studied my ankle for a moment. Then George prodded it with his finger.

I jumped. "Jesus! What did you do that for?"

"To see how swollen it is. Boy, you must have taken quite a fall."

"It definitely was that all right," I agreed.

"I'd have it X-rayed if I were you. It might be fractured."

"It's just sprained."

"You're sure, are you?"

"Sure enough." After all, if I was wrong I could always get it looked at tomorrow. I began hoisting myself up, but George pushed me back down.

"Where do you think you're going?"

"To get an ace bandage and some Advil."

He scowled. "I'll get them. Where are they?"

"In the cabinet by the refrigerator—I think."

George muttered something, which I couldn't hear, as he opened the cabinet door I'd pointed to and pawed through the shelves.

"Bottom shelf," I instructed.

"Do you always keep your first-aid supplies with your cat food?" he asked a moment later when he'd found them.

"Given my cat, it seems a logical juxtaposition," I said while George went over to the counter by the sink, took the bottle of Scotch that was standing there, poured a generous shot into a juice glass, and came back over to where I was sitting.

"Here"—he handed me the glass—"you look like you could use this."

"Thanks." I took a gulp and felt the warmth coming back to my body. I reached for the bandage George was holding but he pushed my hands away.

"Let me. I'm good at this."

Since I wasn't—I'd flunked both Home Ec and First Aid in high school—I let him. George's hands, so big that they engulfed my ankle, were surprisingly skillful.

"You know, it's odd," he said while he worked, "but every Thursday, I keep thinking I'm gonna walk into O'Malley's and see Murphy leaning over the pool table." George shook his head slowly from side to side. "He was an okay guy. Crazy, but okay."

"Nuts," I agreed, remembering the time Murphy had scaled a twelve-story building on the Lower East Side after someone bet him that he couldn't.

"He walked the line."

"Sometimes he went over it," I said, thinking about all the things I'd found out he'd done.

"Definitely. Like with the artillery."

"The what?"

"Murphy's .38."

I choked, spewing Scotch down the front of my shirt. "You knew?" I said after I stopped coughing.

George regarded me with bemusement. "Yeah, I knew. He told me."

"He told you?"

"More or less. One of those, 'I have a friend who . . .' stories. I think he just wanted to know how much trouble he'd get into if he was found with it."

"And what did you tell him?"

"The truth. Not much. Nothing really. He had a clean record. He probably would have gotten a fine and community service. Maybe not even that. But you on the other hand . . ." George let his voice drift off for a moment. "You've accumulated enough trouble for one life . . ."

"Yeah, maybe in my next one I'll do better," I cracked.

"Maybe you will," George replied. His tone was serious.

I was just about to ask George if he believed in reincarnation, when the doorbell rang. Lorenzo. Had to be. One thing was for sure. She hadn't wasted any time getting here.

"I'll get it," George said and started to get up.

I stopped him with a hand gesture. "No, I will." And I told him who I thought it was.

He glanced at me quizzically. "And why do you think that?"

"Second sight?" I answered, trying to be funny.

George pressed his lips together. "Want to tell me what's really going on with you?"

"I can't," I said. "I wish I could, but I can't."

He glared at me. "You don't trust me at all, do you?"

"It's not that . . ."

"Then what is it?" The doorbell shrilled again.

"It's . . ." I stopped, unable to find the words to express my thoughts.

"Fine. If that's the way you want it." His voice was hard as a diamond needle. He nodded toward the door. "Go on, get the fucking thing."

"But what about you?"

"What about me?" Each word was etched in ice.

"You want Lorenzo to see you here?"

"She can see me in the Garden of fucking Eden for all I care," he snapped.

There didn't seem to be anything more to say. I got up and put on a pair of slippers. As I hobbled toward the door, I remembered the advice my lawyer had given me the last time Lorenzo and Cunningham had come by, and I decided I'd be smart to follow it.

Lorenzo was still sitting on the bell when I opened the front door a crack and slipped outside. The cold made me shiver. But it couldn't be helped. I certainly wasn't going to let them inside. The last thing I needed on top of everything else was for them to spot George.

"That certainly took you long enough," she complained. Her glasses magnified the circles under her eyes. Her clothes were rumpled, her hair uncombed.

"I was dozing." From her appearance she had been too.

She pointed to my ankle. "What happened? You look like you hurt yourself."

"I slipped on the ice."

"When?"

"Tonight."

"In front of your store?"

"I'm not saying anything else," I replied, wondering if I had said too much already.

"That's all right. You don't need to." Lorenzo chuckled. "You know this time you've really done it. You have fucked up big time." A grin crept over her face.

My guts twisted into a knot as I thought about my address

book lying on the floor of Sam's bedroom and what would have happened if I hadn't found it. And then I wondered if there had been anything else planted in Sam's house that I'd missed?

"Very big," Cunningham echoed. "Notice," he said to Lorenzo, "how she hasn't asked us what this is about?"

God! Had anybody seen me going in?

"That's because she already knows, don't you?" Lorenzo said, lifting up my chin with her finger. "Don't you? Leaving your car at the crime scene. Very sloppy. Very very sloppy. You want to tell us why you did it?"

I didn't answer.

Lorenzo looked at Cunningham and gave a sorrowful shake of her head. "You know what I think?"

"What?"

"I think she thinks we're stupid."

"I think you're right."

"I'm going to call my lawyer," I whispered. My mouth was dry. I was having trouble swallowing.

"Good idea," Lorenzo said. Then before I knew what she was doing she grabbed my wrists and slapped a pair of handcuffs on them. "We're bringing you for questioning in the murders of Sam Ramirez and John Blount," she announced. "You can call your sleaze-bucket lawyer from the Public Safety Building. In fact I'm going to insist on it," she added as she led me to her car.

"Yeah," Cunningham said from the other side of me. "We want to make sure we do everything by the book."

"Everything," Lorenzo agreed as she opened her car door and shoved me into the back seat. "You ain't walking out of this one on a technicality." And she slammed the door shut.

As we drove away I caught a quick glimpse of George through my front window and shivered when I thought about how I'd nearly told him what had really happened. As it was, he already knew too much. But then I decided that he wasn't going to say anything. Aside from everything else, he'd have too much explaining to do if he did. As I watched the streets whizzing by, it occurred to me that this might be the last time I'd see them for quite a while, but then I stifled that thought and began preparing myself for the ordeal that lay ahead.

Joe and I stepped onto State Street and started walking toward his car. The world looked black and white and gray. As I zipped up my jacket, a garbage truck clattered by, the only thing moving on the street.

Lorenzo had let me go, the way a cat releases a mouse—reluctantly. For five hours, while my ankle had throbbed, we had played Break Robin's Alibi. But no matter which way she'd come at me, I'd stuck to my story, even though I'd kept expecting someone to come into the interrogation room, wave my boots in my face, and call me a fucking liar. But nobody did and finally Joe had told Lorenzo to book me or let me go.

"We'll have another chat," she promised as I brushed past her on my way out the interrogation room.

"She's gonna lean on me, isn't she?" I asked Joe as he fished the keys for his black Saab Turbo 9000 out of his coat pocket and opened the car door.

"She's just doing her job." He slid in. A few seconds later, I heard a pop as the button on the passenger door went up. "I mean what do you expect? After all, you are the prime suspect in two homicides."

"She doesn't have to be so enthusiastic," I grumbled as I studied the car's interior.

Joe had spared no expense. The car had leather upholstery, electronic everything, a cellular phone, and a sound system that a touring rock band would have envied. It was nice to see where my money was going.

I lit a cigarette and shook out the match. "How much did you pay for this thing, anyway?"

"More than you probably make in a year. And be careful with your ashes," Joe warned as we peeled out of the parking lot.

"I'm not a complete slob," I snapped even though I looked a little on the scummy side.

But that didn't mean I burned holes in the upholstery or ground out butts on the carpet. And anyway, Joe didn't look so good himself. Even though he had on the obligatory expensive slacks, Italian shirt, and silk tie, his hair reminded me of a Brillo pad, he needed a shave, and the bags under his eyes were big enough to carry packages in.

We spent the rest of the ride in silence. The paperboy was stuffing the *Post Standard* into my mailbox as we pulled into my driveway. Joe stopped the car about an inch away from the garage door.

"Robin," he said, turning to me, "you'd better find those files."

"I intend to," I replied as I got out of the car.

I limped into the house, dropped my coat on the hall table, and went into the living room. James looked up from the armchair and then closed his eyes again. Like Murphy, he'd never been particularly demonstrative. I grabbed a bottle of Scotch off the sideboard, poured myself a double, turned on the TV, and lay down on the sofa. But before I even had time to take a sip I could feel myself dozing off.

I woke to James chewing on my hair. I checked my watch. It was after one. I had slept seven hours and felt as if I could use ten more, but I made myself get up anyway. My ankle still hurt when I put weight on it, but a little less so than last night.

I decided to wait another day before getting it looked at. I never visit a doctor or a hospital unless I have to, because I don't trust either very much. I was limping into the bathroom when the phone rang. I picked it up. It was Lynn reminding me about the dinner party scheduled for that night. I tried to beg off, but she wasn't having any, so I finally gave in—it was easier than fighting.

I took a taxi to the store and checked my car. It was still where I had left it—I guess the cops hadn't thought it was worth impounding—then I spent the rest of the day working at the shop. Around five, I closed up, went back home, undressed, put my hair up, and passed the next half an hour looking for something to wear that still fit me. But everything was too big. Finally I settled on a short, straight black knit dress. I belted it with my silver conch belt, threw on some silver bracelets, slipped on my cowboy boots, and put on my leather jacket. I was ready to go.

Lynn's husband took my jacket and welcomed me into the house with a sad little hug. Everyone was already there. I perched on the sofa, nibbled at the hors d'oeuvres, and made polite chitchat with the Edwards, the Stones, Lynn, and her husband. The seven of us talked about the weather, the current mayor, world events, and movies we'd seen. Everyone was nice and kind and sympathetic. But that only made things worse. I felt out of place, lost in a world I no longer had an entrance ticket to. If I stayed a moment longer I knew I'd start to cry. So I told Lynn I'd just realized I'd forgotten to lock up the store, and left. I knew she was upset and I felt bad, but there was nothing I could do. I had to get out of there.

I didn't go home though. Home would have been unbearably lonely. Instead I decided to go back to the store and see if I could find Murphy's files. Now would be a good time, because I could work undisturbed. On the way down, I stopped at Nice

'N Easy, tanked up, and bought another pack of cigarettes and the evening paper. Sam's death wasn't announced, but there was a little paragraph about Manuel on the last page of the Metro section. It didn't say much except that he was at St. Ann's and he was still in a coma.

God, I'd have given anything to speak to him, but it looked like I, along with everyone else, was going to have to wait.

Pickles came running to greet me as soon as I opened the shop door. I bent down and picked her up. She clambered onto my shoulder and draped herself around my neck. I reached up and scratched her between her ears. She made mewing noises in my ear. Poor thing. I snapped on the lights and turned up the heat hoping to warm myself up, but the coldness I felt was more than physical. Passing Sam's store had brought last night back: the bedroom curtains billowing; Sam spread-eagled on the snow; my fingers stained with blood.

I pushed the memories back as far as I could, took a deep breath, and steadied myself against the counter. *Find the files,* I told myself. *Maybe there's something in them that could lead to Sam's murderer.*

The only problem was: I had already looked everywhere I could think of. I decided the only thing to do was start all over again. I began in Murphy's office and went through his desk, his file cabinets, his books. I even searched under the rug. When that didn't pan out I looked in the bird room. I cleaned all the cages, moved the supplies, and tapped around the moldings. But the only thing I got for my trouble was a bite on my finger from Fenton, the macaw.

I took a cigarette break and checked behind the cat and dog supplies. No go. I went on to the guinea pig and hamster food. I had moved the boxes off the shelves and was putting them back on when I noticed a last box half hidden behind a carton of doggie biscuits. As I pulled it out, I saw the top of the box had been opened and taped shut.

I said a prayer, took the box to the counter, opened it, and dumped everything out.

A sandwich bag full of folded yellow papers lay among the green pellets.

Eighteen

Very slowly and carefully I took the sheets of paper out of the bag, unfolded them, and spread them out on the counter. There were three in all. I couldn't believe it. I had finally found them. Now, maybe Joe would be able to get Lorenzo off my back. But the moment I took a closer look at them my elation vanished. The handwriting on them wasn't Murphy's. The words consisted of well-formed, precise letters not at all like Murphy's usual scrawl. I felt like crying. And almost did. The whole thing was hopeless. I got up and paced around the store.

After a minute or so I got myself back under control enough to take a second look. And when I did I felt really foolish because I recognized the writing on one of the papers. There was no mistaking the odd way John looped his "b's" and "p's." So things weren't all bad. The problem was: who had written the other two pages? I sat staring at them for a while. The handwriting was familiar. I'd seen it before. But where? I smoked a cigarette and thought. And then, after a few minutes, it came to me. I grabbed a note Tim had left for me a couple of days ago and compared it with the yellow paper. Yes. The handwriting was the same.

It looked as if Tim and I had lots to discuss.

But when I called Tim's flat, he was out. I tried Donna. After all, she worked in the store. She had to know something about what was going on even though she said she didn't. But she was out too. Her aunt told me she'd be back in a few hours.

Great. I went back to studying the papers. This time they were divided into three columns instead of two. The first one named the price, the second named the snakes, and the third listed the buyer's initials. I quickly ran my finger down the third column, but I didn't recognize any of the initials on the first page. Midway down the second one though, I hit pay dirt. KK. Short, I was willing to bet, for Ken Karkoff.

Now, why wasn't I surprised? Was it because Karkoff was, as he would have said, a man of unusual tastes? Judging from the figures I was reading, he certainly had the money to indulge those tastes. Over the past three months he'd spent thousands of dollars on his collection. As I went through the list of his purchases a glimmering of an idea began to occur to me. Suppose John had stiffed Karkoff? What if he'd taken the money and never delivered? What would Karkoff do to get even? Probably something like wrapping up a saw-scaled viper and paying someone to leave it on my counter. He'd probably even think it was funny.

I took a red pen, underlined Karkoff's name, and continued on down the list. DF. LS. KZ. Nothing rang a bell. I turned to the next page. AD. No. PF. No. TM. I sat back.

Maroney?

Thomas Maroney owning a palm viper?

No. Couldn't be. Snakes weren't his style.

But then again . . .

But then again, I wouldn't have expected someone like Lorenzo to own a pair of Jackson's Chameleons.

I put a question mark next to his name and continued on

down the list. Nothing else stood out. I tried calling Tim again. Still no luck. I looked at the list a last time, then folded the pages up and put them in my pocket. Until I spoke to Tim, there wasn't much more I could do. I glanced around the store—one thing was for sure, there was a lot more I could do here—but the problem was, I didn't want to do it. I just wanted to get the hell out. The list had made me think of the viper we'd never found.

I stood up and grabbed my jacket. What I'd do, I decided, was Xerox the pages, drop a copy off at Joe's office, then get some pizza. Not having stayed for dinner at Lynn's, I was hungry. By the time I was done eating, Donna should be home. I'd have a chat with her and see what she knew. Then I'd try Tim's again.

Pickles rubbed up against my legs as I headed for the door. As a sop to my conscience for leaving her alone again so soon, I gave her some cat treats. When I locked up, she was eating one on top of the radiator.

I was debating whether or not I should go home and change before I started driving around—after all the clothes I was wearing, black dress, cowboy boots, and leather jacket didn't exactly suit the weather—when I spotted the patrol car parked in back of my cab. My mind turned blank. My heart started pounding. This, I thought, is what they mean by conditioned response. I wanted to turn around and run back inside, but that would have shown fear—something I couldn't afford to do—because then Lorenzo would think I was guilty and give me an even rougher time. I was almost abreast of the cruiser when the door opened and George got out. My knees almost buckled with relief.

He caught my shoulder and pulled me over to him. Then he began to talk, his words falling in the air like so many staccato notes. "Listen, after the other night I'm going to catch hell if anyone sees me talking to you, so I'm going to make this fast. The ME just completed the autopsy on your friend Sam Ramirez. The bullet that killed him . . ."

"Yes?"

"It was a .38."

My stomach lurched. Murphy's gun had been a .38.

"Tell me . . ." George began, then stopped himself.

"What?"

"Nothing." He gazed at me intently for a minute, before looking away. "They say don't ask the question, if you don't want the answer. So I'm not going to ask." George let go of my shoulder. "You'd better watch your ass," he warned before he got back in his squad car and drove off. "Lorenzo's really gunning for you."

My North Side friends tell me Rocco's hasn't changed in thirty years, and from the way it looks I believe them. I pushed my way through the crowd of people standing in the take-out line and ordered a Coke and two slices with sausage, olives, and pepperoni. A few minutes later, my food came sliding across the counter. I paid and carried everything to the only free booth in the place.

There had never been a time, day or night, when I'd been in Rocco's that it wasn't busy. Word had it that Rocco was part of the Gambino family. Other words had it that there was no Rocco. That the real owner of the place was a guy called Archie Rosenblatt who had correctly figured nobody would buy pizza from a man with a name like that. For all I cared, Rocco's could have been owned by a purple lesbian dwarf with a fondness for pigs. Just as long as the pizza stayed the same, I'd keep coming back.

The first bite burned the roof of my mouth. I sprinkled on some oregano and red pepper flakes and took a second bite.

Even better. While I ate, I thought about what George had said.

Of course, a .38 wasn't an uncommon gun.

But this one was Murphy's. It had to be. The chain of events was too tight. I find the .38. Manuel steals it. Then he turns up unconscious and the gun turns up missing. Next day Sam is shot in the back with a—guess what?—.38 and someone tries to frame me for the murder.

Coincidence?

Not too bloody likely.

I took a sip of soda and began on my second slice. I was almost through when a skinny teenage girl with matte white skin, too much black eyeliner, and ratted bleached blond hair and her black leather-jacketed boyfriend asked me if they could share the booth. I took a last bite of pizza and told them they could have it. It was time I was going anyway. It had been a little over an hour since I'd left the store. Donna should be home by now.

Outside, I cleared another inch of snow off the windows of my car and got in. North Salina, Court, and Park Streets were shut up for the night. A plastic Blessed Virgin Mary standing in a front yard on Vine Street watched me pass by. No one else was out. I parked in the driveway of Donna's house. The path to the front door hadn't been shoveled in the last day and my boots sank into the snow as I walked. I rang the bell and waited.

I could hear somebody yelling inside, another voice answering, then shuffling as somebody came down the hall. The door opened a couple of inches.

"Yes?" The woman standing in front of me must be Donna's aunt.

"I'd like to speak to Donna," I said as I edged my way in.

The aunt started gesticulating. "She no home yet."

Chutes and Adders   **151**

"Maria, who is it?" A man yelled from out back.

Maria answered in Italian, then broke into English. "She wants to speak to Donna. I tell her Donna is out."

Donna's uncle strode out into the hall. "She not here," he told me as he finished tying the belt around his bathrobe with a flourish. "She go to John's apartment."

His wife whirled around. "She never tell me that."

"She don't gotta tell you everything," he snapped.

They were both screaming at each other in Italian as I left. Somehow, I didn't think that Donna's aunt was exactly mourning John's death.

It took me about five minutes to locate the street John's apartment was on—I kept on turning onto dead ends—and fifteen more minutes to find the actual house. Whoever had named Golden Drive had suffered from a bad case of wanna-be's. "End of the Line" would have been more appropriate. Some blocks start off well, then the neighborhood changes and things go downhill. But not Golden Drive. It had started clap-trap and gotten worse. Half the houses had sagging porches and boarded up windows. Tar paper shingles, which are one step up from cardboard, was the siding material of choice. A good third of the houses had no numbers, which didn't matter because you couldn't read the ones that were there anyway. All the streetlamps were out.

By the time I knocked at 1832, I was cold and wet and tired. I rang once and waited. Nobody came, but I knew Donna was there because I could hear her on the other side of the door. I rang again, this time longer. Still no response. In the old days I would have left, but not now. I put my thumb to the buzzer and kept it there. After a minute, the door opened.

"Who is it?" Donna mumbled. Her eyes were unfocused, her speech slurred.

"Mind if I come in?" I asked, even though it was an academic question since she was in no shape to mind anything.

She clung to the door for support. " 'Nother time."

"I'll just take a moment."

She opened her mouth, then shut it. I was in before she could think of anything else to say.

We went into the hallway. The inside of the apartment didn't seem much better than the outside. The oilcloth on the floors was curling around the edges and the dirt-streaked orange walls were punctuated with white splotches that made them look as if they had an exotic skin disease. Wires sprouted out of the dangling light fixture in the hallway. When I followed Donna into the kitchen, the roaches crawling over a congealed hamburger didn't bother running. They were obviously used to company.

Donna took the cup she'd been holding and filled it full of Canadian Club.

"You?" she asked as an afterthought.

"Thanks, but I think I'll pass."

We went back to the living room, leaving the roaches to their own devices.

Donna collapsed on the sofa. A pile of clothes fell onto the floor. I picked up the shirts and pants—all green hospital garb—and put them on a chair before sitting down next to her.

Donna shook her head slowly from side to side. "Gotta take John's stuff back to St. Ann's," she muttered. Then she absentmindedly put her finger in her drink, brought it up to her mouth, and sucked the rye off a scarlet fingernail.

I took out the list I'd found and showed it to her.

"Yeah?" Her head came forward, then snapped back.

"Look at the list."

"Nice list." She pushed my hand away.

Chutes and Adders   **153**

"I want to talk to you about what's on it."

"Sure." Donna took a gulp of rye.

I pointed. "These are price lists."

"If you say so."

"Donna." I could feel my impatience rising. I pushed it back down. "Try and concentrate on what I'm saying."

"Sure." She gave me a lopsided smile. "Anything you want."

"I want you to look at this list again."

"Fine."

But before I could give it to her, she got up, put her hand over her mouth, and ran out of the living room.

By the time I got to the bathroom, Donna was heaving her guts out into the sink. I would have made a lousy nurse, because I walked out before I had to join her.

The sound of retching followed me as I went back down the hallway toward the living room. The door on the left-hand side of the corridor was ajar and I peeked in as I passed. John's bedroom. I stepped in. Barbells, weights, and piles of clothes were scattered all over the place. Socks, underwear, and sweaters were hanging out of opened dresser drawers. I poked around, but it was more for form's sake than anything else. The police had already been here and it was doubtful that I'd turn up anything they'd missed.

I left after a couple of minutes and went into the next room. The door had been closed. But what the hell. When I went inside I did a double take. I could have been in a different apartment. The room was clean and well lit. The walls were painted an off-white. The carpet was light green. But there was no furniture. Just photographs on the walls. And indentation marks in the carpet.

Nineteen

The marks in the carpet looked like they had been made by an aquarium—five, if you wanted to be exact. And I thought John had sold off his snake collection months ago. I had thought this because Murphy had told me John's landlord had given John an ultimatum—get rid of the snakes or get out—and John had sensibly chosen the former. It appeared John had acquired a new collection.

At least, that's what the portraits on the wall indicated. There were twenty in all and whoever had shot them knew what he was doing. The lighting was good, the cropping tight. Most were studies of people I'd seen around the West Side but five featured John and his snakes.

In one, John had a Burmese python wound around his torso. In another, John was feeding a mouse to a fat Gaboon viper. They were the snakes with the two-and-a-half-inch fangs. A third showed John and a black mamba. In the fourth and fifth John was lifting a huge diamondback rattler over his head. In all the photos, John was clean-shaven. Up until two months ago he'd sported a Ghenghis Khan mustache. You didn't have to be a genius to figure out the pictures had been taken recently.

I lit a cigarette, inhaled, then exhaled and went back in the bathroom. Donna was swallowing water from the tap. She'd take a swallow, swish it around her mouth, then spit it out.

"You still here?" she asked, turning her head slightly. Her skin looked yellow in the bathroom light.

"So it appears. What happened to John's snakes?"

"He sold them."

"To whom?"

"I told the cops all this already," she complained.

"Well tell me again."

Donna wiped her mouth with the side of her sleeve and stood up. "I need a drink," she announced and went back down the hall.

"Who bought them?" I repeated.

"Karkoff." I watched Donna pour herself another Canadian Club. "Not that it matters. God, this stuff sucks." She made a face and took a gulp.

"Maybe you should ease off."

Donna shot me a look and I shut up. After all, when it came to this sort of thing, who was I to talk? I was just one step above her.

"John . . ." Donna tapped her fingernails lightly against her glass while she thought. "John was one of those guys that always starts out strong, but finishes weak. Or doesn't finish at all. Know what I mean?"

I nodded encouragingly.

"He always got bored with things. He used to tell me he had a real short attention span."

I thought of the list in my pocket. "Did he get bored with the business he and Murphy and Tim were running?"

Donna burped and covered her mouth with her hand. " 'Scuse me. You keep asking me things the police already asked. I'll tell you what I told them. I don't know nothing about any business other than Noah's Ark."

I took Donna's glass out of her hand and put it on the table.

"Hey!" she protested.

"Just so you'll pay attention."

"Give it back." She made a halfhearted lunge then collapsed back on the sofa.

"In a moment. Now I am in a lot of trouble and I need to know everything that you do."

"And that's minus zero."

"Somehow I find that hard to believe. You lived with John. You worked with him. You mean to tell me you didn't know what the hell was going on?"

Donna cocked her head to one side. "Now you tell me something."

"What?"

"You lived with Murphy. Did you know what was going on?"

Donna's words dogged my steps as I left her apartment. Had I known? Yes and no. I'd known something was going on, but not what it was. The Truth with a capital "t" was that I hadn't wanted to know. Then I would have had to have done something and things weren't that bad that I couldn't ignore them. So I'd just gone along . . . not seeing . . . not hearing . . . not asking. And now the bills were coming due.

"You always pay," my father had been fond of saying. "One way or another, you always pay."

Well, it looked like he'd been right. I just hadn't thought the tariff was going to be this high.

Outside, the sleet had turned back to snow. I shivered as I cleared the accumulation off my rear window and thought about what an unbelievable fool I'd been and how I'd buried myself in my work. By now my hands were stiff from the cold and I could barely feel my knees. I opened the door and was sliding in when I happened to notice a silver Pinto parked down the block. Unlike the other cars it was clean: no snow on the roof, no snow on the hood. But I didn't think anymore about it until I saw it again when I turned onto James Street.

The car stayed about half a block back of me, but every time I turned, the Pinto did too. I got more and more nervous as it went up Park, down Lodi, and around Wentworth with me. Finally, I headed for the Big M, drove into the parking lot, and parked near the store. At least there were people here. A moment later, the Pinto pulled in and began circling the supermarket lot. Shit. I knew they'd see me. The cab stuck out like a sore thumb. But I hunched down in the seat anyway, hoping I'd be lucky. Who knew? Maybe whoever was driving would get bored and leave. But when I saw the Pinto heading toward me I knew that wasn't going to be the case.

I was trying to decide what to do when the car passed under a light and I caught a glimpse of who was in it.

Lorenzo and Cunningham.

My fear turned to rage.

Jesus, what right did they have to do this to me?

They pulled up behind me. I jumped out of my car and started toward them. They got out too. We met in the middle.

"What the hell are you doing following me?" I demanded.

"Were we?" Cunningham asked Lorenzo.

"You know Goddamn well you were," I snapped.

"And I thought we were just coming here to buy juice and cookies," Lorenzo told Cunningham.

"Just lay off me," I said, "or I'll . . ."

"You'll what?" Lorenzo asked.

Good question.

Too bad I didn't have a good answer.

So instead of saying anything, I wheeled around, got back in my car, and roared out of the parking lot.

It took me three cigarettes and fifteen minutes, but by the time I reached Tim's block I'd managed to calm myself down. After circling twice, I parked in front of the fire hydrant and rang his bell. I could tell from the expression on his face when he answered the door that he wasn't exactly happy to see me.

"Don't you believe in calling first?"

I took in the pajama bottoms and T-shirt. "Company?" I asked.

"Studying," he replied.

"I didn't know you were in school."

"Part-time. This is my first semester. So if you don't mind . . ."

He was closing the door when I showed him the list. He changed his mind and let me in.

"Jesus," Tim murmured as I hung up my jacket and scratched Merle behind the ears.

"I don't think he's going to help you now," I cracked as I took a cigarette out of my bag and lit it before sitting down on the sofa. "So," I said, exhaling, "talk to me."

Tim nervously tugged at his ponytail. "You look nice. Did you go out this evening?"

"Cut the bull and talk to me about what's on the list."

"You've seen it. What more is there to say?"

"Plenty."

He massaged his knuckles and thought for a while. "I guess it doesn't matter now anyway," he finally said. "What do you want to know?"

"For openers, how about telling me how the whole thing got started."

"It was Murphy's idea. You know how he was always into these get-rich-quick schemes?"

"Yes." Did I ever. Murphy was into options and commodities. For every win, there was a loss. Usually a big one. But he never learned. There was always a new "hot tip" he couldn't pass up. Maybe that was one of the reasons I never wanted to stop working.

"Well," Tim continued. "We were always getting these people walking into the store asking us for shit we didn't have and couldn't get. And Robin, you shoulda seen these guys. You could tell they were living large. So Murphy figured: hey, what the hell? Why not give em what they want? Only we couldn't because we didn't have a contact, you know, someone who knows who to pay off, that kind of thing. So that was that. End of plan.

"Only people, they kept on asking, they kept on offering money. And then a year ago I went back down to Florida to visit my family and everything changed."

I leaned forward. "What happened?"

"I ran into one of my cousins, right? He'd switched jobs. Now he's working at Herp Inc. Naturally we get to talking and well suddenly everything just rolls along. It's like I'm on a mission from God or something, you know, 'cause everything goes so smooth. And the money, it just starts coming in, because people tell their friends and suddenly everybody starts wanting weird shit."

"What did you guys sell?"

"Everything, man." Tim ripped at his cuticles. "You name it, we had it."

"Venomous?"

He shrugged.

"Endangered?"

"We gave people what they wanted. I don't know." Tim

put his hands up. "We was flying, man. Everything was goin' so good, then it all turned to shit. Murphy dies, John gets done, the cops find the money."

I pointed to the list. "You think maybe one of your customers wasn't satisfied?"

He shook his head. "We never stiffed anyone. We gave good value."

"That's not what Karkoff said," I replied and I told him what he'd said about Rajah.

Tim snorted. "Screw him. That man was never satisfied. With anything." Then he turned and lightly ran his fingers over the statue of the girl on his shelf.

Something about her rang a bell. I got up to get a better look. She was about fifteen inches high and made of plastic. Her hand rested on a gold tower, her bare feet stood on impossibly green grass. Her eyes were deep blue, her mouth a garish rose red. She wore a white tunic and a red mantle bordered with gold. Next to her was a half-smoked cigar and a small glass full of liquid. I picked it up and smelled it. Rum.

"Chango," I whispered.

Tim's eyes widened in surprise.

I was right.

It was all I could do to keep from laughing.

Twenty

For a few seconds after I spoke the only noise in the room was Merle gnawing on a chew bone.

Then Tim said, "Whose this Chango dude you're talking about?" He indicated the statue. "This here's St. Barbara." But his voice was too studiedly casual. He was lying. I could feel it.

"It's both," I told him.

"You don't know what you're talking about."

"Oh, don't I?"

"No, you don't."

"I read a book about Santería. They had her picture in it."

"I read a book," he repeated, mimicking me. "Listen, I don't care what you read. I'm a good Catholic and I'm telling you that this here statue is St. Barbara."

I pointed to the glass of rum and the half-smoked cigar. "I didn't know St. Barbara drank."

"She doesn't. I do."

"Does she smoke too?"

"Jesus," Tim muttered as he put his hand up to his throat and began nervously fingering what looked like a thin strand of beads. The rest of the necklace was hidden under his T-shirt. It was the first time I'd noticed them. A picture in another of the books I'd read about Santería flashed through my mind.

"That necklace you're wearing . . ."

Tim quickly dropped his hand back down to his side. "What about it?"

"Correct me if I'm wrong but does it consist of a double strand of six white and six red beads?"

Tim gave a nervous bark of laughter.

"You've made your *asientos* to Chango haven't you?"

Tim said nothing.

"Haven't you?" I repeated more loudly.

His glance danced over the room.

"You might as well tell me. I already know."

Tim hesitated a moment before looking me full in the face. "So what if I have?" he said defiantly. "It's none of your business."

"Oh yes it is," I replied, remembering my unfinished conversation with Sam.

"How do you figure that?"

"Because I think that somehow this stuff is all mixed up with John's death. And Sam's."

"No."

"No what?"

"No it's not."

I looked at him curiously. "How can you be so sure?"

"Because Santería doesn't have to do with death."

"Oh really? You kill chickens don't you? And goats? What do you call that?"

"A sacrifice."

"I'm sure the animals appreciate the difference."

Tim curled his lip in disgust. "You eat meat, don't you?"

"Yes?"

"Then what gives you the right to criticize us? At least we slaughter our animals quickly."

"Yeah. Well what about the things they do in brujería? I wouldn't call that merciful."

Tim crossed himself. "I don't have anything to do with that kind of stuff."

"Did Sam?"

"What do you think?"

I rubbed my temples. "I don't know what to think anymore," I confessed.

"Well he didn't," Tim said, his voice suddenly grown soft with remembrance. "He didn't hold with witchcraft. He said nothing good ever came of it. He said it gave our people a bad name."

"Our people?"

"Hispanics."

"Isn't McDowell an Irish name?"

"My father was Irish but my mother was Puerto Rican."

"Is that who you learned about Santería from?"

"You know for a long time I didn't do none of this stuff. I thought it was real dumb."

"So what happened to make you change your mind?"

"After my mom died, my dad started drinking and I got sent up here to live."

"It must have been rough."

"Yeah, it was." Tim's eyes glazed over. He blinked rapidly to hold back the tears. "I felt all dead inside. But I don't feel so bad anymore." He managed a small smile. "I guess I have Sam to thank for that."

"How's that?"

"Because Sam told me that if I became a believer, if I

started doing all the rituals and stuff, that my mom would be with me again. And he was right. She is."

"How did Sam know?"

Tim looked at me in amazement. "Haven't you guessed? He was a *bablawo*."

"A what?"

"A teacher." Tim gestured toward the kitchen. "You want a beer. I was just about to get one."

I said yes and we went into the kitchen together and Tim got two beers out of the fridge and handed me one and told me about how Sam was a deeply religious man and how he always tried to do the right thing and how important he was in the community and how he didn't know who was going to take his place.

"Do you have any idea who'd want to kill him?" I asked Tim as we walked back toward the living room.

"None at all."

We sat down. Merle climbed up between us and lay her head on Tim's lap. Tim began scratching the top of her head.

"But he was worried about something," Tim confided after a few minutes.

"I don't suppose he happened to tell you what it was?"

"No. He just said he was going to consult the coconut shells about a problem. Maybe they would tell him what to do."

So much for that line of inquiry. The sliver of hope I'd felt died. I took a sip of beer and switched topics. "How did he feel about brujería?"

"I already told you. He was dead set against it."

I gestured to the list I'd found. "Do you think any of these people practice it?"

Tim shrugged his shoulders. "I wouldn't know. I never

asked. Like I said it's something I don't want to know anything about."

"Well I think I'm going to ask them about that . . . and other things."

"Why are you telling me this."

"Because I need their names."

Tim stopped petting Merle. "I don't know if I should give them to you."

"The way I look at it is, you don't have a choice."

"Why's that?"

"Because otherwise I'm going to give this list to the cops."

"You wouldn't."

But the look on my face must have told him I would, because he got a pen and a piece of paper and started writing.

By the time I got back home it was after one in the morning and I was too tired to think about the information I'd gotten from Tim or about anything else for that matter. I went straight upstairs, peeled off my clothes and crawled into bed. I fell asleep immediately, but then I started to dream. In my dream, the names Tim had given me twisted themselves into strange gelatinous shapes, oozed off the pages, and slithered away. I chased them down a long bristle-filled tunnel that kept folding in upon itself, but no matter how fast I ran, the names always stayed just out of reach.

I awoke at five in the morning with a pounding headache. I took some aspirin, then dozed until the alarm went off at eight. I still had my headache, but I got up anyway—I had too much to do to stay in bed—swallowed a few more pills, opened a can of cat food for James, then ate some yogurt while I pondered what I'd learned last night. I was in the middle of going over my conversation with Sam when Joe rang up. He started in without even a hello.

"I'm calling in regards to the question you asked me the other day."

"What question?" I hadn't asked him anything. I hadn't even seen the man.

"The question regarding disclosure. There's a point of law you might not be aware of."

I told him I didn't know what the hell he was talking about.

"I'm sorry I couldn't get to you before, but I just got back in town and it's taken me a little while to get to my mail."

Suddenly I saw. He was talking about the list I'd found. I'd Xeroxed it, put his copy in an envelope, attached a note, and left it in his office mailbox.

"So what do you . . . ?"

"Let me finish."

"Is something wrong? I don't understand."

"You will if you'd just let me explain," Joe snapped.

"Fine." I shifted the receiver to my other ear. "I'm listening. Explain away."

"Good. I probably should have made this a little clearer but the fact is that if someone comes to me with information that has any bearing on a crime being investigated, no matter how remote, I'm obligated to disclose it to the D.A. as evidence. That's the law. Understand? Now if there is an indictment for this crime then that's another story."

"What other story?"

"If the same piece of information comes to my attention then I can act in a different manner. I can take action."

"So what, exactly, are you saying?"

"I'm saying that in law, as in life, timing is everything."

"Spare me your platitudes," I told him and banged the receiver down.

So Joe wasn't going to do anything with the list I'd given him. He couldn't. That's what he'd called to tell me. Now, why hadn't he told me that before? First he tells me to find Murphy's records and then when I come up with something—even if it wasn't what he or I had expected—he tells me he can't do anything with what I've given him. He has to wait until I'm indicted and then move.

Well, maybe Joe's hands were tied, maybe he couldn't ask questions, but I could. I hadn't gone to all this trouble for nothing. No sir. There was no way I was just going to sit back and see what happened next. That was for sure. Especially when it was my neck on the block.

I washed my dishes, went upstairs, threw on some sweats, laced up my high tops, then came back downstairs, got the list, put on my jacket, and left to go to the store. I figured I'd look up numbers and make calls between customers.

But it turned out I didn't have to bother with the first call I was going to make.

Because when I pulled up in front of Noah's Ark, Thomas Maroney and a man I didn't know were coming out of El Gordito's. I got out of the cab, walked over to them, and asked Maroney what was going on.

He locked the door and pocketed the key before replying. "I'm thinking of buying the place." He smoothed down the lapels of his cashmere coat.

"I didn't know it was for sale."

Maroney indicated the man standing next to him. "Mr. Ramirez, Sam's second cousin, has decided it would be in his interest to sell."

"You really do work fast, don't you?"

Maroney told Sam's cousin he wanted a word with me, then he grabbed my arm and propelled me over to my cab. "Just stay out of my business."

"What did you do, get in contact with the man the moment Sam died?"

"As a matter of fact, he got in touch with me."

"So how much are you giving him?"

"A fair price."

"By whose definition?"

"My own. I'm a businessman and businessmen make money."

"Don't you care about anything else?"

"Considering who you were married to, I find that statement somewhat comical."

To my amazement I found myself defending Murphy. "Listen, asshole," I told Maroney, "even if Murphy did try and turn a fast buck now and then, at least he didn't take advantage of people's bad fortune to do it."

"Yeah, the man was a saint. Anything you wanted he'd get if he could. You know the real difference between him and me?" Maroney indicated himself. "I got a nice house out in the suburbs, a fancy car, and a hot little wife. And Murphy? Well Murphy, he didn't have shit."

Sam's cousin being there was the only thing that kept me from smashing in Maroney's face. For some reason, I didn't want to behave badly in front of him.

As Maroney walked to the car, I wondered why I had gotten so angry. Probably because everything he had said was true. I rubbed my temples trying to make the pounding in my head go away. I felt like I was walking on a tight wire stretched between two buildings. And there was no net underneath. To cross it, I had to just keep going. If I paused or asked too many questions, I'd fall.

All the way down.

I was thinking about how much my life had changed in the past couple of months and about how much my perception of things had altered as I walked to the store. The moment I unlocked the door Pickles ran up and greeted me. She purred with pleasure when I picked her up and rubbed her under her chin. As I carried her over to the counter, I noticed a very dead, half-eaten mouse lying beside the cash register. At least, I decided as I threw it in the garbage, someone around here was doing what they were supposed to.

I turned up the heat, slipped out of my jacket, and began to get ready for the day. But before I even had a chance to count the cash in the drawer things turned busy. And they stayed that way till early evening. Between cleaning cages, taking care of a leaky aquarium, answering the phone, and waiting on customers, I didn't have time to smoke a cigarette, much less do anything else.

Finally around six things slacked off enough for me to close up the store and run down to McD's and grab a hamburger, Coke, and fries. When I came back I got out the phone book and tried putting numbers to the seventeen names Tim had given me.

Surprisingly, most were listed. After I wrote the last number down, I began dialing. The first two people didn't answer, the third, a Rick Dicaprio, had moved to Arizona, the fourth, a Wayne Hart, was in Jamesville Penitentiary for stealing cars, while the fifth had died in an automobile accident three months ago. Very discouraging.

I leaned against the counter. Pickles jumped up and butted my arm with her head. I was petting her when the door opened and Cunningham and Lorenzo walked in. As Joe said, when you're a suspect in two homicides you merit lots of attention.

As inconspicuously as possible, I pushed the list under a pile of order sheets and walked out from behind the counter.

"We just dropped in to say hello," Cunningham said.

"You know, see how things are going," Lorenzo added.

"Well now that you've seen, you can leave."

"In a moment. Did you know," she continued, "that in most murders—maybe sixty to seventy percent—the person who discovers the body is the murderer?"

"I'll be sure and save that statistic for my next Trivial Pursuits game."

"You do that little thing," Lorenzo replied. "Although I hear they don't play that game up in Bedford Hills Correctional Facility too much."

"Funny lady."

"I don't think they're going to like your attitude up there."

"Do you clowns have something to say to me? Because if you don't, get out," I ordered, jerking my thumb in the direction of the door.

"We're going," Lorenzo answered, "for now. But we'll be dropping in again, real soon."

Then Cunningham poked my shoulder with his index finger. "You think that high-priced lawyer can slick you out of this?" he rasped. "Well, you'd better think again."

I slapped his finger away. "Do me a favor. Keep your hands to yourself."

"Sensitive, aren't you?"

I stifled a retort and bit my lip instead. I was damned if I was going to give those two the satisfaction of seeing me lose my temper.

Twenty-one

I called Joe the moment Lorenzo and Cunningham left. Wife number three answered and informed me her husband was out with a client. Knowing Joe, the client was probably twenty-two and stacked. Judging from the martyred tone in the wife's voice, she probably knew it too. I left a message and hung up. Afterward I wondered why I'd bothered. Joe had already made it clear that until Lorenzo arrested me, there wasn't much he could do.

I went back to calling the numbers on my list, but after getting two more no answers I quit. What was the point? Who did I think I was kidding? I stuffed the list in my pocket, went into Murphy's office, and finished clearing off his desk—more to give myself something to do than for any other reason. At least this task was easy and straightforward and the results were visible. I was throwing a bunch of old newspapers in the trash when a picture on the front page of the *Herald*'s Metro section, a picture I had taken, caught my eye. It was Steve Hartoonian.

He was receiving a plaque from a fashionably turned-out woman. Both were smiling the frozen smile people put on for public consumption. The caption underneath read, "Noted religion professor receives Hyman Davis Award for furthering religious understanding in the community."

I reached for the phone book. If anyone could answer my questions on brujería, it was Hartoonian. He was a recognized expert in the field of the occult. He traveled all over the country giving lectures on the subject. Probably, I thought as I dialed, the way my luck was going he wouldn't be home. But he was. I told him my story and he told me he'd see what he could find out. We agreed to meet at R.J.'s the following evening.

After I hung up I smoked a second cigarette and went home. Suddenly I was too tired to do anything else. I spent the rest of the evening watching TV, petting James, drinking Scotch, brooding about what my life had become, and wondering where I had taken a wrong turn.

That night I dreamt about walking on a beach scattered with seashells. A sweet low voice crooned in my ears. The waves broke gently in the distance. I waded out into the water. I was up to my hips when my alarm went off. For a moment, I managed to cling to the vision. Then it faded, leaving me back in my own bed staring out at a gray winter sky. I curled up in a ball and put my head under the pillows, but I felt like I was smothering so I got up, shrugged on my jeans and an old sweatshirt, got the paper from the mailbox, made myself some coffee, and ate two chocolate bars. When I was done I took the list out of my jacket pocket and started dialing. I got two no answers and two answering machines. Probably everyone was at work. But on my fifth try I got lucky. Anita Dembroski, wife of Art, answered.

She was more than happy to chat with me, especially when I told her I was doing an article for a national magazine—unspecified—about people who owned exotic pets. And she assured me that her husband would be pleased to talk to me too. When it turned out that he worked at St. Ann's, which was practically next door to Noah's Ark, I decided to give the lady's statement a try. I called Tim to make sure he was opening up the store, splashed some water on my face, ran a comb through my hair, and drove over to the hospital. I parked my car in the visitor's garage and went inside.

The lobby was empty. It was too early for visitors. The linoleum gleamed under the fluorescent lights as I walked through to the back elevator and took it down to the basement. I was heading for the loading dock. Or trying to. But St. Ann's is two to three square blocks in size and I got lost.

I kept turning corners and finding myself back in the same corridors I had been in before. I was beginning to feel as if I'd stumbled into a maze from the *Twilight Zone* when I spotted an arrow with a sign pointing to the loading area. Five minutes and a couple more wrong turns later, I saw a pair of gray double-hung steel fire doors. The words, AUTHORIZED PERSONNEL ONLY. NO ADMITTANCE were spelled out in big red letters. I pushed the door open and stepped in.

The room was big—maybe thirty by forty feet—and unheated. The walls, the ceiling, and the floor were all painted cement gray. I don't know why the administration had bothered. It probably looked the same now as it had before they painted. Bags of trash, piles of newspapers, and different-sized cartons were stacked along the right-hand wall. In back of me, three sets of push-up doors led to the outside loading docks. I was standing there, congratulating myself on finding the place, when I heard someone asking me what the hell I thought I was doing.

"Looking for Art Dembroski," I said, turning around. A big, burly guy with sandy-colored hair and a beer gut sticking out of his pants was standing on one of the loading docks glaring at me.

"That's me. What do you want?"

"Your wife said you'd talk to me." And I explained about my exotic pet article and as I did I realized that this guy looked familiar. But I couldn't place the face.

"Snakes? You want to talk about my snakes?" He jumped down from the dock and came over to where I was standing. "Sure, I don't mind."

As he did I recalled where I'd seen him. "I remember you." I snapped my fingers. "You were the guy who asked me about John when I brought him into the ER."

"You brought him in?"

"Was he a friend of yours?"

"Not exactly. He worked here part-time. Sweeping up. Washing floors. That kind of thing. How did you come to know him?"

"He worked in my husband's store."

"You're Murphy's wife?" he asked in a surprised tone.

"Was."

"Tough break." Art shook his head as if in wonderment at the unfairness of the universe, then pulled a pouch of Skoal out of his inside shirt pocket, took a pinch of tobacco, and put it inside his cheek before continuing. "I didn't know him too well, but he seemed like a nice guy. Nicer than John by a long shot. Not to speak ill of the dead, but the only time that guy was interested in you was if he could get something out of you. But he did turn me on to pythons. I'll say that for him. And he did know a lot about reptiles. He got me this one king cobra. God, what a beauty."

I thought about my recent encounter with Karkoff's king cobra while I got out my pad and pencil. Several adjectives came to mind to describe Rajah. Beautiful, however, was not one of them.

"Does your wife care?"

"About me keeping snakes?" I nodded as I prepared to jot his answer down. After all, I was supposed to be writing an article. The least I could do was make it look real. "Not really. I think she figures it keeps me out of mischief. Actually she doesn't even see them. I have them in a separate room down in the basement. It's got a lock and everything on it. She insisted on that. That way she don't have to worry none."

"So you don't take your snakes out of their cages and carry them around the house?"

"What are you? Nuts?"

"Some people do," I replied, thinking of Karkoff again.

Art spit on the floor. "Well I just take mine out when I'm cleaning their aquariums and then I wear heavy gloves. I never been bit and I don't intend to be either."

"So what do you do with them?"

"I look at 'em. I have this Lazy Boy recliner down in the room and sometimes I just come down and sit and stare at them. It's kind of like looking at fish. It relaxes me. And I like the challenge of keeping them. It's very difficult. Everything has to be right or they die."

I stopped writing for a minute. "I've read some people use them in religious ceremonies."

"You mean like those Baptists down South that pick up rattlers to show they're God's chosen people? I read about them in *Reader's Digest*. Well, there's no accounting for tastes."

"They also used them in brujería," I added, curious as to the reaction I was going to get.

"Brujería? What the hell is that?"

Art's bewilderment was obviously genuine. He didn't

know what I was talking about. So I explained. As I talked, he reached into his pocket, took out another pinch of tobacco, and stuffed it in his cheek. He was beginning to look like a man with an abscessed tooth.

"Makes you wonder," he said when I was through. "The world just seems to be going crazy these days. Absolutely nuts." And then he started talking about himself.

I wrote down about how he'd found a ribbon snake when he was eight and smuggled it into his house. Only somehow it got loose and wound up in his mother's dresser drawer and he'd gotten the whipping of his life. But that hadn't stopped him. Oh no. It just made him more careful about how he housed the snakes he caught. No, he'd always been interested in them. He liked the way they looked and the way they moved—all controlled energy—and they were better than dogs and cats because you only had to feed them every two weeks and they didn't get hair all over the house. He knew some people thought he was weird, but he knew plenty of others, like Murphy, who didn't.

"Or Dick Higgins," he said, scratching the stubble on his cheek.

"Dick Higgins?" I tapped my cheek with my pencil. The name rang a bell. Yes. I was almost positive that name had been on John's list.

"Now that guy has a great collection," Art mused. "His king cobra is almost nineteen feet long and he has an anaconda that's twenty-five feet if it's an inch. Let me tell you, John made lots of money off of that guy." Dembroski spit a thin stream of brown tobacco juice on the floor. " 'Cause truth to tell, I dropped a couple of dollars with him myself. Too much, according to the wife. But I'm a piker compared to Dick. Now there's someone you should talk to."

"I'd like to."

"He's usually home most evenings."

"Thanks." I closed my pad and slipped it along with my pencil back in my bag. "You've been really helpful."

Art leaned forward. "But if I were you I wouldn't go to his house."

"Why's that?"

"Like I said, he's kind of a weird guy."

"How do you mean?"

"Well for openers he's got his snakes crawling around all over the house." I suppressed a shudder. "That would sure give me the willies, but I guess everyone's got their own ways." Art paused and stroked his chin again. "Tell you what. He comes here every day to pick up the trash. Maybe you can get him then."

I thanked Art for the suggestion and left the way I came in. This time I only got lost once.

On Friday nights, R.J.'s is always jammed. But tonight was Thursday and the place was almost empty. About ten people, split fifty—fifty between college kids and townies—were clustered down at one end of the long bar sipping beer and watching the SU—Seton Hall basketball game. It had been a bad season for the Orangemen and judging from the morose expressions, this game was following true to form.

I ordered a Dos Equis and sat down to wait for Steve. He came in about twenty minutes later while I was in the midst of a heated discussion on who would be named to the Associated Press All Pro Team. I excused myself, bought a beer for Hartoonian, another for myself, and shepherded him off to one of the corner booths. When we sat down, he took off his beret, put it on the table, and ran his hand through his hair. He was wearing jeans and an old black turtleneck sweater. The black highlighted the bags under his eyes and the pastiness of his skin. Maybe the rumor I'd heard about his wife leaving him was true. He had the air of a man on his own and not liking it.

He took a sip of beer and we chatted about all the usual things, the weather, books we'd read, college sports, before we got down to business. Which didn't take long to complete because Hartoonian didn't have much to tell me.

He knew about Santería and he knew about Sam, all right. He spent about five minutes telling me what a great man Sam had been and what a pity it was that Sam had never gone back to teaching. But Hartoonian didn't know about brujería, because the person he thought he could get to talk turned out to be on vacation somewhere out West. He'd tried other people, but they either didn't know anything or weren't saying if they did. Which made sense. I know *I* certainly wouldn't be running around telling people *I* was out in the graveyard last night digging up a body.

"Sorry." Hartoonian apologized again for not being able to help. "There *is* someone else you might want to talk to, though."

"Yes?" I leaned forward.

Hartoonian rubbed his finger across his lip. "Of course, he is a bit of a charlatan."

"That's okay. At this point I don't think I'm in a position to be fussy."

"Well, I just wanted to warn you."

"I consider myself warned."

"As long as you know." Hartoonian rubbed his lip again. "You have something to write with?"

"I should." I began rummaging around in my bag. A moment later I found a pen and a scrap piece of paper. "Ready whenever you are."

Hartoonian took a sip of beer, then gave me the name and

address. As I wrote them down, I reflected that at least now I had something—even if it was slightly dubious—to go on. And who could tell? Why not try and be positive for a change? Maybe this information would actually lead me somewhere.

Twenty-two

Hartoonian and I talked for a while longer, chatting aimlessly about this and that. Then he left and Connie, a friend of mine who moonlights as a bartender when she's not singing, and I exchanged cat stories. It was one of the things we always did: see whose cat had acted worse that week. After about five minutes though, people started coming in and Connie had to get to work.

I passed the time sipping the Scotch I'd ordered and gazing at the name and address Hartoonian had given me. José Ramos, 1385 Oswego Street. They rang a bell, but if you'd asked me, I wouldn't have been able to tell you which one. Disgusted with myself, I slipped the paper in my shirt pocket and went back to watching the Hoyas pound the Orangemen. Halfway through watching Billy Owens score on a rebound, I remembered.

Of course!

Thirteen eighty-five.

That was the house Tim and Karkoff had come out of.

The house Tim's uncle supposedly lived in.

It looked like it was time to pay this José Ramos a visit.

I got Connie's attention and asked her for a dollar's worth of change and the phone book. When she brought it, I looked up the number. There were ten Ramoses listed for the city of Syracuse. My man José was fourth on the list. As I jotted the number down, I reflected on how impossible this job would be in someplace like Miami or New York City. Sometimes there are advantages to living in a small city. Then I walked to the back and dialed. The line was busy. I returned to the bar, watched the game, and sipped some more Scotch. After a few minutes of that, I got up and dialed again. Still busy. Six tries later, my patience gave out. I decided to drive over. What the hell. It wasn't like I had anything better to do.

I was sorry I'd left R.J.'s warmth the moment I stepped outside. The wind tore at my jacket. A scrap of newspaper wrapped itself around my legs, then tumbled across the parking lot. I lowered my head and quickly walked the six feet or so to my car. I put a Stones tape in the stereo and sang along with it on the drive over. I was most of the way through "Jumping Jack Flash" when I hit Oswego Street. I parked in front of 1385, ran up the steps, and rang the bell. A moment later the door opened a sliver.

"Sí?" a voice said.

"José Ramos?"

"Yes?"

"Steve Hartoonian said you might be able to help me."

"You are a friend of his?"

"Yes."

"Just a minute and I let you in."

I heard the slide bolt being pulled back. Then the door swung open and I was face-to-face with José Ramos. He was a slender man in his early to midforties. Average height. Average looks. Neatly dressed in slacks, a white shirt, and a cardigan sweater. His only mark of distinction was the gold bridgework glinting in his mouth. When I stepped inside, I heard giggling, then feet running up a flight of stairs.

"My nieces," Ramos explained. "My wife is watching them for her sister."

So that was why I couldn't get my call through. I looked around. In contrast to the outside, the hallway and the living room were neat and clean, monastically so. Whoever did the housekeeping had a meticulous eye. It wasn't what I expected. But then, the man watching me with birdlike intensity wasn't what I expected either.

"You want some coffee?" he asked.

When I nodded, Ramos took my coat. Then he escorted me into the living room and disappeared into the kitchen. As I waited for his return, I heard the unmistakable beat of rap filtering down from upstairs. The nieces must have turned on the stereo. I shifted uncomfortably on the red velvet sofa.

Nothing I saw, not the glass and chrome coffee table, or the matching red satin loveseat with the plastic cover over it, or the white mantel with the framed high school graduation pictures of dark-skinned boys and girls flashing white-toothed smiles made me think I had come to the right place.

I was wondering if Hartoonian had made a mistake when José Ramos reentered the room. He was carrying a tray with a coffeepot, two cups, and a plate full of chocolate chip cookies.

"My wife made them," Ramos declared as he offered me one.

"They're good," I said, taking a bite as he poured me a cup of coffee.

I took a sip and smiled. It was my favorite kind, strong and sweet. I drank half a cup and studied the crucifix tacked up on the left-hand wall while I tried to figure out how to begin the conversation.

Ramos followed my gaze. "You are Catholic?"

"No, but my husband was."

"So is my wife." Ramos leaned forward. "Now, how can I help you?"

But before I could answer I heard the front door opening and closing. José glanced at his watch.

"My wife, Belicia," he explained as a woman strode into the room.

When she saw me, she came to a dead stop. Her eyes narrowed. "You swore." She turned and shook a finger at her husband. "You promised me no more."

As José made ineffectual shooing gestures with his hand I began to very much wish I was someplace else. "Woman, go," he ordered, "can't you see I am conducting business here."

Her jaw muscles tightened. She folded her arms across her chest, planted her feet on the carpet, and glared at him. Smaller than her husband, her features were finely proportioned, her hair pulled back in a French twist. She wore sneakers, corduroy pants, and a red sweatshirt. Her only piece of jewelry was a pair of round gold earrings. She looked elegant. She would have looked elegant in a K-Mart special. Some women had that knack.

Then I made the mistake of coughing and she concentrated her wrath on me. "And what exactly do *you* want here?" she demanded.

"Steve Hartoonian suggested . . ." I began but that was as far as I got before she cut me off.

"That one." She rolled her eyes toward the ceiling. "Always asking questions. Too many questions. Writing things that give our people a bad name. That make others think we are stupid."

"I don't think that's his intention."

"It is what happens. I tell you something. I work hard," she said in what sounded like the beginning of a well-practiced litany. "Everyday I am at Mathews. All day, I do ladies' nails. Then when I come home at six you know what I find?" I shook my head. "People I do not know in my house. Candle wax on the dining room table. Strange mixtures in my kitchen pots. Sometimes"—Belicia's voice quivered with indignation—"I even find a dead chicken in my sink."

"Mujer"—José's voice rose to a thunderous pitch—"you are shaming me. This woman is not interested in hearing us fight."

"We would not be fighting, if you did not do these things," she snapped. Then she favored me with a sympathetic glance. "You look like a nice lady. Do yourself a favor and go home," she advised before she marched out. "Save your money."

A few seconds later, I heard the sound of opening cupboards and clanging pots. Belicia was in the kitchen.

"It is the priest that makes this trouble between me and my wife," José muttered as he twisted the diamond and gold signet ring on his pinky back and forth. "He does not understand that I do a service for the community, that I help people. That maybe I help you." José sat up straighter, obviously cheered by the prospect.

"Maybe you can," I agreed.

"What you want?" José leaned forward eagerly. "How can I help you? You want advice on money?"

"No."

"Love? The coconut shells . . ."

"Actually," I said interrupting him, "I'm more interested in something else."

"Yes?" José cocked his head and waited for my reply.

"Brujería."

"Dios mío." José quickly crossed himself. "I know nothing about this. Nothing."

"Hartoonian said you might."

José spat into the ashtray. "Hartoonian is wrong."

"Maybe. Maybe not."

He pointed toward the door. "I think you should go. I think maybe Belicia was right."

"And I think you should listen to what I have to say."

And I told him who I was and explained about the airport and the carton I'd received and the call I'd made to my friend down in Fort Myers. As I talked, José got paler and paler.

"This has nothing to do with me," he reiterated when I was done. But he was sweating when he said it and his hands were convulsively plucking at the legs of his pants.

"Yeah, right."

"Why don't you believe me?" he bleated.

Instead of answering I reached into my pocketbook, took out my wallet, extracted four twenty-dollar bills and laid them on the coffee table. "Now you have a choice," I explained to him. "You can take this money and tell me what I want to know. Or I can leave . . ."

"Yes, please," he said quickly.

". . . and some of my friends will drop by. They tend to be a bit short in the patience department, but . . ." Here I shrugged eloquently and allowed my voice to fade away.

Judging from the way José shrank back in his chair, I knew he believed me. Hell, I almost believed me.

"Look," I went on, "I'm obviously not going to go to the police with what you tell me. I can't. All I want to do is get myself out of trouble. And for that I need information. I need to know about the head."

José remained silent.

"Last chance."

He pressed his lips together.

"Or," I said, suddenly inspired, "maybe I'll just ask your

wife. See if she knows something." I began to get up. "You won't mind, will you?"

"Don't." The word shot out half command, half plea.

I sat back down. "Then talk to me," I ordered. "Talk to me now."

José looked over his shoulder, then hurriedly stuffed the bills in his pants pocket.

"Well," I said after a minute of silence, "I'm waiting."

"You swear you wouldn't go to the police?"

I raised my right hand. "I swear."

José looked doubtful. I pointed out that I'd be in more trouble than he would if I went.

"All right," he said after another minute had elapsed, "I will tell you what you want to know." And he began. "Two months ago, maybe more, maybe less, this man appears at my door. He says he hears that I am a grand *palero*. I am about to tell him that this is not true when he offers me money, much money."

"How much money?"

"Fifteen hundred dollars."

I let out a low whistle. "To do what?"

"I am supposed to make a *prenda* and he will take pictures of me doing this. At first, I say no. A *prenda*, it is a serious thing. Most *paleros* do not have them. They are bad things, especially if you lose control. You must be very strong. Otherwise you will bring something up that you will not be able to put back down."

"If you believed that then why did you go ahead?"

José twisted his pinky ring around his finger again. "This man he offer me another five hundred dollars. And I think that Belicia's birthday is soon. And I think that if I give her something nice, like a diamond ring, she would appreciate me more. And I also think that this man is white and he does not know what is supposed to be inside a *prenda* anyway, so I tell him yes. Sam said not to . . ."

"Sam knew?"

"Yes. I tell him when I am buying things at his store. Sam tells me it is a bad idea, that bad attracts bad, and I tell him that he is jealous, that he should mind his own business. Now, I think Sam was right," José finished gloomily.

He picked up his cup and took another sip of coffee. I did likewise. "So what happened?" I asked after a moment.

José sighed and put down his cup. "Everything went wrong. You see, I thought I go to the butcher and get some blood and bones and I use those. But this man, he calls me up and wants to know where I am getting the head from." José extended his hands palms out. "What to do?"

"You could have given back the money."

"I do not want to give it back. I have already seen a ring that I think Belicia will like. So I think and think and finally, I remember my cousin Carlos. Carlos, he always work very hard, always has two jobs. One is with snakes. But in the other, he is sweeping floors in the place where they keep the bodies. I call him up and ask for a favor and he says he will see if he can help me." José stopped and looked down at his cup as if hoping to read his future in the coffee dregs.

"Go on," I prompted.

"A few days later he call back. There is this head, in the trailer where they keep the bodies. It has been there for a long time. Nobody comes for it. Carlos thinks it will not be missed."

Now I knew what it was that I had smelled that night at the Flying Tigers. Formaldehyde. The bag had reeked of it.

"I thought the head was supposed to be from a freshly buried corpse."

José crossed himself again. "God forbid."

"José," Belicia's voice rang out from the kitchen. "It is time to pick up Eduardo."

"My youngest," José explained, pushing his coffee cup away. "I must go."

"But you haven't finished," I protested.

"There is not time. I will tell you the rest later."

"José," Belicia's voice came again, sharper this time.

"Later . . . meaning?"

"Tomorrow."

But I didn't want to wait until tomorrow. "Just one last question."

"Yes, yes," José said hurriedly.

"Who was your customer?"

"I cannot tell you this." José contrived to look affronted.

"Why not?"

"Honor."

"Really?" I extracted another twenty from my wallet and pressed it into his hand.

"This," I said, "is the most honor I can afford."

"No." José shook his head. "I am sorry. But I can not do what you ask. It is not worth it to me."

"Is that so?" And I leaned over, grabbed José's wrists, and pulled him toward me. "If you don't tell me what I want to know," I hissed, "not only will I take back *all* the money I gave you, but I will also march into the kitchen and tell your wife everything you told me."

José's right eye twitched.

"And if I do that, know what?" I sneered. "Your life's gonna be a living hell."

"You won't." José's eye twitched harder.

"Oh, really? Watch me." And I let go of him and stood up.

"Okay. Okay," Jose whispered. "You win. I tell you what you want to know."

Score one for Robin, I thought as I sat back down.

Twenty-three

The name José had come up with didn't surprise me.

After all, anyone who enjoys playing kissy face with a six-foot king cobra has to be bent. In several directions.

The question was: how did that fact relate to everything else? I decided to diagram it out.

When I got home I shed my coat, got a paper and pencil, sat down on the kitchen table, and drew a square. Then I wrote Karkoff's name in the top right hand corner, John's in the top left corner, Tim's in the bottom right, and Sam's in the bottom left. Next I drew lines between John's and Tim's and Karkoff's name and wrote the word "snakes" on top of them. I wrote "Santería" between Tim and Sam and the word "head" followed by a question mark between Tim and Karkoff. Between John and Sam I inscribed acquaintance. Lastly I put a black border around John's and Sam's names, indicating they were dead. Then I sat back and studied what I had drawn.

The first most obvious fact was: out of four people, two were dead. Tim had been connected with both of them, Karkoff with one. In fact Tim was the only person who was connected with the three other players. Which meant—what?

That he was the murderer?

I started drawing "s's" in the paper. Big ones. Little ones.

"S" for Santería.

"S" for snake.

"S" for Sangre.

Then a big "S" with a question mark next to it for "Solution." Something I didn't have.

When I looked at my diagram, logic said Tim was the murderer. The facts were indisputable. But my gut said no. My gut said Karkoff.

I poured myself another Scotch and downed it while I sat at the kitchen table and stared at Karkoff's name and thought about the questions I wanted to ask him. Finally, around twelve, I went to bed.

Giant snakes with gaping mouths dominated my dreams. Murphy was there too, asking me what I wanted. I knew but when it came time to tell him I couldn't remember. I awoke at three, then again at four. At six-thirty I gave up trying, wrapped myself in a blanket, went down to the living room, and turned on the TV. At some point I must have dozed off because the next thing I knew it was after nine and Regis and Kathie were on.

I clicked it off—I'm not a morning TV person—got up, brewed myself some coffee, read the paper, and fed the cat. Then I called the zoo. Karkoff was out and wouldn't be back before two in the afternoon. The conversation I'd decided we had to have was going to have to wait. Terrific. I hung up without leaving a message, put on my jeans and black turtleneck, pulled my hair off my face, and braided it. As I was heading toward the door, I happened to catch a glimpse of myself in the hall mirror. Without makeup I looked sheet-white. The circles under my eyes had turned into dark bruises. What I needed was ten days at the beach. What I was going to get was Lorenzo breathing down my neck and another day of work at Noah's Ark.

I brushed the snow off the cab, started her up, and backed out of the driveway. When I reached Genesee I turned on the radio, but I didn't listen to it. I couldn't. I was still thinking about Karkoff. Not being able to talk to him was bothering me the way getting poison ivy when I was twelve had. I had an itch that I couldn't scratch. And it was making me nuts.

My father, I reflected as I took a right off Genesee onto Fayette, had always said I had no patience for anything. I guess maybe he was right. Five blocks later, while waiting for the light to turn red, I decided that I had to do something and that that something was going to be talking to Sena Perez. Her name was on John's list and the address I had for her, 110 Ohio, wasn't very far away from where I was. It wouldn't be a big deal to run by and have a chat.

Ohio Street was even worse than I had remembered it. The first block was a big vacant lot filled with snow-covered junked chairs, refrigerators, torn mattresses, and other domestic debris. The second block had four standing buildings, each surrounded by their own little plot of trash and debris. A backhoe would have improved the view immensely. The Seward Arms, a yellow brick apartment building with a chimney that was doing a good imitation of the Leaning Tower of Pisa, was the only inhabited place. The next two buildings, Mookie's Garage and Caroline's Seafood Deli, were distinguished by their peeling paint, their busted windows, and the rusted-out FOR SALE signs hanging out front.

One-Ten was down at the end of the block by the DEAD END sign. Small and green, it had pink windowframes and doorsills. Whoever painted it must have been homesick for the Caribbean. The front window was boarded up. Across it, someone had scrawled NED'S HAIR, CLOTHING, AND ACCESSORIES in block letters. Underneath, someone else had spray-painted POWER FOR, NOT OVER, THE PEOPLE in purple. The metal gate across the door was fastened with the kind of padlock designed to foil bolt cutters. No one was in. I scribbled a note, shoved it through the mail slot, and continued on to Noah's Ark.

Tim had opened the store by the time I got there. When I walked in, he stopped what he was doing and scurried over, all abject apology.

"My uncle called to tell me you were over at his house last night," he said as I hung up my coat.

"We had an interesting conversation."

"So he said."

"And what do you have to say?"

His hands flew in the air. "What can I say? I'm really sorry."

"Believe me, not as sorry as I was." I walked over to the aquariums and started feeding the fish. Tim followed on my heels.

"You have to understand. I just felt bad for my uncle. I was trying to help him out. If I had known . . ."

"That I was going to pick up the package?"

". . . I never would have done it." He bit his cuticle.

I went on feeding the fish.

"What did you do with it?"

"You mean the tegu? He's right over there." I pointed to a cage over by the side of the room.

"You know what I'm talking about."

"Why are you so interested? You want the head?"

"Do you have it?"

"No I don't. I threw it out."

"You what?" Tim yelped.

"You heard me."

"Jesus Christ."

"Sorry. Next time I get one in the mail I'll call you."

Instead of replying, Tim grabbed a broom and started sweeping the floor. He used short, vicious strokes and I thought it best not to say anything else. No use getting into a full-scale argument. We worked in silence until the customers started streaming in. It turned out to be a good morning workwise. By twelve o'clock I'd sold one fifty and one thirty-five gallon aquarium with accessories for two hundred twenty and one hundred seventy-five dollars respectively, as well as a three-hundred-dollar rainbow boa. Business held up after lunch, mostly people coming in for fish food, meal worms, and crickets, but by three-thirty it had slacked off enough so that I figured I could leave Tim in charge of the store and go see Karkoff.

When I walked into the zoo, a clot of elementary school students were jostling each other in front of the admissions desk. Judging from their jackets and the souvenirs they were clutching, they were on their way home. I pushed past them and their frazzled-looking teacher and bought a ticket from a woman who only looked up long enough from her knitting to take my money.

I walked down the hallway, went past the anaconda's cage, and opened the door marked STAFF ONLY. The secretary's office was halfway down the first hallway on my left. She was shoehorned into a room that must have been a storage closet in its last incarnation. Her desk was littered with paper, styrofoam coffee cups, and remnants of half-eaten Danish. She looked up. One earring was off. The phone was clamped between her shoulder and her chin.

When I asked for Karkoff's office, she informed me in a clipped tone that he was in the nursery and asked if I wanted to have him paged. I told her no and she gave me directions and went back to her call. I had to walk down two more halls before I got to Karkoff's inner sanctum. The door was ajar. I pushed it open and stuck my head in. No snakes. No closets either. Feeling better, I walked in the rest of the way. From where I was standing, the furnishings looked like standard office issue: a desk, three chairs, a couple of file cabinets, and some bookcases.

The king cobra was not in residence. Unless, of course, you counted the photographs of it on the wall. Actually, the walls were a serpent lover's delight. There were pictures of snakes lying on people's shoulders, snakes draped over tree branches, snakes swallowing mice. The pictures looked like the ones hanging on John's apartment walls. Same subject. Same style. I scanned the bookcases. They were filled with reference books on snakes and birds, photography magazines, and two books on Santería, which I didn't bother thumbing through because they were the same ones I owned. I wondered if Karkoff had gotten them at the Crystal Bookstore too.

I walked over to his desk. The only things on it were a couple of pens, a Rolodex, and one of those "week-at-a-glance" appointment books. I was looking at it when Karkoff came in. I took a step back. Some people take badly to having their personal stuff studied.

"Madeline told me you were here," he said. "Frankly I was surprised."

"I don't see why." I smiled sweetly. "You were so helpful the last time I had questions, I thought I'd try again."

"Really?" Karkoff replied. "I'm glad Rajah impressed you so favorably. Would you like to see him again? I know he'd like to see you."

"Any time."

But Karkoff didn't move. I figured he wouldn't. After all, if

I wasn't terrified, what fun would it be? Instead he told me he was busy. "Say what you came to say and get out."

"I guess we're not doing politeness today?"

"You're being tedious," Karkoff said without looking up.

I swallowed a retort and nodded toward the walls. "You take those photographs?"

"It's one of my hobbies."

"Not bad for an amateur."

Karkoff glanced up from the mail he was opening. "Is there a point to this?"

"I'm getting to it." One thing was certain. This man was never going to win the year's Emily Post Award. "You take the pictures on John's walls?"

He made an impatient gesture that I chose to take as an assent.

"You take pictures of anything else besides snakes?"

"Birds." The word sounded obscene coming from him. Maybe it was the way his tongue darted out when he said it.

"Besides that."

"I shoot what interests me."

"How about rituals? You like rituals?"

Karkoff made a show of looking at his watch. "You're running out of time."

"I think you're going to want to hear what I have to say."

"Frankly, I can't think of anything you would say that could interest me."

"José Ramos." I dropped the name in the conversation the way you dust powdered sugar on French toast—very lightly.

"Don't know him," Karkoff replied a shade too quickly.

"You were at his house."

He shrugged. "I'm at lots of people's houses."

"I didn't know you were so social . . . or so rich." I waited for a reply. When none came, I went on anyway. "I know *I* would certainly remember the name of someone I paid a couple of thousand dollars to."

"I don't have time for your nonsense. You'd better leave."

"I'm not through."

"Yes you are," Karkoff informed me after he talked into his intercom. "I've called security. They should be here any moment."

But I kept going. I'd seen the guards. They were just a bunch of pensioners looking to make a few extra bucks.

"Help me out here. I'm a little weak in the witchcraft department. Now, a *prenda*. Is that the one where they torture a black cat before they boil it alive? No, No. I have it wrong. That's a *nganga*. The one with the head is called a *prenda*."

"Don't push it," Karkoff warned through gritted teeth.

"Push what?" And then I made a connection I should have made earlier. "Tell me," I said, "did Sam Ramirez push it? Did he come to you and demand that you call off your deal with José?"

Karkoff's eyes glittered. They looked as green and flat as one of his snake's. I was just about to tell him that when the security guards came in and dragged me out.

Twenty-four

As I drove toward home I kept thinking about my conversation with Karkoff, or rather I kept thinking about his reactions to our conversation.

When he first saw me, he'd acted bored and impatient. When I'd mentioned José's name, he'd become watchful. When I'd mentioned the *prenda*, he'd been more so. And then, I'd mentioned Sam's name and he'd gone ballistic.

Why?

Scenarios trooped across my brain like ducks in a shooting gallery. I knocked most of them down, but one stayed on its feet.

Fact: Sam knew about Karkoff's deal with José and disapproved of it.

Hypothesis: even though Sam had warned José off, he knew José wouldn't listen—not with two thousand dollars in his hand.

So Sam had done the next logical thing—he'd gone to Karkoff. And Karkoff had told the old man standing in front of him what he thought he wanted to hear because it was easier that way. And Sam had gone away happy. Until I told him my airport story.

I could still see him striding out of the Dominican restaurant. What had he done? Gone home and called Karkoff up? Pleaded with him? Yelled at him? Threatened him? With what? How could Sam hurt Karkoff?

I drummed my fingers on the wheel while I thought about that. Finally as I turned the corner onto East Fayette, I came up with the glimmerings of an idea. Suppose Karkoff had done something, something bad but not terrible, something that might make him lose his job, a thing I was almost positive he valued extremely highly. And suppose Sam knew what the thing was and suppose that he had threatened to tell the proper authorities unless Karkoff backed off. But Karkoff didn't. Karkoff killed him instead.

But had he really? Even I had to admit the scenario I'd just devised was pretty weak.

And what about John? How was his death related to Sam's?

God. What a mess. As I lit a cigarette I wondered why Sam would even have cared about what Karkoff had wanted José to do? José's activities had nothing to do with him. He wasn't involved in any way. Unless, of course, they'd focus attention on him, an attention he didn't want or need.

Maybe. Maybe. Maybe.

Too many damn maybes.

I was itemizing them, when I heard a horn honk and realized the light was green. I put on my turn signal and made a left onto East Genesee. Traffic was heavy with people impatient to get home and I had to concentrate on my driving. Fifteen minutes later I pulled in my driveway. James was sitting in the doorway waiting for me. I let us both in and hung up my coat. He ran ahead into the kitchen. When I walked in he was already perched on top of the refrigerator, waiting for his supper. I opened a can of cat food for him and heated up some canned minestrone for myself, which was the only thing besides chocolate and yogurt I had in the house.

I spent the rest of the evening paying my bills, replacing the door handle on the downstairs bathroom—it had come off three weeks ago—avoiding working on my book, and making lists of things I had to do. The next morning was also pretty much status quo. I opened the store, waited on customers, put away a couple of shipments of dog food, ordered some angel fish from a local supplier, and located a new source of crickets and meal worms. Then around three I ran down the block to buy a pack of cigarettes from the machine at the Laundromat and as I passed "El Gordito's" I got to thinking about Sam and Karkoff and John and John's list and the mess I was in all over again.

For the next two and a half hours no matter what I did I couldn't seem to put the situation out of my head. It just sat there buzzing in mind like a cloud of black flies. By five-thirty I had gotten myself so worked up that I was going to go nuts if I didn't get out of the store and do something, anything. The something I decided to do was take a quick trip down to Ohio Street and see if Sena Perez was in. I told Tim I'd be back in a little while and left.

It was dusk when I walked outside. A few kids wrapped up like mummies against the cold were building a snow fort. I scraped the ice off the front windshield of my cab, got in, and drove out of the parking lot. As I turned onto Ohio, my headlights picked up Go Go Nelson weaving down the middle of the street in the direction of the Seward Arms. I began to get nervous, but as I drove closer it became obvious he wasn't in any condition to chase me and that even if he had been it wouldn't have mattered anyway, since I was in a car. When I was about a foot away, Go Go stopped.

I slammed on my brakes and came to a screeching halt a

little less than three inches away from him. He didn't flinch. I honked. He didn't move, didn't even jump, just swayed gently from side to side in time with some music that only he could hear. Finally, after a minute of waiting for him to move, I edged my way around him, and drove on. He was still standing in the same spot when I reached number 110.

I was in luck. The building was lit up. Someone was home. I knocked. A peephole opened and an eye appeared. When I explained who I was the peephole clicked shut and I heard chains rattling and bolts being pulled back. A moment later the door opened.

"You really writing an article about weird pets?" a woman I assumed to be Sena Perez asked.

"Exotic," I corrected.

She gave me a quick once-over, then motioned me inside and rebolted the door. But I don't know why she bothered doing that. She looked as if she could handle anything that came through it. With her army fatigues, black close-cropped hair, and swagger she was a pint-sized Rambo, all duded up and ready to go. The only thing missing was the web belt around her waist.

As I followed her in I realized I was standing in a store. Then I took a second look and realized the "store" was actually the front room of a house. From where I was standing I could see the edge of an unmade bed peeking out from the open door across the way.

"My snakes are through there." She gestured in the direction I'd been looking. "You want to see them?"

I told her I most certainly did and she started walking. But I stayed where I was because by that time my eyes had adjusted to the dim light and I couldn't believe what I was seeing.

I gestured at the shelves filled with plaster saints, boxes of beads, candles, and stacks of wooden bowls and crockery and iron cauldrons. "This is a *botánica* isn't it?"

When she didn't say anything I told her about what the books I'd read and the clerk at the Crystal Lights Bookstore had said about a *botánica* being a store that sells things that are used in Santería rituals and the stuff she was selling was nothing if not that.

"You've been misinformed." Sena Perez's eyes were as cold and dark as the night outside.

"No. I don't think so."

She crossed her arms over her chest. "Leave. As in now."

Which was the last thing I wanted to do. I began talking. At length. I told her about how interested I was in Hispanic culture and how I'd spent time in Latin America and the Caribbean and that I had great respect for Santería as a religion and that my reaction was due purely to my surprise at finding a store like this in Syracuse and that I was indeed a writer and she could check my credits if she wanted. But she said she wasn't interested, that I was just another pale, white face and that she made a mistake inviting me into her home because she usually didn't talk to people outside of the "community," at which point I said her last comment showed how much she knew because I was a member of the community— at least an honorary one—and she said she didn't believe me so I told her that my husband had run Noah's Ark and that I'd been friends with Sam Ramirez.

At the mention of Sam's name, Sena's expression changed. "He was a good man," she said, touching one of her gold earrings reflectively. "I knew him from Cuba. He used to come to my mother's house on Sundays. They were cousins, my mother and him." Her voice took on a dreamy quality. "I remember sitting on the porch with my brother and sister and listening to the grown-ups talk and watching the palms waving in the breeze. That was a long time ago." She sighed. "Now"—she made a gesture that encompassed the store—"all I have is this. And you know what? It is not the same." And she fell silent.

"I'm sure it's not." I gazed around the room again.

Sena ran her fingers through her hair. "My mother told me that in the town where she was brought up they had stores like this on every street. Then Castro came and everything was gone. Everything. Like that." And she snapped her fingers. "My cousin came with a plane and we flew away. We could take nothing when we left, nothing except suitcases full of clothes. There was no room. I had to leave my dog behind." Her eyes glazed over and she shook her head from side to side as if dispelling the past.

"It must have been very hard," I murmured.

"You have no idea." Then she straightened up and held out her hand. "But we must go forward. Come," she commanded, "let me show you my little island, the one I make for myself."

We walked through the room we were standing in, through her bedroom, across the kitchen, and stopped in front of another doorway. "This is it," she said.

I peeked in. It was enchanting.

The room she was showing me was all heat and enormous plants and lights. It smelled of earth and water and flowers.

"Sam always came here when he couldn't stand your gray skies anymore. He said this place made him feel as if he was back home."

"I bet it did." I pointed to a large aquarium set off to one side. "Are the palm vipers you got from John in there?"

She nodded.

I skirted a corn plant and went over to the tank. The two olive green snakes were wound around a piece of tree branch. Both were sleeping.

"I like to keep dangerous things," Sena told me as I looked at them. "They help to remind me that in this life you must always be careful."

Though I agreed with the sentiment, I wasn't sure I'd pick her way of reminding myself. But I didn't say that. Instead I asked if feeding them was a problem because I knew from experience that sometimes if you had more than one snake in a confined place they'd both go for the same mouse and end up biting each other.

"Not with these two," Sena replied. Then she told me that her other one had given her problems. "That's why I sold him. Otherwise I would have had to put him in his own cage."

"Who'd you sell him to?"

Sena's eyes narrowed at my question. "Why do you want to know?" she demanded, her old suspicions returning.

I shrugged. "No reason really. I just figured maybe I could interview him too."

Sena thought for a moment before she answered. "Yeah. Sure. Why not? I don't think he'd care if I told you. I sold the viper to my landlord."

"You're kidding."

"Why do you say that?"

"Because most landlords aren't that understanding, especially about something like this."

"Well he was the one who suggested I get them in the first place. Before that I had tarantulas."

I shivered. "I don't like those."

"Neither did he," Sena replied and smiled. "You want some coffee?"

"Sure."

We walked into the kitchen. While Sena filled up a battered red tea kettle and put it on the stove, I began clearing away the mail and magazines on the table. I was just about to ask her what she wanted me to do with them when I noticed one of the envelopes was addressed to Thomas Maroney, care of SiMi Trucking, at 110 Ohio.

"You know Maroney?" I asked Sena.

"Of course I know him," she replied, her tone implying that I was an idiot. "He's my landlord. He bought the building a year ago."

"Really?" The man seemed to be on a spending spree.

She turned and faced me. "Why? Is there a problem?"

"No. I guess I'm just surprised. He never impressed me as a snake-owning type of guy."

"Me either," Sena said as she took the mail from my hands. "Me either."

It was really amazing, I thought as I sat down at the kitchen table, what you could learn when you asked the right question. Of course the problem was that you had to know enough to know what the right question was before you could ask it.

Twenty-five

After I left Sena I went back to the store and ended up having a long not particularly illuminating conversation with Tim about her place. He didn't tell me anything I didn't already know or hadn't guessed. At nine I closed up shop and went to see Walt Disney's *Cinderella*. That movie, along with *Casablanca* and *Blade Runner*, has always been one of my favorites, and I was determined to see it before it closed. But instead of making me feel good it made me feel sad, because as I watched it I realized that there was no Prince Charming on the horizon set to come galloping to my rescue and that maybe there never would be. I left the theater with reddened eyes, which was not what I had planned at all, and went straight home.

The phone was ringing when I came through the door. It was Lynn inviting me to lunch. But I didn't want to go. She would be full of helpful suggestions—all of which would be absolutely reasonable and totally inapplicable. I tried explaining that, but she wouldn't listen, and finally I just said I was busy for the next two weeks and hung up. Then I poured myself a shot of Scotch, sat down on the living room sofa, petted the cat, stared at the list I'd found, and thought. Somewhere around one in the morning, I came up with a solid motive for Karkoff killing John.

I knew that some of the stuff John had sold Karkoff was on the endangered species list.

What if John had done a Tangier's dope dealer number, and after selling Karkoff the stuff he'd turned around and blackmailed him?

Karkoff would have to pay.

He'd lose his job.

And have a great deal of trouble getting another one.

The only problem was: I couldn't prove my hypothesis.

To do that I'd have to take a look at Karkoff's reptile collection.

Which, more likely than not, was at his house, a place, given my past experiences with the man, I only wanted to visit when he was gone.

At first I dismissed the idea of breaking in.

It was ridiculous. Ludicrous.

But as the evening wore on the idea became more attractive. And if I was going to do it, now was the time, because Karkoff's desk calendar had indicated he was going to be in Seattle for the next couple of days.

After all, I told myself, if I was a suspect in two murder cases, what difference was a little breaking and entering going to make?

In truth, not much.

But when it came down to the practicalities I realized I didn't have even a glimmer of an idea of how to go about getting into his house.

And then, while I was watching a rerun of an old *I Love Lucy Show*, in which Lucy hired herself out as a maid, I got a flash of inspiration.

My plan was based on two indisputable premises: most people leave their spare keys in predictable places; and nobody notices cleaning ladies. Like meter readers and mailmen, they're invisible.

I went to bed happy, but when I got up in the morning, doubts began surfacing like bubbles in beer. I refused to entertain them, telling myself instead that I really didn't have a choice. Either I turned up a piece of evidence that would send Lorenzo off in a new direction, or I was going to jail. It was that simple. And somehow I didn't feature prison as my new permanent address.

I threw on jeans and another black turtleneck, put my hair up, went down to the kitchen, and made myself a big pot of coffee. Three cups of French roast, a chocolate bar, a handful of vitamins, and two cigarettes later, I was ready to roll. I grabbed my Leica, put on my jacket and boots, scrounged up my vacuum cleaner, and carried it out to the cab.

Karkoff lived over in the Salt Springs section of town. Once Jewish middle class, now mostly black and university, the houses were all small, unremarkable wooden colonials. The drive over took ten minutes. I spent most of it thinking about how if you'd told me two months ago that I'd be contemplating breaking into someone's house, I'd have told you I did articles, not B&E's.

In the beginning, things clicked into place like tumblers in a lock. It took me all of five minutes to locate Karkoff's house key on top of the garage door lintel. And when I opened, the doorbells didn't go off. Sirens didn't blare. Neighbors didn't come charging out of adjacent houses demanding to know what I was doing there. In fact, there weren't any neighbors. They were all out working, a fact attested to by the empty driveways up and down the block.

But once I was safely inside and the door was closed my

legs got the wobblies and I had to sit down on the vacuum cleaner for a few minutes. The words to an Inner Circle reggae song kept sounding in my head.

Bad boys. What you want? What you want? What you gonna do when Sheriff John Brown comes for you?

Lights. Drum roll. And the answer is—ten years.

No, Robin, I told myself. *Lots of people do this all the time. You can too. Just keep your gloves on, do what you came to do, then get out and things will be fine.* I stood up and looked around.

The hallway was dingy. The walls and floor were splotched with dirt. Piles of newspapers sat on a small rickety table. The mirror above it was covered with Post-It notes. I stopped to read them. Most seemed to be of the "don't forget to get" or the "call so and so" variety. I read the names over carefully but I didn't recognize any of them. I opened up the hall closet. No surprises. Just a couple of coats, an umbrella, a pair of galoshes. So far nothing very terrible. I went into the living room.

The sofa, chairs, and coffee table looked as if they had been bought in one of those places that advertise "living room set only $897, for four pieces." I walked around the room quickly. Nothing caught my eye. The room was devoid of personality. No books. No pictures on the wall, odd for a man who was a photographer. No magazines. Nothing. I felt as if I were in a showroom.

I got the same feeling in the kitchen. Green formica on the counters and the walls. Fluorescent light fixtures. I could have been in a lab. Sugar, cans of beets, corn, and Dinty Moore's Beef Stew in the cabinets. A single man's fare. I opened and shut the kitchen drawers. Except for two, which were filled with silverware, the rest were empty. Obviously, Karkoff didn't entertain a lot. Well that was one thing we had in common.

I stepped out into the shadowy corridor and walked slowly down the hallway. There were four doors. The house was a small cape. There was no basement, no attic. Whatever secrets the house contained would be walled off behind those doors. Suddenly, more than anything else, I wanted to go home. All the reasons that had seemed so cogent last night and this morning evaporated before the reality of that first door. I took a deep breath, told myself not to be such a wuss, and pushed.

I was in Karkoff's bedroom. Other than the fact that the walls and the ceiling had been painted black, the room seemed unremarkable. I made out a double bed, unmade, two night tables, a large dresser, and a closet. I began with the tables. The first one was filled with candy wrappers and used Kleenex. The second one was more interesting. It contained a gun. No big deal, I told myself as I closed the drawer. Lots of people had them. Witness Murphy. But for some reason its presence made me uneasy, and anxious to leave, I gave the closet and the dresser a perfunctory going over before walking out and going on to the next room, which turned out to be even less appealing.

The bathroom was small, grubby, and poorly lit. I opened the medicine cabinet door. A half full bottle of Valium, a bottle of nosedrops, aspirin, dental floss, and a grimy-looking comb stared me in the face. Standard stuff. I made a mental note to give my bathroom a good scrubbing. Then I helped myself to some Valium—on the theory that it's one of those things you never know when you're going to need—and left.

In contrast, the next room I entered, the one Karkoff was obviously using as his dark room/studio, was immaculate. It was small, maybe ten by twelve feet. The walls had been painted chocolate brown, the windows boarded over so light couldn't seep in. The effect was rather like walking into a cave. On the right side of the room was a dry bench and a wet unit assembled from kitchen cabinets. A safelight was suspended about four feet away from each unit. All the supplies were neatly laid out. It was a good, tight setup, not unlike the one I employed in my house.

I turned my attention to the mounted portraits hanging on the walls. For the most part they were high-key vignettes. There were snakes sleeping, snakes about to strike, snakes striking, snakes digesting their prey. Then there were the portraits of people and snakes. Go Go Nelson held up a small indigo, John had a Burmese python wrapped around his waist, while Maroney displayed a large, angry bushmaster. Maroney again.

I took a couple of steps back and studied the photographs. They were definitely shot by the same hand as the ones in John's apartment. One thing was for sure, I thought as I turned the light back off, whatever else I thought of Karkoff, the man was a good photographer. Somehow that fact didn't please me.

When I opened the door to the third room tentacles of heat reached out and embraced me. Next came the smell, heavy, fishy, with an undertone of rotting flesh. I recoiled, then forced myself to step inside. A large space heater sat in the middle of the room. Next to it was a long, white table. On one side were bowls and tubing, on the other a large yellow, plastic bag. But my eye was caught by the shelving, rows and rows of it reaching from floor to ceiling. They were filled with aquariums and the aquariums were filled with reptiles. I walked in a little more and stopped dead when I realized what was in the aquarium in front of me.

A Komodo dragon.

I couldn't believe it.

They were only found on a couple of small Indonesian islands.

Their exportation was strictly controlled by the government.

And here I was staring at one.

My hypothesis of John blackmailing Karkoff began to gain credence. The penalties for being caught with a Komodo included jail and a whopping fine. I took the lens cap off my Leica, checked the exposure and started snapping.

How much had the dragon cost? Twenty thousand? Thirty?

Had John and Murphy arranged the buy?

God.

How had they managed to have it smuggled out?

And why would Karkoff want it?

As adults, Komodo dragons grew to nine feet and weighed over two hundred pounds.

And they'd been known to kill people.

After I had taken half a roll of pictures I decided I had enough and moved on. As I walked through the shelves I spotted copperheads, cobras, mambas, bushmasters, and over twenty different kinds of vipers. The man's collection was incredible. He was truly obsessed, as all great collectors are. Turning the corner of the second row of aquariums, I accidentally brushed against a Gaboon viper's cage. He reared up and struck the glass in his rage. I raised my camera.

"Gotcha," I said as my shutter clicked.

As long as we were on opposite sides of the glass he could do anything he wanted.

Then I stopped dead. In a corner were a group of cages that had been hidden by the other aquariums.

And they were full of spiders—large ones.

My skin began crawling. I lowered my camera.

One—it must have been at least nine inches in diameter—was splayed out on the glass. Its sign said PINK-HAIRED-BIRD-EATING-BRAZILIAN TARANTULA. I took a half step forward and it waved two of its hairy legs in my direction. My nerve broke and I ran toward the table. I don't mind snakes, but I loathe spiders, especially ones that jump.

I had been standing there for less than thirty seconds when I became aware of an unpleasant smell coming from the yellow bag lying next to my hand. Probably just dead mice for the snakes, I told myself. Then I did something moronic, something that to this day I find totally inexplicable. I opened up the bag and peered inside. The fetid smell of rotting meat washed over me. I gagged. I felt faint. Then as I put out a hand to steady myself, I accidentally pushed the bag off the table. It landed with a splat. The smell got worse. I looked down. A newly born dead puppy was lying on the floor by my feet.

I swallowed my nausea and was focusing my camera—people had to know what Karkoff was like—when a stream of something warm hit the top of my head and ran down to my chin.

I glanced around.

Nothing was there.

But I heard a low, long hiss coming from over by the spider cages and caught a flash of movement over by the pipe attached to the wall. I strained to see, but couldn't.

Then when I did see, I wished I hadn't.

A spitting cobra was sitting less than five feet away from me.

Barbara Block

Twenty-six

The cobra's mouth was opened, its hood flared, its body poised to strike. A moment later he did. I ducked just in time. The strike hit the aquarium beside me. A stream of viscous, yellowish venom oozed down the glass. One look at that and I turned on my heels and raced out of the room slamming the door behind me. When I got into the kitchen, I stuck the side of my face into the sink and turned on the cold water and started scrubbing, all the while trying not to think about what would have happened if the poison had gotten into my eyes.

I'd be alone in a world of permanent darkness. The thought made me shudder and I scrubbed harder. My skin felt numb when I finally shut the water off and straightened up. Little beads of moisture dripped down off my chin and onto the front of my sweater. I was looking around for a paper towel when I sensed something behind me.

I spun around.

A skeletal, small brownish red dog stood regarding me. Its tail was tucked between its legs. Its teats hung down toward the floor. The poor thing was probably the mother of the pup in the snake room. I wondered what had happened to the rest

215

of her litter and then, after a moment's reflection, I stopped wondering because I knew. My eyes filled up. I blinked back the tears. She'd lost her babies and I'd never have any. Suddenly I had to get out of Karkoff's house.

I was almost at the door when the phone rang.

One ring. Two rings. Three rings. The noise pressed against me, filling the room like an overinflated balloon. Finally on the fourth ring, the answering machine clicked in. Karkoff's disembodied voice floated onto the air telling the caller to leave their name and message.

There was a beep. Then a woman spoke. "Ken," the voice said. "I'm leaving the package in the garage. Call me if you have a problem."

That voice. I was ninety-eight percent certain I recognized it, but to be one hundred percent sure I went over and pressed the replay button. After I'd listened to the message a second time I was absolutely positive. It was Donna. And her voice held that particular hum a woman's voice gets when she's interested in a man. John had been dead for what? Less than two weeks? Here was a lady who moved fast.

Unless, of course, she'd been seeing Karkoff while John was still alive. A whole new area of speculation opened itself up. I thought about the different possibilities as I grabbed the vacuum cleaner, locked Karkoff's door, and walked over to my car. I was getting in when I spotted a flash of brownish red over by the blue spruce in the center of the yard. I looked again. Karkoff's dog. She must have slipped out with me. I'd been too engrossed thinking about Donna to have noticed. On impulse I went over, grabbed her by the scruff of her neck and put her in the cab. She scrambled onto the floor in the back and cowered there till I got home.

Even so, I was positive I'd done the right thing. Nobody— be they man or animal—deserved to live in that house. Of course James might not feel that way, but he'd adjust—in time.

I shouldn't have worried though. James sat on top of the refrigerator and looked baleful, while the dog trembled under the kitchen table. I put down some food and water and laid an old blanket on the floor. After I'd gotten a safe distance away, the dog crept out and began eating. She gulped her food down, then slunk back under the table, curled up on the rug, and went to sleep. I decided to name her Elsie Too. As I watched her my mind kept going back to the message I'd heard.

Donna and Karkoff?

Karkoff with any woman?

I couldn't picture it. At all.

I'd been reading things into Donna's voice that weren't there.

Karkoff and Donna knew each other. They would. As I said before, Syracuse likes to think of itself as a big city where, in reality, it's a small town. So what? Donna had simply ordered something for Karkoff, something like a book, and was dropping the package off. It was that simple, I decided as I went upstairs and unloaded the Leica. Or was it? And then I stopped caring because as I developed the film, I got tireder and tireder till even the fillings in my teeth were aching.

By the time I hung the roll up on the line to dry, the only thing I wanted to do was sleep. My eyes were stinging with fatigue. I was too exhausted to even glance at the pictures I'd taken, much less study them. The moment I hit the bed, I went out and I stayed that way until the next morning when the dog woke me up out of a dead sleep by barking in my ear. She'd evidently gotten over being scared of me pretty fast.

I stumbled into my sweats, slipped my feet in my boots, put on my parka, and took her outside. She didn't have a collar on and at first I was afraid she'd run away, but when it became apparent she was going to stick close to me, I decided to take her for a walk around the block. She slunk along beside me, her tail between her legs, jumping at the sound of every slamming door and passing car. Halfway around the block I began wishing I'd brought my gloves and by the time we got back to the house my fingers were tingling from the cold.

I collected the morning newspaper off the front porch and went inside. James was waiting for me in the kitchen. I fed him, refilled Elsie's dog food bowl, then made myself a big steaming mug of café au lait. I cradled the cup in my hands, savoring its warmth, as I took it over to the kitchen table. While I sipped the sweet, milky brew, I ate a chocolate bar, a couple of slices of French bread, and scanned the local paper, after which I lit a cigarette and watched a blue jay pick little blackberries off a bush in the side yard. I was in no hurry to go upstairs and look at the prints I'd made last night.

I wanted to stretch out the anticipation of my triumph for as long as possible, so to delay the moment even more I picked up a pen and did the crossword puzzle. Then I went upstairs to get dressed. While I slipped my favorite sweater, a light blue cashmere, over my head and pulled on another pair of jeans, I savored the expression on Lorenzo's face when I handed her the photos I'd taken. I couldn't wait to hear what she had to say. I walked into my studio all happy expectation. Maybe that's what made what I saw when I looked at the prints doubly bad.

They were underexposed. Every single one of them. All you could make out were vague outlines. I held the negatives up to the light. They weren't any good either. So much for my showing them to Lorenzo. They were totally worthless. God. I raked my hair with my fingers. All the risks I'd taken had been for nothing.

I punched the wall in frustrated rage.

The pain was immediate and sobering.

I brought my hand up to my mouth and sucked my knuckles and thought about what a screw-up I was.

Somehow I managed to mess up even the simplest of tasks.

I wanted to go into my bedroom, throw myself down on the bed, and bury my head in my pillow, but I couldn't. I had to go to work. Several deliveries were due at the store around nine. Somebody had to be there to sign for them and that somebody was me. So instead of doing what I wanted to I went downstairs, put my parka back on, told Elsie to guard the house, and went off to Noah's Ark.

The shipments arrived not too long after I did and I spent the rest of the morning putting away bags of dog food, hanging leashes up on the wall, and straightening out the shelf with the cat care products. Tim joined me about ten and we cleaned the aquariums and the reptile cages. Around twelve I hopped in the car and got us both some food from Burger King. Neither one of us talked much as we ate. After the morning's disappointment I wasn't feeling very conversational and I guess Tim wasn't either. When we finished our lunch we started on the bird room.

That should have taken us about an hour, but Tim forgot to secure the door of the parakeets' cage and before we knew it we had twelve of the little birds doing loop-di-loops around the store. The cat was thrilled. But I wasn't. And neither was Tim. It was a little after three-thirty when I got the last one down from the rafters.

"You close up," I told Tim as I put the parakeet back in his cage. "I've got some errands to do. Then I'm going home."

But that's not what happened.

I had just finished up at the post office and was heading toward the bank when I saw the garbage truck pulling out of St. Ann's loading dock. And I remembered. I remembered what Art Dembroski had told me about the guy behind the wheel. He had a king cobra. One he'd gotten from John. Just like Karkoff had. Both men probably knew each other. I'd be willing to make book on it. How could they not? Maybe this guy could tell me something about Karkoff, something I could use.

Before I realized what I was doing I'd put on my signal light and made a U-turn in the middle of on-coming traffic. But by now the truck was a block away. I tried catching up, but I kept on getting stuck behind slow drivers and red lights. But even so, I managed to keep the truck within sight. We drove up Arbor Street, turned onto Oswego, then took a right at the Lucky Dog Thrift Shop. At this point we were near the C&S Social Club. I couldn't figure out where the truck could possibly be headed until I remembered the road in back of the clubhouse. Tyler was a deeply rutted three-block street that led up to the Blasmeyer Candle Factory.

In better days, the place had employed a hundred people and supplied all of upstate New York with candles. But five years ago it had joined the long list of manufacturers that couldn't compete in the new international market and had gone belly up. The bank had tried to auction the building, but when there were no takers, they'd boarded up the windows and walked away. Nobody ever went up there.

I followed the truck up the road, but although I could see the tracks they had made, I couldn't see them. I hung a left, ignored the NO TRESPASSING sign tacked to a telephone pole, and bumped my way up the narrow path. The road pitch was extremely steep. In the summer, that wouldn't be a problem, but now with the snow I was slipping and sliding all over the place. I made it to the top, but when I crested the hill, I skidded half off the road. I threw the car in reverse, but it didn't move. The more I tried to extricate myself, the deeper in the snow I went. I was stuck good and proper. Finally, I bowed to the inevitable and got out to get my shovel. But it was in the trunk and the trunk lock was frozen. I was holding a lighter to it when I heard the roar of a motor starting.

The truck was coming back.

Good.

Maybe they'd be able to pull me out.

A minute later it came into view.

I began walking toward it.

It took me a moment to realize that it was coming straight for me and it wasn't slowing down.

Twenty-seven

As I jumped out of the way, I tripped and fell into the snowbank. Maybe this hadn't been such a good idea after all.

The truck screeched to a halt a couple of inches from where I'd been standing. The driver got out and ran toward me. "Can't you read?" he snarled. "This here is private property."

His eyes were a wintry blue. His chin sported a three-day stubble. He was wearing a plaid shirt with a hunter's Day-Glo orange vest over it. He had the build of an ex-line backer. An aura of suppressed violence clung to him like a cloak.

I got up and dusted myself off. "I can read all right," I replied, too angry to be cautious. "But what the hell is the matter with your driving? You nearly ran me over."

"Is that a fact?" he said in a voice that didn't ask for an answer.

But I gave him one anyway. I don't enjoy taking a dive in the snow, especially when it's fifteen degrees out.

"Yeah it's a fact."

He reached over and grabbed my arm. "Shut up."

"Fuck you." The moment the words left my lips, I wanted to take them back. But it was too late. They were already out.

Mottled red patches erupted on his cheeks. "I told you to shut up," he growled. And he shook me so hard my teeth rattled.

Then the second man got out of the truck and strolled over to where we were. He was a smaller, thinner, younger version of the one holding me.

"See, Pete," the first man said, "I told you Maroney was watching us. But you said I was nuts. Well, how nuts am I now?"

"I don't know." The other guy looked dubious. "She don't look like one of Maroney's to me."

"I don't have anything to do with Maroney," I insisted as I tried to wriggle out of his grip.

He drew me closer. I could smell the beer on his breath before he turned his head. "If she's not one of his, how come she knows his name?" he demanded triumphantly of the other man.

"He wants to buy my store."

"What store?"

"Noah's Ark."

"You're Murphy's wife?"

I nodded.

"I don't believe you." But his grip loosened so I guess he did.

"Why don't you tell me exactly what it is you think I'm supposed to be doing here?" I suggested.

Surprisingly he did. He explained about how Maroney thought he and his brother were holing up somewhere on their run to have some beers and how Maroney had been trying to catch them at it for the last couple of months. As he talked I happened to glance at the garbage truck they had climbed out of and as I did I noticed the letters SIMI painted in blue on the side and I remembered the envelope I'd seen at

Sena Perez's place. It had been addressed to SiMi care of Maroney. So Maroney owned SiMi. And then I also recalled where else I'd seen those letters. On the zoo dumpsters. I didn't know if that meant anything or not, but it was an interesting fact and I filed it away for possible further use.

"So what do you have to say for yourself?" he said when he was finished.

Instead of giving him a smart-assed answer I did the sensible thing and told him about the story I was writing, about Art Dembroski giving me his name, about spotting the truck at the hospital, following them here on impulse, and getting myself stuck in the snow.

"He gave you my name?"

"That's what I just said, didn't I?"

Dick's partner looked at him with exasperation. "I told you you worry too much. I told you when I first seen her that she was okay. But you don't listen worth shit. You never did. Not since the day you was born."

Dick cocked his head to one side and studied my face. "You're a writer?" he asked in astonishment. I don't know what he expected one to look like, but it obviously wasn't like me.

"Yes, I'm a writer," I repeated.

"For a magazine?"

I nodded.

"And you want to hear about my snakes?"

"Yes."

"Okay. But if you're lying . . ."

"I'm not lying." *A lot*, I silently added.

He let go of my arm, but I could still feel where his fingers had been. I'd have some nice black-and-blue marks by the end of the day.

"I don't know why you want to write about his snakes," the

guy Dick had called Pete whined. "I don't know why anybody would want to read about something like that. It's got to the point where I don't even go in his house anymore and I'm his brother. He was like this regular guy until John got hold of him and turned him on to all this weird shit."

"That's exactly why I want to talk to him," I told Pete before I turned to Dick and asked him about the king cobra Art had told me he owned.

Dick smiled for the first time. He held his hands out toward his sides. "He's a big boy."

"As big as Karkoff's?"

"Wider. And he's got his fangs."

"Who got it for you? Murphy or John?"

"Murphy. Boy he was one fuckin' great guy."

And we went through the usual litany about what a shame it was that he had to die so young, but as soon as I could I changed the topic of conversation back to John because I really didn't want to talk about Murphy. At all. I mean what was there to say? It was all too complicated. Yes, I was very sorry the man was dead. I still missed him. A lot. But I also hated his guts. He'd lied to me. He'd left me in an incredible mess. If he were here now, knowing what I know, I'd probably kill him.

"Murphy got me a wild-born bushmaster before he died," Dick said, interrupting my train of thought. "God is he a beaut."

"I bet."

"Well he is. Say what you want but he's better company than lots of people I know."

"You must know some unpleasant people."

He shrugged. "They're different is all. Like John." He chuckled at some private memory. "God, that guy sure was one crazy motherfucker. I used to know guys like him in 'Nam.

They'd do anything. Anything at all. He ever show you his bracelet?"

"He had lots of them."

"This one was made out of human bones."

"Sorry, I must have missed it."

"Let me show you what I got. You can put it in the article you're writing."

"Dick," Peter said hurriedly, "she don't wanna see."

"Sure she does. She likes snakes doesn't she?" He reached under his shirt and pulled out a long black leather thong. Something brown and shriveled dangled on the end of it. "Know what this is?"

I shook my head.

"It's a gook's ear. Souvenir from the war."

I repressed a shudder.

"Dick, put it away," his brother ordered.

"I just thought she'd be interested, that's all." Dick stuck his lower lip out. He was pouting like a five-year-old told to go to bed when a party was going on.

"She wants to know about your collection," Pete continued. "She ain't here to listen to your war stories."

"Fuck you too," Dick said to his brother. Then he ostentatiously tucked the thong back in his shirt, walked over to the cab, and inspected my tires. "You're stuck pretty good," he observed after a few minutes.

"I know."

Dick turned to his brother. "Pete, we still got those chains?"

Pete shook his head. "Don't you remember? Charlie borrowed them a couple of days ago."

Dick cursed under his breath and straightened up. "Maybe there's something we can use in the factory."

"Might as well take a look," Pete replied. "We ain't getting out of here till she does."

Even though we were only fifty yards or so away, the factory loomed up, all gray cement and broken windows. The snow sucked at my boots as we trudged up the hill. When I looked up, I saw dark gray clouds scudding across the sky. It looked like another storm front was moving through. I put my hands deeper in my pockets and tried not to think about the chill seeping in through the soles of my shoes.

The first door we came to was padlocked. I turned to leave, but Dick threw his shoulder against it. There was a shudder, a crack, as the hinges pulled out of the frame, then a crash as the door fell inward. A cloud of dust billowed out and we retreated, coughing. As we walked over the door to get inside, I couldn't help thinking about the damage Dick's hands could do to me. I saw myself lying on the snow with my legs spread apart, my face beaten to a pulp. I shuddered and concentrated on my surroundings.

We were in the factory entranceway. The time clock was still on the wall, its hand permanently stopped at four-forty-five. To give me something else to think about, I read some of the names off the cards as we went by. Kalwinski. Metroka. Candowski. Mastronoi. Vallalonga. Lorenzo.

Lorenzo!

I pulled the card. Guissepe Lorenzo. I wondered if that was Lorenzo's father? I pictured him working here thirty, forty, fifty years ago dipping candles, a neat precise man, while Lorenzo's mother polished and scrubbed at home. Or had her mother worked here while the father did something like masonry work and the grandmother, who only spoke Italian, stayed home to take care of the children in a dark house that smelled of beeswax and furniture polish? Just like my grandmother had. Only she had spoken Yiddish. I stuffed the card in my pocket and hurried on.

Paper crunched beneath my feet as I walked. The air smelled of dust, rodent droppings, mold, and wax. The daylight flickering in through the windows provided the only light. But even through the gloom, I got a sense of a large space, football field-sized. At the far end, I spied a group of towers rising up and then I realized they were probably kettles that had been used to melt the wax. I ran my hand over the conveyor belt and tripped the switch. Nothing happened. I don't know why I expected it would.

"Got something," Pete called out.

I turned to look. He was fingering a length of thick metal chain. It was holding one side of a shelf full of small, white boxes onto the wall. There was a similar chain on the other side.

"We could use this," he said, giving one of the links an experimental tug.

A few of the boxes slid off and clattered to the floor. I jumped back as one fell open, expecting to see what? Another dead puppy? But it was only lengths of string. In the dark, they looked like white worms.

"What was that?" Dick yelled.

"Nothing. I got some chain we could use. See if you can find me some bolt cutters, so's I can get it off the wall."

"Okay," Dick replied, and moved off into the back of the factory.

"Now"—Pete turned to me—"how about telling me what you're really doing up here?"

"I told you."

"I just want to make sure."

"All I want to do is talk to your brother about his snake collection. What's the big deal?"

"Because if you're from Maroney . . ."

"Jesus. You said it yourself. Do I look like somebody that would work for him?"

"You'd better be telling the truth."

"I am."

"Because I don't like liars."

"Neither do I," I said.

Then I noticed the bones. Immediately I thought of the head that had been sent to me.

My mouth went dry.

My heart started to hammer inside my chest.

Then I took a second look and realized that they weren't human after all.

My heart rate went back to normal; I thanked God for small favors.

And reminded myself that biology had never been my strong suit.

Twenty-eight

They were arranged in a little white gleaming pile on the floor. The remains of a ritual? I walked over. Pete followed. We stopped a couple of inches away. Now that I was closer I saw the bones looked small and light.

"Chicken." Pete pointed to the feathers stuck to a wooden bowl next to them.

"How do you know?" I hunkered down to get a better look.

"That's what they always use."

"They?"

"The spics," Pete said impatiently. "Hey, don't touch that thing," he warned as I reached my hand out to the bowl. "You'll get blood all over your fingers."

As I stood up I wondered how Pete knew about this kind of thing, but before I could ask him he answered my question for me.

"We used to come across this stuff all the time down in New York City when I worked for the Parks Department," he explained. "We had to clean up pig guts, bowls of blood, goat heads. You wouldn't believe the crap we used to find down there. Damn spics," he repeated and kicked the bones with his shoe. They looked like pick-up sticks spread out on the floor.

"You shouldn't have done that," a voice in back of me warned. I startled. Then I realized it was Dick. I'd been so engrossed in what I'd found that I hadn't heard him approach. "It's bad luck."

His brother snorted. "Don't tell me you believe in this shit?"

"Just leave those things alone." Dick moved the clippers he was carrying from his left to his right hand.

"I might have known," Pete sneered and spat on the floor.

"I just don't think it's right to go messing with another person's religion is all."

"This isn't a religion. Going to Mass is religion. This," Pete said, indicating the floor, "is crap." And he turned on his heels and marched away leaving Dick and me to contemplate my find.

"Is he really that religious?" I asked Dick as he clipped the chains holding up the shelves. They clattered to the floor. I jumped back just in time to avoid getting hit by them.

"Naw." Dick grabbed the chain and wrapped it around his hand. "He hasn't been to Mass since Mr. High and Mighty made Holy Communion. It's what happened with Rosa that's making him talk like that." He jerked his head in the direction of the door. "Come on, let's get out of here."

"And what was that?" I asked as we walked.

"I shouldn't be telling you this." A big malicious grin spread over his face. "But it is kinda funny." Dick half turned toward me. "See, Pete used to go out with her."

"Rosa?"

"Yeah. Rosa Servales. She was a real hot little number. First six months everything's fine. Then one night Pete has a few too many beers at the bar, goes home and slaps her around a little—nothing too serious you understand, just a couple of whacks—but she gets pissed. So what does she do?"

"Shoot him?"

"No. She tells him she's gonna put a curse on him."

"A curse?"

"That's what I said but I guess she must have because you know what?" I shook my head. "God's honest truth." Dick raised his hand. "I swear the guy ain't had a day's luck since then."

And with that we stepped out of the factory. The wind lashed out at us. I tucked my chin into my jacket as we hurried back to the cars. The sky was getting grayer. What little daylight there was was fading. Soon it would be dusk. Pete watched from inside the hauler as Dick wound his end of the chain around the bumper of the truck and I wound my end of the chain around the cab's bumper. When we were done Dick gave the signal and Pete started the truck's engine up and put it into reverse. For a moment nothing happened, then ever so slowly the cab began to move out of its bed of snow and back onto the path. When it was completely on it, Pete stopped the truck and I went over to my cab, unwound the chain, and handed it to Dick.

"So," I said, "now that John's gone you think you're going to be getting anymore snakes?"

"As a matter of fact I'm getting an albino monacle cobra next week."

"You're kidding." Those things were extremely rare. And deadly. "Who from?"

"Karkoff."

"He doesn't want it? Somehow that doesn't sound like him."

"He's got two. But they're both female. See, he thought when he bought them from John he was getting one of each sex."

"That must have pissed him off," I said, suppressing a smile. Anything that pissed that man off was okay with me.

"Yeah. John really took him for a ride. I heard Karkoff wanted his money back, but John wouldn't give it to him. He told him to go kiss his ass." Dick fashioned the chain into a ball and began passing it from one hand to another. "I never figured John out," Dick continued. "He was okay for a while, but after Murphy died it was like he couldn't be bothered with anything anymore. All he could talk about was how he was getting out of this town."

"Well he did leave." I rummaged through my pocket for my car keys. "It just wasn't the way he planned."

"That's for sure," Dick replied. "Oakwood Cemetery and Hawaii definitely ain't the same thing."

"No they're not."

Then Pete leaned on his horn.

"Well, got to go." Dick gave me a half salute and started for the truck. I returned the gesture and headed for my car.

As I drove back down the hill I thought about what Dick had told me about John.

So John had been getting ready to leave. To Hawaii no less. Probably bankrolled by the fifty grand Lorenzo had found in the air shaft. Only he'd been killed before he could get out. So was that money his? It certainly looked like it. Or had it been Murphy's? Or Tim's? The only thing I was sure of was it wasn't mine.

At the bottom of the hill I took a left and briefly considered asking Donna what she knew, but I quickly abandoned the idea. She hadn't told me anything the last time I'd spoken to her and there was no reason to think she'd act any different now. But I might have better luck with Tim. I spent the rest of the drive over to the store going over the conversation I was planning to have with him.

Unfortunately, he wasn't there. The store windows were dark. The parking lot was deserted. He'd closed the place up early and left. I made a U-turn and headed across town to his hangout, Louie's. I knew that sometimes he stopped in there for a couple of beers before heading home.

Louie's was this lowlife bar and grill located on the fringes of downtown. It sat like a squat box between a shoe store and a motorcycle repair shop. It was one of those places that was always turning up in the news. As in, so and so was raped after she had been drinking at Louie's. Or so and so was arrested after a knife fight broke out. The guy who owned it must have paid big bucks to the boys downtown, because in spite of the drugs, the fights, and the after-hours drinking the place was never closed down.

But if I didn't know its reputation, I would never have guessed it from what I saw when I walked into the bar ten minutes later. The place was dead. Aside from a few drunks muttering to themselves over in the corner, there was no one there. I turned to go, but the aroma of barbecuing ribs and chicken made my mouth water and I decided to have a bite to eat first. I was just about to place my order with Marge, the bartender, when the door opened and Art Dembroski, the guy who had worked with John down at St. Ann's, came wondering in. He spied me and came over.

"What are you doing here?" he asked as he sat down next to me.

"Grabbing a bite to eat. And you?"

"Getting a beer," he said.

Then Marge came over and we placed our orders.

"Now, there's somebody I wouldn't like to tangle with," I half whispered once she'd moved down to the other end of the bar.

"Me neither," Art agreed.

Marge was a bull dyke whose attire ran to orange bowling shirts and black chino pants. Although she was only five feet three inches she weighed over two hundred pounds. The ax handle she used for settling disputes was prominently displayed on the cabinet in back of the bar. Rumor had it that once upon a time she had been a doctor's wife living a comfortable middle class existence, but she'd fallen in love with a biker and roared off with him into the sunset on the back of his Harley hog. Only it hadn't lasted. Nothing ever does. When the biker left her, Marge had done three things in rapid succession: gotten a job tending bar, gone on an eating binge, and developed a liking for sweet young things. I don't know if the story was true or not. But it really didn't matter. Because it was a good one and that, after all, was what really counted.

I downed my first Scotch and as the liquor worked its way down me, I began to really appreciate why Murphy drank and I wondered if I wasn't doing a little too much of it myself. Then Marge slid a plate of ribs in front of me. I pushed the plate between Art and myself. For a while we sat alternately gnawing on the huge mound of ribs and licking red glob off our fingers.

"I spoke to Dick," I said when I'd finally had enough. I was so stuffed I couldn't have eaten another thing.

"What did you think?" Art asked as he wiped his fingers off with a couple of napkins and signaled for another Miller. No imported beers here.

"The man's off the wall."

"I told you he was. But he does have an impressive collection. If you like poisonous stuff."

"And you don't?"

"I have one venomous snake, but that's it. And I'm kind of sorry about that one. Especially now with the grandchildren coming over."

Chutes and Adders   **235**

"Lots of people do."

"They're mostly assholes. People who collect snakes for the wrong reasons."

"Like John."

"Like John," Art agreed just as Marge plunked his beer down. The foam slopped over the side and ran under my plate. I ignored it. Art got out his pouch and stuffed a plug of chewing tobacco in his cheek.

"I don't have no use for men who knock their women around," he said after a minute.

"Who does?"

"If you ask me John did too much of that."

I suddenly remembered the bruises on Donna's arms, the black eye, and her limp all of which she claimed to have acquired falling down the stairs.

"There's never any call for that. Even if they're screwing someone else. I mean if a woman wants to leave you, I say let her go." I watched Art fiddling with his napkin and wondered if he'd done a bit of that himself. "Good riddance. You get rid of garbage, you don't keep it."

Art broke off talking to watch two bikers come in. The chains on their leather jackets and boots rattled as they sauntered past. They sat down on a couple of stools away from us and ordered boilermakers in too-loud voices.

"Damn trash," Art said, turning back to me.

"If you don't like them why do you come in here?"

But instead of answering me Art drained his mug and pointed for another. "You know what I don't like about my job?" he asked me suddenly.

"No. What?"

"All the trash I have to deal with." Art emptied his glass again and slammed it back down on the counter.

"Don't you think you should slow down?"

"I'm fine," he insisted as he ordered another beer. Then he let go with a stream of brown tobacco juice. It hit the floor and spread out, a brown puddle among the cigarette butts.

"Hey," one of the bikers yelled, "what the fuck you think you're doing?"

Art straightened up and turned around. "You talking to me?"

I laid a ten on the counter, got up, and put my jacket on. It was time to go. I'd seen enough violence recently. I didn't want to see anymore. On the way out, I noticed Marge reaching for her ax handle. I heard a crash, followed by a moan as I reached the front door.

I didn't bother to look. I figured I'd seen enough unpleasantness for one day.

But I figured wrong. Because as I was getting into my car, Lorenzo pulled up beside me and got out.

I slammed the cab door shut and straightened up. "What do you want?" I demanded as she walked over to me.

She shrugged. "Nothing much. I was just passing by when I saw you, so I thought: why not stop and say hello?"

"Well now that you've said it, how about moving your car so I can get out of here?"

"In a minute," she replied, resettling her glasses on the bridge of her nose. "By the way, how many beers have you had?"

"Why?"

"I just don't want you to drive drunk."

"Don't worry. And now that we've got that straightened out, I'd really like to go home."

"You know," Lorenzo said, nodding toward Louie's, "I'd have figured you for someplace fancier. See. It just shows to go. You never really know what people do."

"So they say," I replied, trying to keep a lid on my temper because I knew that losing it would just make things worse.

Lorenzo studied my face under the lamplight. "You're looking a little tired. Not sleeping well?"

"I'm sleeping fine, thank you very much."

"It must be tough."

"What?"

"Walking around with what you did on your conscience."

"I didn't do anything," I said through gritted teeth.

She leaned forward. "You know we *will* get you. If not today, then tomorrow. If not tomorrow, then next week. Or next month. Or next year. There is no statute of limitations on murder." I could feel my stomach twisting in a knot as her voice fell to a whisper. "Why not tell me what happened? Just between us. Woman to woman. Trust me. You'll feel better. What happened? Did you and John have a fight? Was it over money? A lover's quarrel? Or was the snake a joke that went bad? I bet you didn't even mean to kill him. It was probably an accident," Lorenzo's voice crooned. "It was an accident, wasn't it?"

"Leave me alone," I screamed, my self-control breaking in spite of my resolve.

"Of course." Lorenzo smiled. She'd gotten what she wanted. "I wouldn't want to be accused of harassing you."

Then she left.

After watching her disappear from sight, I took a deep breath and got in my car.

"I will not let her get to me again," I repeated over and over as I drove home. By the time I pulled into my driveway I almost believed it.

Twenty-nine

Elsie was waiting for me by the door. I could tell from her expression that I was late. I apologized and took her for a quick walk, then went straight upstairs to bed. But I couldn't sleep. I was too cold, I was too hot. I had a cramp in my leg. My nose itched. My ankle throbbed. I kept thinking I heard noises downstairs. I guess my encounter with Lorenzo had bothered me more than I thought it had.

Finally around one o'clock I conceded defeat, got up, turned on the light, and ran a bath. As I slipped into the warm water I kept on thinking about what Dick had told me about the way John had stiffed Karkoff on the albino monacle. I wondered how John had thought he was going to get away with it? And then I wondered how mad Karkoff had been? Mad enough to kill?

I leaned my head back on the porcelain and watched the water running out of the tap. After a few minutes I felt myself relaxing. I stopped thinking about John. I stopped thinking about anything at all. My eyes began to grow heavy. I closed them for what seemed like just a minute. But when I opened them again I found myself shivering in a tub full of cold water.

I clambered out, toweled myself off, and went to bed. This time I slept. My alarm went off at eight o'clock. As I dragged myself out of bed and worked the kinks out of my back, I decided it was time I went back to the gym. Most eighty-year-olds probably felt better than I did at the moment.

I slipped into my sweats, took the dog out for her morning walk, made myself a cup of café au lait, and called Tim at home. But he wasn't in. I started to get angry but then I looked at the kitchen clock and realized he wasn't at his flat because he was on his way to open the store. I debated about calling him there, but decided to drive over instead. The questions I wanted to ask him were better asked in person. I went back upstairs, put on my jeans, slipped an olive green turtleneck over my head, laced up my running shoes, grabbed my leather jacket, and headed out the door.

A couple of inches of snow had fallen during the night. The powdery flakes had dusted the walkway and turned the hedge along my driveway into a frosted wedding cake. One of my neighbor's kids had built a snowman and its black marble eyes watched me as I brushed the cab off. I couldn't help remembering that Murphy and I had built snow forts when we first got married. But then, somewhere along the way, we'd stopped playing. Was that when things had started going wrong. If we had still been making snow angels would Murphy have ended up dead in the front seat of his car?

It was one of those unanswerable questions, the kind that could own you if you let it. I turned on the radio and listened to Golden Oldies instead. It seemed like a more productive thing to do. Fifteen minutes later, I turned into the parking lot at Noah's Ark, shut off the engine, and climbed the steps to the store. Pickles trotted up and proceeded to wind herself around my feet. I picked her up and petted her as I walked over to Tim. He was standing behind the counter counting out the change in the cash drawer.

"I have something to ask you," I said.

He stopped counting and looked up. One of the macaws let out an ear-piercing shriek.

"It's about the business you, Murphy, and John were running."

"What about it?"

"How did you divide up the money?"

"We split it three ways."

"No. I mean when you got paid. Did someone hold it or did you divide it up right then and there?"

"What are you? Nuts? Then and there of course. Why are you asking?"

"I was thinking about the fifty thousand Lorenzo found in the heat vent."

"What about it?"

"I was just wondering where it came from."

"Not from me, that's for sure."

"John?" I asked, recalling what Dick had said about John telling everyone he was going to Hawaii.

"I doubt it."

"Why do you say that?" The cat started to wiggle. I put her down.

"Because John was the type of guy who always liked to keep all of his stuff close to him. He wouldn't have stashed it away in a pipe."

"So you think the money was Murphy's?"

"Who else's?"

I looked Tim square in the eyes. "It could be yours."

He snorted. "Get real. If I was making that kind of money do you think I'd be standing here doing this?" And he made a gesture that encompassed the store.

"No."

Tim absentmindedly tugged on his ponytail. "Maybe Murphy was keeping two sets of books."

"He could have been," I conceded.

It was a possibility. It was just one I didn't want to think about. Especially in regard to the IRS. I began wishing I'd read the tax returns Murphy had filled out before signing them.

There didn't seem to be anything more to say so Tim and I went back to work. I spent the next hour setting up the new salt water aquarium and cleaning out the hamsters' cages. Then I took a cigarette break and went into Murphy's office to go through the mail. There was nothing important, just a few bills and some promos for upscale items like all natural gourmet dog food and herbal flea collars, things that wouldn't sell here because they were twice the price of regular items. As I was throwing everything away Tim stuck his head in the room.

"Hey, Robin," he said, "got any stamps around? I need to mail something."

"Just leave it here"—I indicated a spot on the edge of my desk—"and I'll drop it in the postbox with my stuff."

"Thanks." Tim handed me the envelope. "Can't be late with the rent."

"Definitely not." I was tossing it in the pile with my other letters when I happened to glance at the address. Maroney Realty. Of course I had known that. Tim had told me. But this time something clicked.

I weighed the envelope in my hand while I thought about how busy Maroney had been buying property. He'd bought Sam's house, he'd tried to buy this place, did, in fact, own Tim's. I began to wonder what else he owned around here?

Suddenly I had another idea about where that fifty thousand in the heating vent might have come from. It was a long shot, but what else had I been playing these days? Eventually one would have to pay off.

It was time to do a little research at the courthouse.

There were a few facts I needed to check out.

When I came out front Tim was in the process of explaining to a woman and her teenage son why they wanted an iguana instead of a monitor lizard as a pet. I interrupted to tell him I was leaving and that I'd be back soon. He gave me a wave indicating everything was under control and went back to his customers. I walked down the steps, got into my car, and drove downtown, where I lucked out and found a semilegal parking space in front of the Civic Center. Then I skirted around the fencing erected to protect pedestrians from the bricks falling off the facade, and went into the courthouse.

I bought a pack of Camels at the kiosk in the lobby, climbed the marble steps to the second floor, turned left, and went into the record room. Three hours later I'd confirmed my suspicions. Maroney Realty, along with SiMi Trucking, had been buying up all the property around the store. I wondered if the fifty thousand the cops had found could have been tied into Maroney's real estate dealings in some way. I put down my pen, pushed the wooden chair back, and stretched. It looked like James Maroney, Esq. and I were due for a tête-à-tête.

The traffic on Genesee was moderate. The drive out to Maroney's office took a total of twenty minutes—ten minutes to get to the DeWitt fire station and another five to get out to Lyndon Corners, where I turned right. Then I went three blocks and made another right and there it was. Maroney's office turned out to be one of those hypermodern glass brick and aluminum jobs that looks like a fancy shack but costs a king's ransom to build. The inside followed suit.

Everything was beige, teak, and expensive, a far cry from Maroney's mail drop on Ohio Street. The receptionist's desk had three telephones, a Rolodex, and nobody sitting there, so I marched into Maroney's office without being announced. His head was down, the light glinting off his bald spot. He was writing something. When I coughed, he put his pen down and looked up.

"What are you doing here?"

"I want to talk."

"Have you ever heard of calling for an appointment?"

"I believe I read about that once."

"Then I suggest you try it," he said and went back to writing.

"I want to talk about the store."

"Ah"—he drew the word out—"I see. So you've finally gotten some sense in that thick head of yours."

"I want to make a deal."

"Go on," he prompted, "I'm listening." And he folded his hands over his stomach and leaned back in his brown leather chair.

"Give me one hundred fifty thousand dollars and it's yours."

He snorted. "You've got to be kidding."

"Not at all."

"That house is at least sixty years old, it needs a new roof, a paint job, and God only knows what else. Not to mention the fact that it's in a shit neighborhood."

"True, but you're not buying the house, you're buying the land."

Maroney took a mint from the cut glass bowl on his desk

and popped it into his mouth. "Why would I want it?" he finally asked in a bored tone.

I wanted to tell him that if I knew the answer to that question we wouldn't be having this conversation in the first place. But of course I didn't. Instead, I took the pages I'd Xeroxed at the courthouse out of my pocketbook and threw them on his desk. "These are copies of all the real estate transactions your two companies have been involved in in the past year."

Maroney glanced at the papers, then tossed them to one side. "So what's your point?"

"You've been buying up all the buildings around the store."

"I buy and sell buildings for a living. That's why the company is called M-a-r-o-n-e-y R-e-a-l-t-y."

"Thanks for the spelling lesson, but I think I can figure that out."

"The way you've been acting, I wasn't sure." Maroney half rose out of his seat, then seemingly overcome with the effort of it all sat back down.

I wandered over to the far wall and read the plaques hanging on it. There was one from the Syracuse Chamber of Commerce, another from the Kiwanis Club, a third from Catholic Charities, and a fourth from St. Ann's. All of them lauded Maroney's civic responsibility.

"You're very charitably inclined," I observed. I was about to say something else when it hit me. I had my answer. I pointed to the plaque from St. Ann's. "Aren't they going to be building a big sports medicine complex?"

"I wouldn't know."

"That's funny, because it's been all over the news for the last six months."

"I don't watch TV."

"If I remember rightly, the complex is going to be big, it's going to be state of the art, and it's going to serve the entire upstate region. Only nobody is saying where it's going to be located."

Maroney licked his lips.

"Now why am I getting the idea that it might be built where the store is. After all, St. Ann's is only a couple of blocks away."

"So you think I'm buying up all the land so I can resell it to the hospital?"

"Something like that."

"Even if that were true—and I'm not saying it is—there's no way in hell I'd give you one hundred and fifty thousand dollars for your property."

"I don't think you have much choice. You need it."

"I shouldn't have even offered you sixty thousand dollars."

I picked my next words with care. "I bet you figured that since you already gave Murphy fifty thousand dollars we're quits. Well forget it. The cops have that money and I'm not getting it back."

"What are you blabbing about?"

"You gave Murphy a down payment on the store. He was going to sell, but he got killed before the papers could get signed."

Maroney rolled his eyes in disgust. "Do you really think I'd be stupid enough to do something like that?"

I had to admit that the answer was no. When put like that no other conclusion was possible.

He slapped his desk with the palm of his hand. "If I really wanted you out, you'd be long gone."

"Is that so?"

"Yes that's so."

"What would you do, torch the place?"

"I'm a little more subtle than that."

"I'm not so sure."

"Seventy thousand. That's my final offer. Take it or leave it."

"I'd be a fool to take it. If I'm going to sell, I'd be better off dealing with the hospital board directly."

Maroney shrugged. "Do whatever you want. I'm a businessman, not a gangster."

"I'm glad you see it that way." I placed both my hands on his desk and leaned forward. "Just so we get one thing straight. Anything happens to that store and I do mean anything and I'll . . ."

"You'll what?" Maroney sneered.

I smiled. "I'll call up the DEC and tell them you're dumping stuff out behind the factory."

Maroney's eyelids started twitching like they were doing the St. Vitus's Dance.

It was good to see that at least one of my hunches had turned out to be correct.

Thirty

I was in a good mood when I left Maroney's office. Just seeing that last expression on Maroney's face, knowing I'd gotten to him, was enough. Maybe it was that I wanted to bask in my moment of glory a bit longer or maybe I needed to reassure myself that I'd read Maroney's reaction correctly, but when I turned off Genesee Street I found myself headed up Blasmeyer Road toward the candle factory instead of continuing on West Geddes to the store.

At first I saw nothing. Then as the road curved around the factory I made out a structure lying about four hundred feet off to the left. It was gray and blended in with the color of the sky. As I got closer I could see the building was actually a large trailer. When I was a little less than ten feet away I killed the motor and got out. As I stood there with the wind tugging at my clothes, it occurred to me that I'd better make this fast because I'd have a lot of explaining to do if some of Maroney's guys showed up.

I hurried toward the trailer. Walking was easy because the snow underneath my feet had already been trampled down to a hard-packed surface. There'd been a lot of traffic on this particular spot. But that observation turned out to be the limit of what I could discern. The trailer's one door was barred with a heavy bolt and there were no windows to peek through. I did a quick circuit of the structure but all I saw was snow and bare tree branches.

For a moment I was disappointed, but then I decided I really didn't need to go inside to confirm my suspicions. The fact of the trailer's existence was enough to do that. I hurried back to my car, started it up, and drove back to the store. It was too late to call the DEC now. The office would be closed. But I would tomorrow. Even though I knew it would be a waste at least my conscience would be satisfied. Because the truth was that by the time a DEC agent got out there the trailer would be long gone. In fact Maroney had probably started making arrangements for its disappearance the moment I walked out his door.

Tim's VW was the only car in the store's parking lot. It looked like it was going to be a slow evening. I entered the store through the side door. Tim was reading a magazine when I walked into the front room. He put it down just long enough to inform me that our charge card machine had been offline for the last three-quarters of an hour. I threw my jacket on the counter and called the company, only to be told that they were having technical difficulties with their computer—surprise, surprise—and that they were hopeful the problem would be resolved soon. Till then it looked like it was either check or cash.

That could have been a problem, but it wasn't because we didn't have any customers. The only sale I rang up for the whole afternoon was for a $1.98 can of tropical fish food. I passed the rest of the time playing with the cat and going over order forms with Tim. After we were done, he left for his class at OCC and I washed down the floors. Then I turned off the lights, locked the doors, and drove over to R.J.'s for a drink. The place was packed, mostly with people in their twenties trying to pick each other up, and I had to inch my way past them to get to the bar. Connie was on. We exchanged a quick greeting, but she couldn't talk. The place was too busy.

I ordered a beer and amused myself by eavesdropping on some Nottingham High School teachers discussing how a kid had punched the principal in the jaw and how they'd wished the kid had hit him harder. I would have listened longer—it sounded like an interesting story—but when I lit my cigarette one of the group gave me the evil eye, so I picked up my beer and glass and moved down to the end of the bar. I'd had enough hassles for one day.

As I emptied the rest of my Dos Equis into my glass I considered Maroney's reactions at our meeting yet again. He'd cared when I'd mentioned the dumping behind the factory because that had been real, but he hadn't been at all upset when I'd told him what I'd found out about his real estate dealings.

And he hadn't been pretending either.

In fact, he'd thought my little revelations had been funny.

But really, when you thought about it, why shouldn't he have?

I'd come charging in all puffed up, to accuse him of what?

A real estate scam.

No wonder he had laughed his ass off. So what if people found out that he was buying up the land around St. Ann's so he could resell it at a whopping profit? It's not as if that wasn't done all the time. As Maroney said, the worst that could happen to him was a slap on the wrist and a fine.

I drained the last of the Dos Equis and ordered another one. It seemed like it was time to cross Maroney off my list of murder suspects. Come to think about it, realistically I couldn't imagine Maroney killing anyone. He had too much to lose and nothing to gain. He had the fancy house, the expensive car, the younger, blond wife. He hobnobbed with Syracuse's elite—such as they were.

Connie slid the Dos Equis across the bar and as I poured it into my glass for some reason I remembered the first one I'd ever had. Murphy and I had been sitting inside a roadside shack twenty miles outside of Vera Cruz listening to the rain beat down on the tin roof, eating shrimp, and drinking Dos Equis. By the time the storm had passed he'd been too drunk to drive and I hadn't known how to handle a shift. We'd ended up spending the night curled up on the dirt floor. God, I'd been pissed, but Murphy hadn't been able to stop laughing. That was one of the differences between us. I took things too seriously and he didn't take them seriously enough.

I took another sip of beer and thought about us for a while longer and then gradually my thoughts worked their way back to Maroney, and I found myself tugging on the strings of the problem again.

No, there was no reason to suspect him. . . .

Unless . . .

Unless he was leveraged out. New scenario. What if he had borrowed everything to buy all the property on the block? What if my refusal to sell put his fortune in jeopardy? Then he'd stand to lose everything. Maybe the snake *had* been meant for me. Maybe Sam had been killed because he wouldn't sell.

But if that were the case, why hadn't Maroney tried for me again?

For a moment I toyed with the idea of trying to check out his financial standing. The information was in a computer somewhere and if it was in a computer it was accessible . . . if you knew the right person.

The only problem was, I didn't.

I took another sip of beer and watched the TV screen above the bar. MTV with the sound off. Not that they needed it with the stereo blaring. Two girls dressed in leather and chains were crawling on the floor toward some guy with long hair playing a guitar. Perfect. Just what I wanted to watch. I was stubbing out my cigarette preparatory to leaving when George sat down next to me. He was wearing a black T-shirt, black jeans, and a black leather jacket.

"Off duty?" I asked, indicating his attire.

"Undercover."

The idea of George undercover was so ludicrous I laughed despite trying not to. I mean this was a man who stood out from the crowd. Any crowd.

"So," he said, signaling to Connie, "how are things going?"

"Given the circumstances as well as can be expected."

"You should let me help," George said as he walked over. He ordered a draft, then turned back to me.

"You know you can't."

"Why the hell not?" he demanded. His voice held an angry undertone.

"Because you'd lose your job," I said, explaining the obvious.

"Who gives a fuck?"

"You do."

"You're nuts."

"Am I?" I looked into his eyes. He turned his head away.

"No," he finally conceded after a moment's silence.

I didn't reply. Instead I watched the SU students Connie was now waiting on. They were whooping and hollering and carrying on. I'd done that too in college. But that was a lifetime ago in a different universe.

"Is your lawyer doing anything?" George asked. Somebody had turned the sound system up even louder and he had to shout to make himself heard over the sounds of Bruce Springsteen.

"No. He says there isn't much he can do until I'm arrested."

George took a sip of beer, then put his mug down. "It's not so bad."

"What?"

"Being arrested."

"Boy, that's reassuring."

"No, really. The women's side isn't that bad."

"Somehow I don't think I want to find out."

Was I crazy or what? The only person who seemed to think being arrested was a big deal was me.

George took a quarter off the pile of change Connie had left him and spun it. The coin whirled around for a few seconds. Then it began to wobble. "Murphy certainly left you in a mess," he said, flattening it out with his hand.

"No kidding."

"If it's any consolation I don't think he meant to," George continued. "He just wasn't thinking."

"He never did."

"That wasn't his strong suit," George agreed.

Wrapped up in our separate memories we were both silent for a minute. Then he broke it.

"Did you know Murphy was doing cocaine?" George asked abruptly.

"No. Did you?"

"No."

For some reason the fact that George hadn't known either made me feel marginally better. After all, he was a professional. If he had missed the signs, how the hell was I supposed to have seen them.

George stroked my cheek with his hand. His fingertips lingered by my lips. "I wish there was something I could do. . . ."

A jolt of longing surged through my body, surprising me with its intensity. I jumped up.

"What's wrong?"

"Nothing." I slipped on my jacket. "I just remembered I have something I have to do at home." Then I started to walk away.

"Wait," George called after me.

But I didn't. What I was feeling scared me too much.

So I stood out in the parking lot with the snow blowing in my face, cleaning off the car windshield, and talking myself out of what I had felt. By the time I opened the cab door, I'd almost succeeded.

But not quite.

I was still wondering what it would be like to sleep with George when I pulled into my driveway.

As I trudged up my path to the front door, little clumps of snow worked their way down my boots. I was about to put my key in the lock when James came darting out from the bushes and rubbed against my legs. Which was odd, because I distinctly remembered he'd been asleep on the sofa when I left.

Then I noticed my door. It was opened a crack. I was positive I'd locked it when I left, but then I reminded myself I'd inadvertently done that kind of thing before. I went inside. Nothing seemed to be amiss. I took my boots off, walked into the kitchen, and checked for messages on my answering machine. There weren't any. A fact which depressed me. Even though I wasn't in the mood to speak to anyone, I wanted someone to want to speak to me. Go figure.

I poured myself a Scotch, went into the living room, and turned on the news, but I couldn't concentrate on what the announcer was saying. I kept feeling something was wrong. I got up and walked through the kitchen and the dining room again. Nothing was out of order. It was just my nerves, I told myself. The past weeks were getting to me. Considering what was going on it was to be expected. But my little speech to myself didn't help. I was still jumpy as I went up the stairs.

I was almost to the second floor landing when it hit me. The dog hadn't come out to say hello. I started calling for her. No response. I checked my bedroom. She wasn't there. Then I went into my studio.

The moment I stepped inside, I knew somebody had been there.

The light was on. I'd left it off. My heart started beating faster. I took another step in. Even from across the room I could tell that the negatives of the pictures I'd taken inside Karkoff's house were gone. I'd left them lying on the counter and now they weren't there.

Then I noticed the sheet of white paper clipped to the drying line.

It swayed slightly as I walked across the room.

I took it down.

"You lose," it read.

Karkoff.

I crumpled up the paper and threw it on the floor.

Thirty-one

That slimeball.

For a moment I was so angry I couldn't even move.

So angry I couldn't even think about how Karkoff had known I'd been in his house. So angry I couldn't think of anything at all. Then I remembered Elsie and that was enough to get me going.

I jumped in the cab and sped over to Karkoff's house. As I pulled over to the curb, I caught a glimpse of his car through the garage door. Karkoff was home. I hadn't made a mistake. I strode up to the door and pounded on it. Hard.

It took a moment, but he answered. He looked surprised to see me. He was even more surprised when I punched him in the stomach. For that matter so was I.

"You fuckin' son of a bitch," I said as he doubled over.

Then I brought my foot back. I was about to kick him, my foot was already in motion, when I heard someone say, "Don't move."

I glanced up. Donna was standing in the doorway. She had what looked like Karkoff's gun in her hand and she was pointing it in my direction.

"You okay?" she asked Karkoff, not taking her eyes off me.

"Fine." He straightened up.

"You know, you really aren't a good loser," he said to me as he rubbed the place where I'd socked him. "That's an aspect of your character you should work on."

"Screw you." I was still angry, but that anger was draining away—fast. I wondered if Donna would actually shoot me. Then I decided she wouldn't, especially not here, not in public.

"Plus you have a foul mouth," Karkoff continued. "And you're careless. Not a good combination. I mean if I were going to break into someone's house and I had a car as distinctive as yours I certainly wouldn't park it in the driveway of the house I was burglarizing."

I didn't say anything.

"For your information, not that I think you're going to need it in the future, my next door neighbor saw you coming out and called me out in Seattle. Red hair. A camera. A camera?" Karkoff tsk tsked. "Robin playing Nancy Drew. How quaint. Then when she told me you put the dog in the car I knew it couldn't be anyone else. Robin, you really are hopelessly sentimental. Animal shelters across the nation are killing hundreds of unwanted pets a day. I'm not doing anything worse than they are. In fact I'm doing better, because these animal lives are going for a worthy cause."

"Ah. Karkoff's ontological view of the universe. Life is just an endless food chain. Eat or be eaten."

"Oversimplified but essentially correct."

"Which is why," I continued, "I suppose it's okay to kill someone."

Karkoff arched his eyebrows. "Come again?"

"I may be careless, I may be sentimental, but at least I'm not a murderer."

"Don't you think the term murderer is a little strong for what I've been doing?"

"What other term would you use?"

"Feeder."

"I'm not talking about your snakes."

"I get it." Enlightenment flashed across Karkoff's face. "You think I killed John and Sam." Then he did something I didn't expect. He smiled, a big broad grin. "Your lack of observational powers never fails to amaze me. You think you see everything and you see nothing at all."

"I see enough."

"Not of what counts."

"So you're telling me you didn't kill John?"

Karkoff looked at me scornfully. "I'm not telling you anything at all."

"So you did kill him."

"You're becoming tedious." He moved next to Donna and held out his hand. "Give me the gun."

"Don't," I cried as she handed it to him.

"Sorry, but I always do what my boyfriend says."

My stomach twisted. I remembered what I had thought when I'd heard Donna's voice on Karkoff's machine. My instincts had been right. I should have listened to them.

Donna smirked. "Ken and I have been together for a while now."

"Good for you."

"We have mutual interests," Karkoff explained.

"And he doesn't hit me like John used to do."

"Nothing like having high standards," I couldn't keep myself from cracking.

"Or keep promising to marry me like your husband did," Donna added.

"What?" I hadn't heard right.

"Oh sorry," Donna said, her voice syrupy with phony apology. "I thought you knew. Everyone else did."

"The problem with you," Karkoff chimed in, and he was smiling too, "is, as I said before, that you don't see what's in front of you. Which is quite odd considering you're a photographer, though from the pictures you took in my house, not a good one."

"We were together six, maybe seven months," Donna mused. "Eight at the most. But then Murphy started seeing someone else. Not that I really cared. He always had an eye out, if you get my meaning. It wasn't like I had to twist his arm or anything to get him in bed."

Karkoff gave a slight cough and Donna stopped talking. "I think it's time you came inside," he said to me.

"I think not," I replied. Whatever happened I wasn't going back in that house. That much I knew.

He waved the gun. "You're not in a position to argue."

"You wouldn't shoot me out here in the open."

He opened his eyes wide in astonishment. "Why ever not? You're a burglar. You robbed my house once. You came back and assaulted me. I'm merely protecting myself."

"You do that and the police are going to want to come in to your house and take a statement."

"Let them."

"They'll see what you have."

"I'm a respected curator. I'm entitled to keep a collection in my home."

"They'll see the dragon."

Karkoff chuckled. "So what? They wouldn't know a Nile monitor from a Gila monster." He waved the gun again. "I'm done talking. Now get inside."

But I didn't move. "If you're going to kill me you're going to have to do it out here."

Karkoff arched his eyebrows again. "Kill? Who said anything about kill. I just want to show you my collection. Introduce you properly."

"I'll pass."

"You don't have the choice."

"I'm not moving." I figured if I was going to die at least let it be over quickly. But as it turned out apparently I had figured wrong.

Karkoff pulled the trigger back. The click eclipsed all the other sounds. "Look around. There's nobody out. Now either you move or I kneecap you and then I drag you inside."

As I looked at him standing there, I knew he meant what he said. I turned to Donna. "You'd let him?"

She gave a half shrug and studied the needles on the fir tree by the house. She'd go along with whatever he wanted, her shrug had said. Even if she didn't think it was right. I judged the distance to my car—about one hundred feet. Could I make it? Maybe. If Karkoff was distracted. It was a big "if."

"Well?" Karkoff's voice was heavy with impatience.

"I'm coming." I took a small step forward. Then another. "Tell me," I asked, stalling for time, praying an idea would come to me. "What happened to the dog?"

"You're worried about the dog?" Karkoff choked down a laugh, spewing saliva around him. "I love it."

"She's here," Donna answered. "Back where she belongs."

"Come on," Karkoff ordered. "I'm tired of waiting."

I took another step and another. Suddenly there was nothing but me, Karkoff, and the doorway to the house. All my senses were sharpened. I was aware of everything. I saw the lights from Karkoff's house shining on the snow, saw each distinct needle on the fir tree, smelled the cold damp air, the faint aroma of burning wood, heard the scrabble of what?

Elsie. Her nails were scratching the wood floors of Karkoff's hallway. She'd heard me. She was coming to the door. Coming to see me.

Suddenly I was blessed with an idea. I increased my pace. Now I was on the doorstep, right next to Karkoff. He pushed the barrel of the gun in my shoulder. His first mistake.

"Hurry it up," he ordered.

But instead of going forward, I pushed back into him. Hard. He lost his balance. As he stumbled, I hit his wrist with the side of my hand. The gun fell onto the stoop. Karkoff bent to get it, but I kicked it onto the ground. He straightened up. I was getting ready to knee him, when I felt an arm across my throat pressing against my windpipe, cutting off the air. It was Donna.

"Hold her," Karkoff instructed as he ran down the steps to get the gun.

Thirty-two

But if I knew one thing, it was that I wasn't waiting for Kark-off to come back. I took one of my elbows and jabbed it under Donna's rib cage as hard as I could. She grunted. Her grip loosened. I wrenched away and took a flying leap down the steps. My momentum carried me forward and I smashed into Karkoff as he was straightening up. The gun was in his hand. We both went down. The gun flew out of his grasp and landed in the snow. He grabbed for it, but I managed to get there first.

"Okay," I said, scrambling up and motioning to him and Donna with the gun, "you two up on the porch."

"What are you going to do, shoot us?" Karkoff scoffed as he brushed the snow off his shirt. "I bet you don't even know how to pull the trigger."

I told him I thought I could figure it out and ordered him to get moving.

Karkoff took a few steps back, then stopped and crossed his hands over his chest daring me to do something. So I explained the situation to him. Just so there'd be no confusion.

"You're probably thinking that I won't be able to hit you

and Donna even if I do fire this gun," I told him. "Well maybe that's true: But maybe it's not. Maybe I'll end up hitting you someplace really bad—like your face. Or your dick." At that Karkoff's skin turned blotchy. I continued. "Not that I'd want to do that, you understand, but guns in the hands of people who are nervous, who don't know what they're doing, tend to be very dangerous."

"Ken"—Donna's voice floated down from the porch on a wave of anxiety—"maybe we'd better do as she says."

Karkoff put his head down and started walking again.

"Very good," I said when they were both where I wanted them. "Now open the door and let the dog out."

Karkoff did as he was told.

"This isn't going to help your situation," he said as Elsie streaked across the yard toward me.

"Ask me if I care," I replied as I backed up toward the cab.

I reached behind me and opened the door. Elsie and I got in and I started the engine. When the motor was running, I threw the gun in the direction of the pine tree, slammed the door shut, and put my foot on the accelerator. I careened down the block, took the turn onto Delray way too fast, and almost went into a telephone pole. Elsie went flying off the seat. As she scrambled back on, I told myself that I'd better slow down. Otherwise I'd end up in a ditch.

I went down Seeley and up Beatty. By the time I reached Mountain View I was hyperventilating and my hands were shaking so badly I could hardly drive. I pulled over to the side of the road and started taking slow, long deep breaths to clear the carbon dioxide out of my system because that was what was making my hands shake. After a few minutes they had returned to normal and I was able to drive home.

When I saw my house I wanted to cry out in relief. I pulled into my driveway and practically ran onto the porch. As I was putting my key in the lock I spotted a package jammed into my mailbox. I took it out and read the label: J. P. Menlow. The shirts I had ordered for Murphy two months ago had finally arrived. Just a little late. I hurled them into the snowbank by the driveway and went inside.

The house was quiet, too quiet. The only noise was the *tip tap* of Elsie's paws as she ran into the kitchen. I turned on all the lights, the TV, and radio. Then I grabbed a glass from the sink and poured myself a Scotch. Liquid sloshed over the rim as I carried the glass, along with the bottle, up the stairs.

I went into my studio and stared at the pictures I had taken of Murphy over the years. Murphy with our dog. Murphy in front of our first house. Murphy holding out our wedding ring. We were going to be the perfect couple. What a laugh. I took a giant swallow as I thought about what Donna had said. I shouldn't have cared. It didn't matter, I told myself. The man was dead. He had done worse. But it did matter. The alcohol burned going down. I wanted it to burn. To burn clean through my insides.

I turned and walked into the bedroom, then stopped, ensnared by my reflection.

How could I have been so stupid? I asked it. So blind? So God-awful dumb?

About everything.

I had seen nothing.

Nothing at all.

Had Murphy loved me?

Had he cared?

Even a little?

I picked up the clock radio on the night stand and hurled it. A hundred reflections of me danced, splintered, and crashed to the floor. The dog yelped and ran out of the room. Good. Let her. Nobody wanted to be around me anyway. I washed down a Valium with the rest of the Scotch and refilled the glass. Then I emptied it again. What I was doing was really bad. I knew it and I didn't care. In fact that thought gave me a perverse pleasure.

Half an hour later I was puking my guts into the toilet bowl. When I was done, I slipped onto the bathroom floor and lay there, too spent to even clean myself up. I was so tired I felt dizzy. I remember counting the tiles on the floor and asking myself what would my friends say if they came in and saw me like this? But I don't remember what I told myself because I passed out. The next thing I knew I felt something warm on my face. I opened my eyes. It was Elsie licking my cheek.

I grabbed hold of the sink leg and pulled myself up. Then I stripped and stumbled into the shower. The water pummeled me as I leaned against the tile wall. I closed my eyes and let the spray wash over me. Finally I turned it off and stepped onto the bath mat. The whole room reeked of puke. Filled with self-loathing I grabbed a towel, walked out of the bathroom, closed the door, and went into my bedroom. I'd clean up the mess I'd made later. I couldn't face it then.

I toweled myself off, crawled into bed, and immediately fell into a deep sleep. But half an hour later I found myself sitting straight up. My heart was racing. I was covered with sweat. I was terrified. I'd been dreaming about Karkoff, only this time he had the gun. I lay back down and put my hand on Elsie's back for comfort. She lifted her head for a second and then dropped it back down. I tried closing my eyes, but every time I did I kept replaying my fight with Karkoff. Finally I got up and got dressed. Sometimes when I got like this it helped to walk.

Elsie watched as I put on a heavy pair of leggings, a long-sleeved T-shirt, my big heavy blue turtleneck, wool socks, and boots. She was right behind me wagging her tail when I went downstairs and donned my jacket and gloves.

"Okay," I said, "let's go." And we went outside.

The sky was overcast. No stars were visible. It was very still. The only sounds were my footsteps crunching on the ice and Elsie's snuffling as she smelled each tree, bush, and lamppost. I walked half a mile past row after row of sleeping houses while my thoughts hopped around in my head like so many Mexican jumping beans. By the time I reached Barry Park my thighs were chafing with the cold and my ears were burning. I turned around and went back home.

As I climbed my front steps, I spotted the package I'd tossed on the hedge earlier. Might as well give it to Good Will, I decided. I was in the process of retrieving it when I realized something.

Something I should have realized earlier.

In all my attempts to figure out what the hell was going on, I'd forgotten a cardinal rule: when stumped, always go back to the beginning.

Only I hadn't done that. I'd gotten lost in a maze instead.

John's death, Sam's death, everything had started with the package.

The package that someone had dropped off in the store.

And I realized I knew who that someone was.

I had known for weeks. I just hadn't known that I knew. The guy had told me himself.

Twice.

When he'd demanded his money.

Only I hadn't paid any attention, because drunks are like elevator music. You tune them out.

I looked at my watch. It was three-thirty in the morning. I'd have to wait until it got light out before I went looking for Go Go Nelson. The Seward Arms wasn't the kind of place you wanted to go into during the day, much less at night. I went upstairs, set my alarm for eight, and went back to bed. Tomorrow's horoscope had said, "A chat with an acquaintance will bring interesting results." It would be nice if that were true.

I awoke to another gray winter morning. When I stepped outside, the taste of snow hung in the air like a sullen promise. I took the dog out for her morning pee, then headed down to the 7-Eleven and bought myself coffee, the paper, and a couple of packs of cigarettes. The coffee was weak and bitter, but I'd managed to finish it by the time I got to the liquor store, where I purchased a bottle of Thunderbird. Then I drove over to the Seward Arms.

As I walked across the street and scrambled over the curbside pile of snow I felt a little like Gary Cooper in *High Noon*. The door to the Seward Arms was painted lavender. Someone's idea of a joke? It was a flimsy, plywood affair, the kind you could punch through without damaging your knuckles. There was a hole where the lock had been and the doorknob wobbled when I turned it.

The interior hallway was lit by a bulb that couldn't have been more than twenty-five watts, but even that couldn't hide the dirt-streaked walls or the garbage-strewn floor. I kicked an empty forty-ounce bottle of malt liquor out of the way and read the names on the mailboxes. They were written in smudged black pencil and it took several minutes before I could decipher Nelson's name pasted over the box for room 305.

I pushed the interior hall door open and went inside. The smell hit me immediately. Composed of unflushed toilets, stale beer, and rotted food, it was the odor of despair. I stopped and lit a Camel. One thing about smoking—it may give you lung cancer, but it's great for masking odors.

Nelson's room turned out to be at the end of a short, dark hallway, last on the right. I knocked. No answer. When I knocked again, the door swung open a couple of inches. I peeked inside. Daylight streamed in through two dirt-caked windows illuminating the empty bottles, the plates of half-eaten food, the piles of rags.

"Nelson."

A groan came from the corner of the room over by the windows. Cautiously I crept over to where the sound had come from. Nelson was lying on a stained, mildewed mattress. He looked almost as thin as Karkoff's dog. His mouth was open, the three teeth left were brown, rotting stumps. Every time he took a breath, his cheeks sunk in.

The left side of his face was a yellowish purple, no doubt a remnant of a fight or an accident. I nudged him with my foot. He didn't move. I nudged harder. Nothing. I kicked him in the shins. He jumped up. As he moved I caught a glint of something metallic in his right hand. Then that hand came up and I saw what was in it. A butterfly knife.

Not wanting to crowd him, I held out the bottle of Thunderbird while taking a half step back. "Look," I crooned, "see what I brought you."

Nelson stared at the bottle for a good moment, but the hand with the knife stayed up.

"Now, how about putting the knife down."

But instead of doing what I'd asked he lifted it a fraction higher.

"I said put it down."

This time he listened. His hand opened and the knife clattered to the floor.

Trying not to show the relief I was feeling, I kicked the knife aside, then twisted the cap off the Thunderbird bottle.

"All I want you to do is answer a couple of questions," I said as I looked around for a glass.

"I don't. . . . It's too black." Nelson stopped and shook his head. Spittle sprayed out of his mouth and down his shirt.

"Easy ones," I reassured him. There were no glasses. But then why should there be. There wasn't even a sink. I found a paper cup, dumped its contents into a bowl on the table, filled it half full with Thunderbird, and handed it to Nelson.

He gulped it down and held the cup out. Poor guy. I hope I never get like that I thought as I poured a little more rotgut in his cup and closed the bottle. "You'll get the rest when you tell me what I want to know."

"Wha's that?"

"Last month somebody gave you a package to deliver to Noah's Ark. Do you remember?"

He nodded.

"I want to know who that someone was."

Nelson gave me a blank look. I held up the bottle. "Try and think," I urged.

He scratched his hair. A louse walked onto his hand. I shuddered and controlled an impulse to run out the door. "Was the person who gave you the package a man or a woman?" Better to start simple.

He pointed at me.

"It was a woman?"

Nelson nodded eagerly.

"Are you sure?"

"Yes." He reached out for the bottle.

"Wait." I pulled it back. "What else?"

"She was red."

"She was wearing red clothes?"

"No."

"Then what?"

He looked down at my hands.

"She had red nails?"

He wore a big grin as he bobbed his head up and down.

"What else?"

"Don't know." He looked at the Thunderbird longingly.

"Try and recall."

He scrunched up his eyes while he thought. "She was a stick," he finally said.

"A stick?"

"Yes. And she had a black spot. And wings. And she drove a blue chariot that went down into the ground."

I gave up and handed him the Thunderbird.

This had been a bad idea from the beginning.

The guy had wet brain.

To have expected him to tell me anything, when half the time he couldn't even remember his own name, was a little like expecting an ant to climb up the Twin Towers.

Thirty-three

My grandmother always used to say that you got what you paid for. Maybe, I reflected as I drove toward my house, I should have bought Nelson a bottle of Chivas Regal, because the Thunderbird sure hadn't gotten me very much.

The morning had turned out to be a total waste of time.

I lit a cigarette as I made a left onto Butternut.

I might as well have stayed in bed, I decided, as I pulled out the ashtray and flicked my match into it. I could have used the extra sleep.

But then I saw a guy on crutches crossing the street and that got me thinking about what Nelson had said about the woman who paid him being a stick. Maybe he had meant she used a stick—like a cane.

Maybe Nelson didn't have wet brain after all.

Maybe he did remember. And he was trying to tell me. He'd just gotten his words mixed up.

Because Donna had been walking with a cane when I'd run into her at Fay's.

And then there were the black circles under her eyes.

Were they what Nelson had meant by the black spot?

And she definitely had long, red finger nails.

And most important of all—she'd never shown up for work the day John died. She'd told her aunt she was going to work, but she'd never made it.

Was it because she knew what was going to happen at the store and she didn't want to see it?

I hit the wheel of the car.

It was Donna. It had to be.

Now that I thought about it, in the past few weeks her name had hovered off in the wings like an understudy waiting for her break. She'd been involved with John. With Karkoff. With Murphy. With everyone, in fact, except Maroney. She was the link, the person who connected everybody to everybody else. I made a U-turn and started back to my house.

The lady had both the motive and the means.

Art had given me Donna's motive back at the bar. Revenge. John had beaten her up. Regularly. Maybe the last time was one time too many.

And she certainly had access to the means—the snake. And she wasn't afraid to handle it.

Then I thought about Manuel and my elation vanished.

What about him? I tapped my fingers on the steering wheel while I considered possible explanations. Okay. What if the money and the gun were really Donna's—Murphy was just holding them—and Manuel knew it? And what if he wanted a finder's fee? And what if Donna had agreed to his terms and arranged the payoff at the store? But then something went wrong and they'd ended up fighting. Donna had hit Manuel over the head, taken the money and the gun, and gotten out of there. Then she'd used the gun to shoot Sam.

Why that? Simple. Because Sam had suspected Donna was the killer. That's what he had wanted to talk to me about the night he died. That's why he'd written Donna's name on the paper lying on his desk. But because it had been surrounded by doodles I'd assumed it hadn't meant anything. Bad assumption. Somehow Donna had found out what Sam knew and killed him.

I lit another Camel and thought through everything again. The explanation, I decided as I pulled into the driveway, held. Sure there were holes. So what? Lorenzo and Cunningham could fill them in. That's what they were being paid to do anyway. The important thing was that I was off the hook, that I had somebody else to give them.

I stubbed my cigarette out, tore into the house, and called the PSB. But Lorenzo was out. I almost spit in frustration. She'd been dogging my steps for the past weeks and now when I wanted her she wasn't around.

"Tell her to call me," I instructed the desk officer, giving him my name and number. He said that he would and I hung up.

Then I headed straight for my studio. I'd cleaned up one mess. It was time to tackle another. Murphy's pictures were going in the trash.

He didn't deserve to be on my wall.

He'd never liked me taking pictures of him anyway.

Down came the picture of Murphy sitting on his motorcycle. Down came the snaps of him walking along the beach at Montauk, the one of him dressed in a cap and gown holding up his master's degree. By the time I was done I'd have nothing to remind me of him. It would be like he hadn't existed.

I got to work on the next batch.

Murphy in front of Noah's Ark.

Out.

Murphy holding up a ball python.

Out.

Murphy at his desk.

I was wadding it up when something caught my eye.

Something on his desk. Something half covered by the mountain of junk.

I looked closer. Held the picture up to the light.

Glasses. Frames that looked familiar. Frames that had no business being there.

None at all.

I was still staring at them, still not believing what I was seeing when I sensed a presence behind me.

"What's this?"

A hand reached out and snatched the photograph.

I half turned.

"It looks like I got here just in time," Lorenzo said. She was holding a gun and it was pointed at my chest. "Downstairs."

I did as I was told, hoping that, like Karkoff, she'd make a mistake I could take advantage of. But she didn't. She knew better. She took care to stay far enough behind me so that there was no way I could back up and smash into her without getting shot. As I reached the bottom step I began considering how much of a chance I'd have if I ran. I just decided that I'd have almost none when I saw Elsie. She was lying stretched out in the hallway. Even from there I could tell she was dead.

"Stay where you are," Lorenzo ordered as I started toward my dog.

But at that moment I didn't care enough to listen. "Why?" I cried as I got down on my knees and stroked Elsie's fur.

"Because I didn't want her to bark," Lorenzo said.

Then before I could do or say anything a burst of pain, so deep it took my breath away, exploded in my head. Whorls of light danced in front of my eyes. Everything went black.

*   *   *

I awoke to the smell of dust and dirt. Something raspy tickled my nose. I sneezed. A poker point of pain shot through my head. I groaned then opened my eyes. Greens and blues swirled in front of my pupils. I blinked. They were still there. Then I realized that that was because I was lying face down on the rug in Murphy's office. I turned my head slightly and experienced another stab of pain. My hands were in back of me. I tried to move them, but I couldn't. They were tied together. So were my legs. I heard the door open. Heard footsteps coming toward me.

"Time to rise and shine, sweetheart."

Lorenzo yanked me up. The room went spinning. Nausea overwhelmed me. I broke out in a cold sweat.

"Here." An armchair appeared underneath me. Lorenzo pushed me down into it. I felt something being wrapped around my waist. I looked down. Lorenzo was duct-taping me to the chair.

"You know," she informed me as she wound, a spider securing me in her web, "this is all your fault. If it wasn't for you none of this would have happened."

"How do you figure that?" I whispered.

"You should have let him go."

"Who?"

"Murphy, of course."

Of course.

"Why'd you tell him you wouldn't give him a divorce?"

"He never asked me for one."

Lorenzo studied my face. "You're lying," she finally said after a moment.

"If that's what you want to think."

"I can tell from your eyes. You know you shouldn't have done that. We were good together. We fit. He and I. I knew from the moment he came to my house to set up an aquarium for my Jackson chameleons that we were meant to be to-gether." She straightened up and tossed the tape on Murphy's desk. "Didn't you realize something had changed?"

"Yes. But I didn't know what it was."

"I thought wives were supposed to know everything," Lorenzo sneered.

"Evidently not."

"You know he and I had something."

"So you said."

"Something special."

"Like blow?" I asked, taking a wild guess.

Lorenzo's face tightened.

"You started him on it, didn't you?"

She didn't say anything.

"Didn't you?" I insisted.

"Lots of people use it. It's no big deal."

"Is that a trace of guilt I detect in your voice?"

"Be quiet."

"What were you two doing, taking a snort in the car when he dropped dead?"

"Shut up."

"You were, weren't you? And then he collapsed and you just walked off."

"He was dead when I left."

"God, you really are cold."

"Listen, sister"—Lorenzo brought her face close to mine again—"some people don't have the luxury of doing what they want. Some people have to operate in the real world. If I had called an ambulance, I would have had too much explaining to do. I could have eaten a felony manslaughter charge. I would have lost everything. And for what? Nothing was bringing him back." She resettled her glasses. "He was gone. Anyway," she added a touch defensively, "I went to the funeral."

"And that's supposed to make everything better? You killed him just as sure as if you'd pulled the trigger."

"You and John are a pair."

"How do you mean?"

"Because that's what John said to me at the cemetery. 'Trying to atone for your sins?' "

"Is that why you killed him?"

"The stupid shit was trying to blackmail me." Lorenzo's voice shook with indignation. "Murphy shouldn't have bought blow from him. I told him to come to his mama if he wanted any, but he didn't listen."

"He never did," I murmured. "To anyone."

Lorenzo continued on as if she hadn't heard me. "You know John saw Murphy and me together."

"And added everything up."

"He should have kept his nose out of our business."

"So how much did John want?"

"Twenty thousand."

"Or?"

"He was going to turn me in to Internal Affairs. I've worked too hard to get where I am to let some two-bit punk bring me down."

"Too bad you didn't know about the money in the heat vent, but then I guess Murphy didn't tell you everything either. Not that it would have made any difference to John," I continued. "You probably would have murdered him anyway. I mean you couldn't risk having somebody with that kind of knowledge walking around, now could you?"

"I wasn't trying to kill him, you idiot. I was trying to scare him. The snake was supposed to be a warning. I figured he'd end up in the hospital for a couple of weeks. And even if he didn't, even if the snake didn't bite him, he'd get the message.

Chutes and Adders   **277**

How the fuck was I supposed to know the little prick's asthma was that bad?"

"Bad luck for you."

"No," Lorenzo corrected me. "Bad luck for Sam. And you."

"You mean if John hadn't died, then Sam wouldn't have figured out you were the killer and you wouldn't have had to shoot him, right?"

"Not exactly. Sam made the same mistake you did. He thought Donna was the murderer."

"So why didn't you arrest her?"

"I couldn't. I can't. She has an alibi. She was with some friends over at a bar on the North Side. And anyway I just knew from the way Sam was staring at my hair when he came down to the PSB to tell me about Donna that it wasn't going to be too long before he remembered that the last time he'd seen me my hair had been red."

God. Nelson had meant my hair not my nails. He'd pointed at one, but meant the other. No wonder he'd come after me the night I was chasing Manuel. He'd seen my hair and thought I was Lorenzo. He'd wanted to get paid. And then as I looked at Lorenzo I realized something else. The black spot Nelson had been talking about wasn't the circles under Donna's eyes. It was the mole on top of Lorenzo's lip. And the stick he'd mentioned wasn't a cane it was Lorenzo's nightstick. And the blue chariot must have been a squad car. I wondered if Sam had spoken to Nelson too and come to the same conclusion I had.

"See, the way I look at it," Lorenzo went on, "is that since you were the one that started this whole mess I figure it's only poetic justice that you take the fall."

"And you know what I think?"

"What?"

"I think that's bullshit. I think you're framing me because you're jealous of me."

"That's crap."

"Is it? You know Murphy lied to you about divorcing me. He had no intention of leaving me. Hell. You even dyed your hair red so . . ."

"Shut up."

"You just can't stand to hear the truth, can you?"

Lorenzo balled her hand into a fist and pulled her arm back.

I saw the blow coming, but there was nothing I could do to avoid it.

A cluster of pain exploded on the left side of my face when the punch landed. Something warm and salty trickled down from my nose and into my mouth.

"Jesus, you really are Looney Tunes," I muttered.

Lorenzo punched me again. This time I felt my jaw snap.

"You're going to see exactly how nuts I am," Lorenzo promised. Then she walked out the door.

Thirty-four

No matter how much I twisted and turned, I couldn't loosen the tape. I sat trussed up in the armchair, listening to Lorenzo walking back and forth in the other room, going up the stairs, coming down, wondering what she was doing. Then I smelled gasoline and in a dreadful flash I knew.

My heart began to hammer. Blood rushed to my head. The overhead light seemed to shimmer and blur. I was going to faint. I knew it. But I couldn't. Not now. I pressed my nails into the palms of my hands as hard as I could. The pain was enough to allow me to get myself back under control.

I stretched my fingers out as far as I could and tried unsticking the tape around my wrists. But they were so thick, so engorged with blood, so numbed I couldn't feel anything with them.

"Don't bother," said Lorenzo from behind me. "Duct tape is much harder to get out of than rope."

"What were you doing?" I asked even though I knew. She reeked from gasoline.

"You'll find out soon enough." Lorenzo lifted a clump of my hair, fingered it meditatively, held it up to the light. Just like a butcher, I thought, stroking the sheep's throat before he slits it. I flinched, tried to contain it. "I used Clairol's Ginger Snap on my hair. But I could never get it to look like yours. I don't know why I dyed it. I guess I thought Murphy would like it."

I turned my head slightly. Lorenzo let go of my hair. "You knocked Manuel out, didn't you?" I heard myself ask her. Terror had made me dissociate. I was hovering near the ceiling looking down at her and me, and thinking—how odd that a part of me still cares about the answers when they won't make any difference at all.

She snorted. "That lousy spic. Stealing my money."

"That twenty thousand was yours?"

She pinched my cheek. "Very good."

"And the gun?"

"An extra. Just in case."

"What was the money from? Drugs?"

"Favors."

"Payoffs?"

"Favors. People paid me to do them favors."

"You must have done a lot of them."

"No more than anyone else on the force."

"How did Manuel know the money was yours?"

"He didn't."

"I don't get it."

"No, I don't suppose you do." She stroked my hair again briefly. This time I was unable to contain my shudder. She smiled when she saw it. "I was tailing you the day Manuel took off with the bag. When I saw you chasing him, I got curious enough to want to know what was going on so I followed him. I finally nabbed him over by Bryne Dairy. The dumb shit was standing outside the store drinking chocolate milk. Chocolate milk? Jesus. Then I made a mistake. I didn't cuff the little prick before I checked out the bag. What can I say, I got careless. He punched me, grabbed the bag back, and ran. I was going after him when I got a call. There'd been a homicide on the corner of Teall and East Fayette I had to check out.

"It turned out to be nothing, just one alkie taking out another one. By the time I got done with all the paperwork it was after nine. But I figured, what the hell. I'd go looking for Manuel anyway. Turned out nobody had seen him. Not his mother, his grandma, his friends. No one. I was about to give up when I remembered something Murphy had told me. 'Sometimes when Manuel gets in trouble,' Murphy had said, 'he uses the store attic as a hideout.' So I decided to take a look-see. Sure enough. The attic window was wide open. I climbed up and there he was. Boy, let me tell you, was he surprised to see me. He thought I was going to arrest him."

"Yeah, stupid kid. How was he supposed to know you didn't want to do any more paperwork that night."

Lorenzo backhanded me and I could feel something crack at the base of my neck. "What the fuck do you know? Miss High and Mighty Liberal. What gives you the right to say things like that? My father came over from Italy. He worked on the line at the candle factory all his life. He died when I was seven and we had to go live with my mother's parents. They were from the old country too. I had to fight to go to school. They thought I should stay home and help with the housework. I didn't get trips to Europe. I didn't get to go waltzing off on photography tours of Central America snapping pictures of the downtrodden."

"Screw you." My anger overcame my fear. If I was going to die at least let me set the record straight. "So your father died when you were little? Big fucking deal. So did mine. My mother had to go to work. I was raised by my grandmother too. She couldn't speak English. So what? Those trips you're talking about? I paid for them cleaning houses. I went to school on a scholarship. I worked weekends at a restaurant washing dishes. So don't give me that sob sister stuff. You had choices just like everyone else. You just made the wrong ones. Nobody made you go into the police. Nobody made you take payoffs. Nobody made you fuck another woman's husband. Nobody made you kill people."

Lorenzo poked my breastbone with her finger. "Murphy always said you had a big mouth. Well, talk now. Because you don't have much time left."

"Wait," I cried. My fear came back.

"It's a shame the fire engines won't get here in time."

"It's not going to work," I argued. "They'll find me tied up. They'll know something's wrong. And then they'll start looking."

"So what? Somebody broke in, tied you up, robbed the place and then burned it down. Just the way they did on Ashworth last year."

I thought of the ruined house six blocks away. The cordoned-off block. The firemen in their yellow coats scurrying around in the flame-lit night, the smell of burning wood that lingered for months afterward, the sightseers coming up to gawk.

"I've even hung the balloons full of gasoline from the ceiling just the way Maroney's guy did."

"You can't."

"Watch me." Lorenzo turned and started walking. Then she stopped and turned. "Who knows? Maybe you'll be lucky. Maybe you'll pass out from the fumes instead of burning to death."

"Come back." I started rocking back and forth in the chair, trying to loosen my bonds.

"Have a better next life," Lorenzo called out from the next room. "Your balloon is about to go up."

For the first few seconds I heard nothing. Then came the sound I'd been dreading: a *whoosh*. Next the door slammed. Lorenzo had left. I was all alone in a burning building.

I went hot and cold. I was sweating, but inside I was so cold my bones were aching. I heard a voice screaming no over and over again in a shrill falsetto, then I realized it was mine. But I couldn't stop.

Even though I knew it was a waste of time.

Even though I knew that nobody would hear me.

Then I felt something sharp digging into my leg. I looked down. Pickles had panicked. She was climbing up my leg. The pain sobered me.

I tried loosening the duct tape around my hands again, but it was no use. It wouldn't budge. I kept rocking back and forth trying to loosen the tape that bound me to the chair anyway. I couldn't think of anything else to do. But it didn't help. I tried standing up. I couldn't. The chair was too heavy. Then I looked down and realized that my rocking had moved the chair forward. I tried some more. Progress came in quarter inches. I concentrated on that and tried not to think about how old the house was, how dry the wood was, how fast it was going to burn. I tried not to hear the screams, not to smell the burning flesh of the animals in the other room.

Finally, I was at the door. I closed my eyes, took a deep breath, and tried to stand. I couldn't. I tried again. This time I made it. But when I tried to go through the door the chair wouldn't fit. No matter which way I twisted and turned, the chair was too wide. Damned old house. I swung my body around and smashed one of the legs against the door frame over and over.

Nothing happened.

I did it again and again. An eternity of times. Finally I heard a crack. I looked down. The chair leg was folding inward. I twisted and inched my way through the door and into the hallway.

Then I stopped. Dead. The front room was engulfed. Flames licked at the walls and the ceiling rafters, claimed the windows and the front door. I heard a cage full of parakeets screech, watched them become a bright ball of light.

The heat nibbled around my shoes, touched my skin. Heat seared my lungs with every breath I took. I went back a step. I had thought I could go out the side door. But I couldn't. The fire had beaten me. I retreated back inside the office and stood there, while I wondered what to do and listened to the cat yowl. Then I remembered the boarded-up door on the other side of the office. Murphy had closed it up a couple of years ago after some kids had snuck in through it and stolen his Walkman. The door wasn't really necessary and it had been cheaper than connecting it to an alarm system. I only hoped he had done his usual slip-shod job.

Tendrils of flame were licking at the office door as I turned around. Smoke was everywhere. Black. Dense. Making my eyes sting. Clawing at my throat. Every breath was an agony. I had to get out. I hopped forward, landed on something, stumbled, and fell. I tried to get up, but the weight of the chair pinned me down. I crawled along the floor like a beached whale, while Pickles, panic-stricken, clawed at my face. I could hear crackling behind me. But I couldn't turn to look. I began coughing. Big wracking coughs, the kind where you coughed up your insides. My eyes were streaming from the smoke, but I kept going. Halfway to the window I made out the indistinct shape of a carton on the floor. I wiggled over. Maybe I could use it to help lever myself up.

I was just about to put my arms on the carton when I saw the viper. It was coiled next to the box ready to strike. So it hadn't died. Manuel had been right. It had been living in the heat ducts all this time. The fire had flushed it out. I would have laughed if I wasn't choking to death. I couldn't go back. It was too late for that. But if I went forward the snake would bite me. Then as I tried to decide what to do I heard a crash and felt a searing pain in my leg. I glanced around. A charred, smoking piece of wood lay on the floor just a few inches from my leg. The ceiling was giving way. Embers were dropping like shooting stars. I made my mind up—getting bit was preferable to burning—took careful aim, and landed square on the viper. It gave a convulsive shudder, opened its mouth, then shut it again. The thing was dead.

And that's the last clear memory I have. Somehow I got over to the door. And then I was standing up. Somehow I had managed that. I do remember, though, turning around and using the chair as a battering ram as I watched the fire consume Murphy's desk. Then the fire was around me. Flickering. Red. Hungry. I recall hearing the sound of cracking wood, then feeling something cold on my back. The next thing I knew I was being pulled backward.

"Cut her loose," someone was saying.

"Careful lifting her up," someone else said.

I was cold, so cold.

Then I passed out.

Thirty-five

The next thing I knew I was lying on the ground. Snow was swirling around me. Watching the flakes melting on my fingers reminded me of my grandmother's paperweight. When I was little I'd spend rainy afternoons lying on the sofa, shaking the little globe up and staring at the white flakes as they landed on the farmhouse and the pine tree.

"Is she going to be all right," a voice I recognized as George's asked from somewhere out of my line of sight.

"Yeah she'll be fine once we get her to the hospital."

"Can I talk to her?"

"If you make it quick."

Suddenly George was hunkered down beside me. I made out something wiggling around in his arm. Then I heard a meow.

"Look what I found." He held out Pickles. I felt a surge of relief. So we'd both made it. "She's going to be fine, just like you." He stroked my cheek. His hand was dark against my skin. "Who did this to you?"

"Lorenzo," I whispered. It hurt to talk. My throat felt like it had been sandpapered.

George looked puzzled. "Lorenzo did what?"

"Tried to kill me."

"Are you sure?" Only the fluttering of his eyelids betrayed his confusion.

"Yes."

Then before George could say anything else one of the paramedics clapped a hand on his shoulder and told him he had to go. They were getting ready to take me to the hospital.

George gave my hand a squeeze. "Hang in there kid. I'll see you at St. Ann's."

"What about the cat?"

"She's coming with me," he replied as he stood up.

One of the paramedics took his place. He stuck a needle into the crook of my arm. But I didn't feel anything. I was too busy watching the store burn. The flames, scarlet and yellow, billowed out of the roof and danced up toward the heavens, lighting up the night. The spumes of water arcing down gleamed in the fire's reflection. For a moment I was caught up in the fire's beauty, then I thought about everything dying and tears welled up in my eyes and rolled down my cheeks.

"Let's do it," somebody up above me said. And I felt myself being rolled onto a board and carried to an ambulance. Just like Manuel, I thought as the doors clanged shut.

After that I passed out. The next thing I knew I was smelling burnt chicken feathers. It was disgusting. Then I realized that smell was me. And then I stopped smelling, I stopped thinking because the pain came, waves of it that wound around my feet and legs, lapped at my face.

As I clenched my hands, trying to contain the onslaught, my fingers brushed against something cold and round. Bars. Bars? I turned my head.

And realized I couldn't see.

I reached up and pawed at my face—touched something around my eyes.

"It's just gauze," a voice said and gently took my hands and put them down.

"My eyes . . ." I croaked. My throat felt even worse than it had earlier.

"Are going to be fine. I'm Dr. Powers. You're in the ER at St. Ann's."

I raised my hands to my face again.

"No. Don't touch. I've put an antibiotic ointment in your eyes to guard against infection—just as a precaution." I felt a prick in my arm. "There. This should help ease the pain." He patted my hands. "Everything's going to be fine. Really."

I wanted to believe him. I had to believe him. Then I did believe him because the pain was receding. I was floating. Pinpoints of light exploded in front of my eyes. I was cocooned in wads of cotton wool, my mind drifting over turquoise water, over the palm trees. I heard clicking, saw little round holes appear in the sand.

"Doctor, do you need any help?" a scallop asked a clam.

The "y" in the "yes" winked at me.

Other voices rose and fell, a stream that carried me further and further away into the brush. Then I was back walking on the beach. Only this time Sam and the dog he had never had were there. He was showing me where he was going to build his hut and how you thatched the roof.

"See." He waved his hand around, indicating the water, the white sand. "The gods provide."

Which gods? I wanted to ask—there were so many of them—but before I could open my mouth the other voices came and took me off to somewhere cold and white.

"We're going to be moving you upstairs just as soon as they have a room ready."

But instead of answering I began to hum. The humming turned into a rope. I scrambled along it till I got back to the tree. I sat down under it and ran my fingers through the sand, lifted it up, watched it fall back.

"It's beautiful here," I said.

"Yes, isn't it."

I looked up, shading my eyes with my hands, trying to identify the familiar voice. It was my father.

"You always did like Jones Beach," he remarked.

I laughed. "Remember when I buried you in the sand. How old was I? Five?"

"Six."

"And I decorated you with shells."

"So you did."

Then the light on the beach turned a sickly yellow. Something bad was about to happen.

Lorenzo.

My God. How could I have forgotten her?

She'd know I was alive. All she had to do was listen to the police radio.

And then she'd come here and get me. I had to leave.

I struggled to sit up.

"What are you doing?" Dr. Powers demanded as I reached up to take the bandage off my eyes.

"Getting out of here."

"You can't. You're going into shock."

I pulled the gauze down anyway. Everything in the room looked blurry. Then things started to sway. I concentrated on a fixed point as I worked my way toward the edge of the gurney.

Powers tried to restrain me while he told me why I couldn't do what I was doing. But I wasn't listening. I was too intent on leaving. I was taking the IV needle out of my arm when George appeared.

"What the hell are you doing?" he screamed as he strode across the room.

"Leaving."

"You can't."

"That's what I just told her," Powers said.

"I have to. Lorenzo is going to come looking for me."

"No she won't. I've just gotten off the phone with the D.A.'s office. They're sending someone over to take your statement."

"You told them my story?"

He nodded.

"About her trying to kill me?"

"That's what I just said."

"So are they going to arrest her?"

"Here," George said, "sit back and let the doctor reband- age your eyes."

"Damn you. Answer my question."

George studied the sink.

"Well?" I insisted.

Reluctantly he told me that she'd be relieved of her active duties and transferred to a desk job pending the outcome of the investigation into my allegations.

"That's fucking great. She'll still be out walking around."

"It won't matter. There'll be a twenty-four-hour guard sta- tioned outside your room until this situation is straightened out."

"To keep me in or to keep her out?"

George lifted his hands up to the heavens. "Why don't you try looking on the positive side for a change?" he demanded.

I was about to tell him what I thought of his comment when I felt another prick in my arm. A moment later I was back in La La Land again. Monkeys chattered in the trees. A scarlet and blue macaw flew into the coconut palm. It was a nice world, one I liked a lot, and I visited it frequently over the next four days.

When I wasn't there I was talking to the D.A.'s people. They came several times because the nurse wouldn't let them stay too long. I gave them as detailed a statement as I could. But it was hard because my mind kept on wandering back to the parrots and the hibiscus.

George said they believed me, but since it came down to my word against Lorenzo's I wasn't too sure.

Then at some point when I was supposed to be asleep I was positive I heard him talking to the guard outside my room and telling him that Lorenzo had taken off and no one knew where she was and that he should be careful.

But when I asked George about that, he said the Demerol was getting to me. I'd imagined the conversation. Everything was fine. There was nothing I needed to concern myself with. I should just think about getting better.

I took him at his word.

It was easier and I was in too much pain to think anyway.

Time just passed.

I was lying in bed tracing the cracks in the ceiling for the thousandth time when I heard the fire alarm shrieking.

At first I thought it was a drill. But after it went on for a while I began to have my doubts.

I pressed my buzzer.

But nobody came.

I had to know what was happening.

It took a lot of effort but I managed to get myself out of bed to hobble across the room.

I opened the door.

The guard wasn't there.

His chair was empty.

That's when I knew that something was wrong.

People were running this way and that down the corridor.

"There's a fire in the east wing," I heard someone say.

But suddenly I knew with absolute certainty that there wasn't.

Lorenzo was here.

Somehow she'd managed to kill the guard and set off the alarm.

And now she was coming for me.

She had to.

Without me the police didn't have a case.

I hesitated for a second trying to decide whether I'd be safer locked in my room or out in the hallway with everyone else.

But I hesitated too long.

Because by the time I'd made up my mind to leave Lorenzo was beside me. At first I didn't recognize her. She'd cropped her hair and dyed it blond and she was wearing a nurse's uniform.

"Back in the room," she ordered. Her eyes traveled downward. I followed their path and saw the gun she was holding. The barrel was peeping out from under a pile of towels.

Fear rose up in my throat like nausea.

I did as I was told.

She came in after me and shut the door.

"What did you do to the guard?"

Lorenzo raised her gun. "Let's just say that he won't be interrupting us." She smiled. "God, you've been a pain in the ass, although maybe I should thank you for my new hair style. What do you think?"

"I think I liked you better as a brunette," I managed to get

Chutes and Adders   **293**

out as I played for time. All I knew was that I hadn't gone through everything that had happened to die now.

Ever so slowly I inched my IV pole closer and closer to me. Lorenzo didn't seem to notice. The days she'd spent on the run must have tired her out and made her careless.

She raised her revolver just as I got my two hands around the pole and swung it at her. I felt a searing pain in my shoulder and ignored it. The pole connected with her hands and the gun dropped to the floor. I kicked it under the bed.

She dove after it.

I tried to drag her out. By now every part of my body was screaming in agony.

When I finally succeeded, I wished I hadn't. Because when she turned around she had the gun back in her hands.

I grabbed for it. We wrestled.

Then somehow the gun went off.

I heard a pop.

A red hole appeared where Lorenzo's cheekbone had been. She fell back.

The wall behind her was splattered with red and gray, graffitied with Lorenzo's brains.

The door flew open a few seconds later. George came running across the room. "Jesus, are you all right?" he asked as he scooped me up off the floor.

"I'm fine," I said, looking down at Lorenzo. "But I don't think she's doing too well."

Thirty-six

They found the guard almost immediately. Lorenzo had shot him and stuffed him in one of the hospital supply closets. It wasn't exactly an inconspicuous place, but it was convenient and sometimes convenience matters. Lorenzo must have figured she'd be in and out before anyone had a chance to discover the body.

As for me, in the fracas I somehow managed to reopen my burns and the one on my leg got infected so they're pumping me full of antibiotics.

And of course they moved me to a new room.

Especially after I announced I wasn't staying in the old one.

This one has peach wallpaper and a newer bathroom. I like it better.

The police and the D.A. are still coming in. They always have some new question or other to ask. I try to do the best I can to answer, but it's hard for me to focus on what they're asking. I feel like I'm talking to them across a great chasm.

My editor called. It seems she read about what happened to me in *The Post*. She wants me to do a book on my experiences. She'll pay well. Which is good, since it turns out there was no fire insurance on the store. Murphy had let it lapse.

The doctors come in and talk to me too. I know what they're saying is important, but as soon as they leave their words go straight out of my mind. George listens to them though. He keeps telling me that I'll be able to go home soon, though he says I'm going to need physical therapy and even with that I'll probably walk with a limp.

Lynn and Connie and Tim have dropped by, but since I don't have much to say, they shift around uncomfortably in their chairs, leave their offerings, and depart.

Which is okay.

A couple of times, I've even managed to make it upstairs to visit Manuel. He's out of his coma now and it looks like he's going to be okay—eventually. But it's going to take a while.

But mostly what I do is stare out the window and watch the snow melting on Irving Avenue or study the bouquet of gerberas and baby breath George brought me. For some reason I find myself thinking a lot about a board game my father and I used to play before he died.

It was called Chutes and Ladders. You threw the dice, then moved your piece the requisite number of squares. Sometimes you got to climb up the ladder, other times you slid down the chute.

It sounds like what happened to me.